Roy's gaze fastened on her gown, making her cheeks glow with heat.

His eyes roved from the cheap eyelet trim of her simple muslin nightgown, up each cloth button until he reached her breasts, where his attention stalled. Ellie flushed with embarrassment, wishing she'd gone ahead and buttoned her gown right up to the top. She only prayed the gathered folds of her nightgown hid her six months' swollen belly.

The sooner she helped him get a blanket, the sooner Roy would be out of her bedroom. His bedroom. She felt a little twinge of uneasiness to think that she would be sleeping in his bed, a fact that hadn't seemed to register until she saw him staring at her in it. That slightly different scent, fragrantly musky… The sheets and blankets that covered and warmed her were the same ones that also performed the same service for him. The realization made sleeping in his bed seem almost inappropriately intimate.

Dear Reader,

The sleepy little town of Paradise, Nebraska, is turned on its ear when abandoned and pregnant Geraldine Fitzsimmons moves into town, but her lively humor and friendly nature soon win over the staid townspeople and disarm confirmed bachelor Roy McCain in author Liz Ireland's delightful new Western, *Trouble in Paradise*.

In keeping with the season, don't miss *Halloween Knight,* complete with a bewitching heroine, a haunted castle and an inspired cat, by Maggie Award-winning author Tori Phillips. It's a delightful tale of rescue that culminates with a Halloween banquet full of surprises! *USA Today* bestselling author Margaret Moore returns with her new Regency, *The Duke's Desire*—the story of reunited lovers who must suppress the flames of passion that threaten to destroy both their reputations. And in *Dryden's Bride,* a Medieval by Margo Maguire, a lively noblewoman en route to a convent takes a detour when she falls in love with a noble knight.

Whatever your taste in historicals, look for all four Harlequin Historicals at your nearby book outlet.

Sincerely,

Tracy Farrell
Senior Editor

TROUBLE
IN
PARADISE

LIZ IRELAND

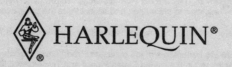
HARLEQUIN®

TORONTO • NEW YORK • LONDON
AMSTERDAM • PARIS • SYDNEY • HAMBURG
STOCKHOLM • ATHENS • TOKYO • MILAN • MADRID
PRAGUE • WARSAW • BUDAPEST • AUCKLAND

ISBN 0-373-29130-2

TROUBLE IN PARADISE

Visit us at www.eHarlequin.com

Printed in U.S.A.

Available from Harlequin Historicals and
LIZ IRELAND

Cecilia and the Stranger #286
Millie and the Fugitive #330
Prim and Improper #410
A Cowboy's Heart #466
The Outlaw's Bride #498
Trouble in Paradise #530

Other works include:

Silhouette Romance

Man Trap #963
The Birds and the Bees #988
Mom for a Week #1058

Please address questions and book requests to:
Harlequin Reader Service
U.S.: 3010 Walden Ave., P.O. Box 1325, Buffalo, NY 14269
Canadian: P.O. Box 609, Fort Erie, Ont. L2A 5X3

Prologue

New York City, 1892

Mrs. Louisa Sternhagen's large green eyes, which, in her youth, had been renowned for their pleasing appearance but now were protuberant in her aged, gaunt face, widened almost to popping when she realized, quite suddenly, one morning over her customary breakfast of coffee and dry toast, that her downstairs serving maid was *with child*. Quite!

"Good Lord!" the venerable woman exclaimed.

Since Mrs. Sternhagen wasn't one to mutter an oath even in front of servants, Ellie Fitzsimmons started in surprise, her quaking hands nearly dropping the weighty silver coffee service on her employer. She didn't have to look into the woman's face once more to know what exactly had caused Mrs. Sternhagen's outburst. A knot formed in the pit of her stomach. This was the moment she had been dreading for months.

"Heavens, Eleanor! What have you done?"

Placing the coffeepot down on the sideboard, Ellie turned back to her mistress, took a deep breath, and announced belatedly, "I'm going to have a baby, ma'am."

Mrs. Sternhagen paled. "I can see *that* for myself." Having recovered from the first blow of surprise, she reverted to the clipped tone she customarily used when addressing her servants. "You should have come to me sooner."

"Yes, ma'am." *So she could have the privilege of being sacked sooner,* Ellie thought, biting her tongue to keep from voicing the thought.

Silence stretched in the opulent dining room, broken only by the grandfather clock in the marble-floored hall chiming a quarter past eight. Ellie had no idea what to say next, but for some devilish reason, she had the terrible urge to giggle. Maybe it was the way Mrs. Sternhagen's thin lips puckered into a sour line of disapproval. The lady had never so strikingly resembled a bug-eyed old prune.

Finally, Mrs. Sternhagen took a sip of coffee and glanced up at her again. "And what are your plans, young woman?"

"Plans?" Ellie replied, blinking innocently.

"Yes, plans!" the old lady repeated impatiently. "Come, come. Don't you intend to find a father for your child?"

Ellie's cheeks heated with indignation. She had expected a lecture. She fully anticipated that she would be let go. But Mrs. Sternhagen couldn't be so obtuse that she didn't see what had happened under her own roof!

She squared her shoulders. If she was going to lose her job and, because she was live-in help, her home, she couldn't see the point in sparing her employer's feelings. "I had no trouble finding him, ma'am, since he lived under the same roof as me."

An iron-gray eyebrow shot up warningly. "Indeed?"

"Yes, but when I told him that he was going to be a father, he caught a sudden chill and decided to go on holiday to South Carolina."

Recognizing her son Percy's autumn itinerary, Mrs. Sternhagen froze. "Is this blackmail, miss?" she asked icily. "Because if it is, I warn you I'll have none of it."

Fury coursed through Ellie's veins. She looked down at the coffeepot, wishing now that she *had* spilled some burning liquid on the old biddy's lap. She had to keep her eyes focused on the Persian rug to calm herself. "I merely thought you might wish to be informed that you're going to have a grandchild."

"Outrageous impudence!" thundered the deep voice. It appeared the great lady might faint, but she soon gathered her breath and glared blisteringly back at Ellie. "I *have* grandchildren. Eight of them—my own flesh and blood."

"But—"

Before she could be given that lesson in biology, Mrs. Sternhagen continued, "Frankly, Eleanor, when you first came here, I was concerned. But you seemed intelligent, and quick enough. A little too dreamy, perhaps. I often worried where your mind was. Now I know. It was in the gutter."

Now Ellie feared *she* might faint. To be called "quick enough" by a woman who could barely write a bread-and-butter note without assistance was too much to bear. She had read twice as much, knew twice as much, as most of the guests who passed through the marble foyer! But then to be told that her mind was *in the gutter*...

Mrs. Sternhagen's expression turned unspeakably

grim, silencing Ellie before she could hurl the insult the old woman so richly deserved. ''This is a respectable house, Miss Fitzsimmons, and as such, there is no longer any place for you here.''

Chapter One

"It's a fine mess you've gone and got yourself in, Ellie," Mary O'Malley, one of Mrs. Sternhagen's upstairs maids, lectured. "Not that I couldn't see it comin'. First day you came around to the house, I says to myself, 'Lord, if that one ain't gonna cause herself a load of trouble, thinkin' she's better'n everyone else—with her books and her letter-writin' and her absentminded ways.' And that's just what you done, ain't it? Caused yourself a load of trouble!"

Ears already numb with lecturing, Ellie nodded. The only load she could think about at the moment was the one she was carrying in both hands. The two battered grips held all her possessions in the world, including beloved but weighty books that had belonged to her father. For a moment she blocked out the terrible cacophony on the busy street—most of it coming from Mary—by imagining what her favorite novelists might do with a character in her predicament. Say, Mr. Dickens or Victor Hugo. Then she shuddered. They would surely make her out to be one of those characters who came to a bad end—either washing up on a storm-tossed rocky shore, or worse, marrying some toothless old farmer who owned a deep well to toss herself down some blustery day. She tried to think about Anthony Trollope instead. Or better yet, Jane Austen. They might be a little kinder…or at least funnier. Everything was bearable if she could laugh, although right now she didn't feel like she had so much as a chuckle in her.

"And if you ask me," Mary said, "that coffee you spilt on Mrs. Sternhagen's finest Persian rug weren't no accident, neither!"

Ellie reluctantly pulled herself out of fiction and back to her real biography. She shrugged sheepishly. "I was upset, naturally…."

"Pride goeth before the fall, don't it? Lucky for you that I'm the charitable type," Mary rattled on, heedless of the dust kicked into their faces by a passing carriage. "Fergus and me's happy to help you. Your room's no more than a closet but I daresay you'll be lucky to be havin' it, since you won't be able to pay us nothin' and will likely be a terrible burden."

"I'll do what I can, Mary." But the promise rang hollow even to Ellie's own ears. She had little money saved, and what she did have would probably be gone before the baby came, no matter how tightly she economized. Mary was right. She *was* lucky someone would take her in for a little while, at least until she could find another situation.

But how was she going to achieve that feat? The only work she had ever done was as a domestic, but no decent family was going to take in a pregnant girl. She was lucky not to have her condition show too much, but a maid's uniform was not very forgiving. Besides, her potential employers would soon learn that she had been dismissed by old Louisa Sternhagen, and it would inevitably become known, in the way things always became public knowledge in the small world of New York society, that her downfall had been caused by a liaison with her ex-employer's son.

She would have to leave New York. But where would she go? Philadelphia? Things were probably no better there for a young woman with a child. She couldn't imagine anywhere being very promising. Except...

For a brief moment, her mind blotted out soot and dust and noise and she imagined the grassy rolling plains of a place far west, as they had been described to her in letters. Parker McMillan had written that Nebraska was a more informal place than the east. He'd also said there weren't too many spare women out west, which had to mean that practically any woman could find work there. Even a woman with a baby, perhaps.

"Here we are," Mary announced, steering Ellie into the door of a dreary brick building. Once inside, they were met by a dark narrow staircase.

"Top floor." Mary bustled up the stairs with barely a glance back at Ellie. "Lord, you look a thousand miles away!"

Ellie laughed. "I was."

Mary frowned her disapproval, as if laughter weren't allowed a fallen woman like Ellie. "Thinking about some fella, I suppose. As if you hadn't had enough trouble with men!"

Ellie stiffened defensively. "I only write to Mr. McMillan about cultural subjects."

"McMillan? Ha!" Mary rolled her eyes, obviously shocked that Ellie could be so misguided. "What would a *Scotsman* know about culture?"

Three flights later, they arrived at the O'Malley apartment, which felt nearly as gritty as the street had. The front room was narrow, with a kitchen stuffed right in the middle. Laundry hung on a line zig-zagging the room, assaulting the occupants with patched worn garments and gray drawers that made Ellie want to avert her face as she passed. Mary escorted Ellie to her "room," little more than a section of a hallway marked off by a cloth screen.

Mary gauged her reaction. "Don't like it, do you?" Her voice held a challenge.

Ellie shook her head, not wanting to be impolite, or to give Mary another chance to call her high and mighty. "No, no, it's very nice. I just…" She swallowed, feeling despair overwhelm her. "I think I might write a letter before supper."

"Letters!" Mary scoffed, retreating. "I might've known. Well, suit yourself—as long as you know dinner don't make itself!"

Ellie flopped onto the cot, sending a cloud of dust billowing up from the mattress. Dust or no dust, her living conditions would be easier to endure than Mary's charitable nagging. Wasting no time, she reached into one of her bags and found her writing paper.

Nebraska. She mouthed the word, familiarizing herself with the feel of it on her tongue. It sounded so foreign, so far away. Yet the name of the town was comforting. Paradise. What more could she ask for?

She could probably just scrape together enough money for a train ticket there, and even then she would probably have to sell some of her father's nicer books. She looked down at her bags and frowned. Her father's treasures, his legacy to her. They were practically all she had left of him. Her mother had died when she was still a baby, and her father, a coachman, had raised her in the tiny rooms furnished by his employers. These books had been his joy in life, his one extravagance, and they'd read them together. In a way, those pages had been their real home.

And yet she needed them now to provide for her own child.

Her child.... For a moment, she tried to imagine her own boy or girl, growing up somewhere unfettered by the strict rules that governed the society she knew. Why, in Nebraska it might not be so terrible not to have a father.

She shook her head. No place on earth was that unfettered!

But then again...who in Nebraska would have to know her child had no father? After all, even Parker McMillan, whom she had written to for almost a year in response to an advertisement in the paper seeking a correspondent on cultural subjects, knew very little about her. And what little he did know wasn't entirely accurate. When he had mistaken her for an educated lady of leisure after receiving her first letter with its impressive return address, she had embroidered her dull life with just enough fabulous detail to appeal to her own sense of fun, not to mention her love of fiction. She had never dreamed that she would actually meet Parker McMillan from Nebraska.

But there was absolutely no reason now, when her need was so desperate, that she couldn't embroider her tale just a little more. For instance, if she told him she was recently widowed...

"When you goin' to open that letter, Parker? Christmas?"

Ike Gray, tickled by his own wit—Christmas was nearly three months away—burst out laughing at what was supposed to be a joke, not caring that no one else joined in the merriment.

In truth, at the reminder of Parker's letter-writing

proclivities, Roy McMillan was annoyed. His younger brother always tightly guarded the mail he received from a certain New York City address, then pored over the letters by the fire after dinner. What the heck were he and that lady writing about all the time? Roy couldn't imagine. He himself had barely written five letters in his entire lifetime, and most of those had been for business. What could anyone have to say to a girl on paper, especially one who was a thousand miles away?

Parker, accustomed to their farmhand's ribbing, pushed his chair away from the dinner they'd just demolished, leaned back, and smiled broadly. "Is it my fault that I like to talk about other things besides hogs and wheat sometimes? Or that I have to go halfway across the continent to do it?"

Ike smiled broadly at Roy and winked. "You sure all you're doin' with this Eleanor woman is talkin', Parker?"

Roy scowled at the idea that it could be anything more. His brother's correspondence with a woman plumb across the country was his own business, but he hated to think of Parker getting carried away. For a McMillan man, Parker was uncommonly susceptible when it came to matters of the heart. All last winter, Roy had had to deal with Parker's moping over fickle Clara Trilby—and last winter had been unusually long and severe, giving Parker ample opportunity to stare endlessly into the fire, letting out occasional breathy lovesick moans. How irritating that had been! With November just weeks away, Roy certainly didn't care for a repeat of last year, especially if all that groaning was going to be over a woman Parker had never even clapped eyes on.

"Not like you can talk in a letter anyhow," Roy

pointed out. "Not really. It's certainly no way to carry on a romance."

Ike practically howled at that statement. "Since when were you a romance expert, Roy?"

Roy shrugged, perturbed. Whose side was Ike on? He'd been here last winter, too. Didn't he remember the *moaning?*

Besides, everybody knew the McMillans were a family of bachelors, with the singular, albeit vital, exception of Roy and Parker's father, whose marital gambit had turned out to be a disaster. The woman he'd married had been able to stand only five Nebraska winters before she'd bolted, leaving her husband and toddling babies behind. As far as Roy knew, their father had never heard from his mother again before he died three years later. Roy and Parker were subsequently reared by three bachelor uncles, and Roy could remember thinking, even as a boy, how companionable they all seemed, how much more free and happy their lives were than their father's short, disappointing life had been. Even now their last surviving uncle, Ed, was still living on the old McMillan homestead five miles away, alone and happy and productive, an example to them all of the joys of bachelor life.

Unfortunately, Parker appeared to forget the McMillan bachelor creed sometimes, opening himself up to unnecessary suffering.

Roy kept his gaze focused on Ike, but directed his words to his brother. "I just don't see the point in getting all tangled up with a woman in Paradise, much less one in New York City."

His brother's eyes, which could stare right through a person with disarming intensity, focused on him. "Then who was that gal I saw you all tangled up with at the Lalapalooza last Saturday?"

"You know what I meant," Roy replied curtly, squirming a little under his brother's gaze. "Saloon girls don't count."

"They'd count if you'd married one," Ike interjected. "Yessir, if you married one, she'd sure count."

"Well I'm not going to marry one," Roy replied.

"Wilber Whitestone did—that pretty yellow-haired girl named Marie." Ike crossed his arms as if he'd just won an argument.

Roy rolled his eyes. "But *I'm* not going to marry anybody."

Parker laughed. "Don't worry, Roy, I'm not embracing matrimony. Even if I wanted to, I doubt Miss Fitzsimmons would have me."

That assurance didn't soothe Roy any, either. In fact, it made him downright mad. "Why? Does this Fitzsimmons lady think she's too good for you?"

Parker shook his head. "She's not like that. But from what she's written me, I know that she lives pretty well. A big house in a neighborhood where all the richest people in New York live. You should hear the parties she's described—the food and the dancing and the people! Do you know that the Vanderbilt family visits her home?" He continued to shake his head, clearly impressed with such opulence. "A fine society lady wouldn't be interested in moving to a dusty four-room house in western Nebraska."

"Sounds pretty hopeless, all right," Ike admitted.

"Good," Roy said. "Women are more trouble than they're worth."

"I don't know…" Ike put in. "My mama was an awful hard worker, and so were my sisters. In fact, Roy, a woman can be a handy thing to have around the house. They can do all sorts of things that you probably never think about."

"Like what?"

"Well…they can cook, for instance."

"We can all cook just fine," Roy argued.

Ike and Parker's gazes subtly surveyed the remains of their dinner, which, incidentally, Roy had prepared. He knew what they were thinking. He himself had to admit that the corn bread had tasted leathery, and all right, he'd charred the ham a little. Personally, he *liked* that smokey flavor. The beans had come out mushy—but that was just because while he'd been cooking them, he'd also been working on sharpening the blade on the old plow. Time had gotten away from him.

"Most of the time, we do just fine," Roy reiterated.

"Oh, sure," Ike agreed. "Not to mention, it's folks like us what keep the indigestion-pill salesmen in business. But cooking aside, women can also mend things, and keep a house tidy, and help out with chickens and churn butter." His gaze took on a faraway look. "If you could have tasted my mama's butter…."

Several times a month they were treated to rhapsodies on the subject of Ike's sainted mama. At times like these, the only thing to do was either nod politely or change the subject.

Roy changed the subject. He still couldn't stop worrying about the highfalutin' female writing Parker letters. "If this Fitzsimmons woman is so busy with these Vanderbilts all the time, what's she writing to you for?"

Parker lifted his shoulders. "She's curious about the west, and she saw my advertisement for a correspondent. That's all. We talk about books, and music, and things of that nature."

Ike grinned. "Knowing this Miss Fitzsimmons is better than goin' to college, it sounds like."

"Much better," Parker agreed.

Parker had a reputation in Paradise of being something of a self-taught intellectual. He'd given a Fourth of July speech once on Thomas Jefferson that had impressed everyone it hadn't put to sleep. Roy didn't mind having an intellectual as a brother. He was proud of his little brother's smarts. A lovesick intellectual, however, was a trial. "As long as you're sure that's all there is to it."

Parker laughed. "Don't worry, Roy. The McMillan bachelor tradition will continue."

Ike scratched his scraggly beard and turned to Roy. "How long is this so-called tradition gonna last, if'n you and Parker don't have kids? Where's the next crop of bachelors supposed to come from?"

Parker looked over at Roy, a mischievous smile on his face. "He has a point, Roy. Looks like we're the end of the line."

Roy shifted uncomfortably, hating to be caught in a quandary. Not that it mattered one way or another to him about what happened to the McMillan line…except that there *was* the farm to take care of. He and Parker had worked hard to turn this parcel of land into something. Hard to think of it passing on to strangers after they were gone….

Quandaries! That's what came of letter-writing and gabbing at dinner about hypotheticals. "All I know is it's about time we finished yacking and decided who's going to clean up."

The three of them always decided that issue of dishwashing by a game of chance. And when it came to the nightly draw for the privilege of that chore, Roy was lucky and drew high. Pulling the ace of hearts off the top of the deck, he smiled broadly and let out a sigh. "Leisure at last," he gloated, propping his feet on the table as he watched his brother draw. Parker looked worried when he drew a five of clubs.

Roy's smile disappeared. Good Lord, was Parker so eager to read a letter that he couldn't spare a half hour?

Of course, *he* didn't want to clean up the supper dishes, either, and he didn't even have a letter waiting for him. Just a snooze in front of the fire.

"Oh, hellfire!" Ike cried as he slapped the three of hearts down on the table. "I've cleaned up the durned dishes three times this week!"

"Bad luck, Ike," Roy said, feeling little remorse for his good luck. "You want some help?"

"Heck, no," Ike replied quickly. Grumbling and arguing came naturally to the three men, but accepting help for work that was rightfully theirs wasn't their way. "I'll do 'em. I just wish my luck was a little better."

"It all averages in the end," Roy assured him philosophically. "Chances are that next month you won't have to do the dishes but once or twice."

"If'n one of you would marry, we wouldn't none of us have to do dishes ever again," Ike said.

Roy shook his head. "You're following a cold trail, Ike."

Parker, he noticed, didn't say anything.

Roy stood and followed his brother out of the kitchen into the sitting room. Parker was immediately absorbed in that letter. The fire had dwindled to a red glow, and Roy threw another log on, jumping back as the embers flew up.

"Good lord!"

Roy remained distracted by the new log, which he poked crossly with an iron, until he looked back at his brother. If shock had a face, it would have been Parker's.

"Is something wrong?" Roy asked, alarmed.

"She's coming here."

Their almost identical blue eyes met and held. *She* could only mean that Fitzsimmons woman—but that was impossible! "Here?" Roy asked, his voice a bullfrog croak. "To Nebraska?"

"Here," Parker corrected, "to *our house*. Mrs. Eleanor Fitzsimmons will be paying us a visit."

"Mrs?" Roy repeated. "You never said she was married."

"I never knew until just now."

That was peculiar. "Well why the heck doesn't she stay in New York with her husband where she belongs?"

"Her husband just died."

"A widow." Roy shuddered with dread. Widows were the most hazardous females there were. A man really had to be on his guard around widows. "B-but she can't come here!"

"But she is," his brother assured him.

"Oh, no," Roy said, gesticulating with his poker. "She can't do this. Where would we put her?"

Parker smiled, almost as if he found Roy's panic amusing. Amusing! "In the barn?"

Roy didn't appreciate the humor. Especially since, more likely than not, *he* would be the one sleeping in the barn. "Write her back and tell her…"

Smiling patiently, Parker waited for his suggestion.

Did he *want* the woman to come here? Roy couldn't tell. Sometimes Parker was hard to read. "Well, tell her it's not a good time. We've barely finished the corn harvest, and now we've got to get the sorghum cut. We don't have the leisure to mess with a woman!"

"I'm not sure the sorghum would hold much significance to a woman like Mrs. Fitzsimmons."

"Hell, I don't care. Tell her that the damned house burned down!"

Parker shook his head. "It doesn't matter. It's too late."

"Why?" Roy asked.

"Because by now she's left New York. According to the dates she gives in this letter, Mrs. Fitzsimmons is already on her way."

Chapter Two

"I knew there would be trouble," Roy grumbled, stomping his feet as he stood outside waiting for the train. A cold blast of air had rolled over the plains the day before, and the wind was bitter. There was no end of work to be done on the farm, yet here he was, one-half of the greeting party for some hare-brained society lady. "I knew there'd be trouble the minute you told me you were writing some woman you'd never even met before!"

Parker, unperturbed by the imminent invasion of their bachelor paradise, kept his eyes on the tracks. "You should have stayed home, Roy."

That had been unthinkable. He grumbled through his muffler. "I had some things I wanted to do in town."

A knowing smile crossed Parker's face. "And you wanted to get a gander at Mrs. Fitzsimmons."

Roy crossed his arms but said nothing. As if Eleanor Fitzsimmons wasn't going to look like every other woman in the world! He never had been one to be swayed by women anyway—especially rich, high-toned, pampered city women.

But Parker was. Take Clara Trilby. That girl was a

menace. Oh, maybe she wasn't rich like Mrs. Fitzsimmons, but she was the daughter of the most successful merchant in Paradise, and she put on airs as if she were a duchess. And she'd left Parker's battered and spent heart drowning in her wake.

"Admit it, Roy. You wanted to make certain Mrs. Fitzsimmons didn't drag me off to a preacher on the drive home."

"I won't even bother answering *that*," Roy said. Then, after a moment of silence, he couldn't help adding, "Your trouble is, you give women too much credit. I never met a woman yet who was half as interesting as a good poker game."

"You haven't met a girl outside of the kind you meet at the Lalapalooza in years, Roy," Parker pointed out. "Look, instead of fidgeting out here in the cold, why don't you go run your errands while I wait for Mrs. Fitzsimmons?"

"*Mrs.* Fitzsimmons!" That was another peculiar thing about this woman. Why had she chosen two days before her planned visit to announce to Parker in a letter that she was recently widowed? Why had she written to Parker for a year and omitted to mention the fact that she was a married woman? "You have to watch out for widows, you know. They're the real sneaky ones."

Parker nodded, pretending to soak in his brother's wisdom.

"They've had time to figure men out—and they aren't above using subterfuge to finagle another man into marrying them. Especially by using the pity card!"

"Of course you know all about widows," Parker said.

"Just look what happened to Al Drucker!" Roy reminded him. "*He* felt sorry for that one widow woman with four kids, and before he knew what hit him, she'd up and stolen all his money and run off to California to be with her lover, leaving Al with the four kids!''

"So it follows that Mrs. Fitzsimmons will be just that underhanded.'' Parker raised a brow at his brother and sent him one of those piercing gazes that unnerved Roy. "They aren't all like Mama, Roy.''

Roy recoiled, which was always his reaction when he heard his brother use this endearment in reference to the woman who had abandoned them. He barely remembered her—just her sweet, violet scent, her merry laugh, and the soft sound of her voice as she sang at night.

He shook the unsettling thoughts away, and turned back to the subject at hand. "I tell you, there's something fishy about Mrs. Fitzsimmons, and I intend to watch her. She isn't going to leave my sight for a moment.''

"Why, Roy, you sound downright intrigued.'' Parker laughed. "And you said all women were dull!''

"I didn't say they weren't crafty, though.''

A whistle sounded in the distance, and Parker walked over to his brother's side to watch the train's approach.

"She's bound to have quite a few bags with her,'' Parker said. "I'll bring the wagon around.''

The thought of the woman arriving with too many belongings panicked Roy. How long could she be planning to stay? He turned to stop his brother, but Parker was already out of earshot as the train chugged noisily toward the small depot.

Roy grumbled to himself. This was going to be a nuisance! What if Parker didn't get back in time? How was he supposed to pick out a woman he'd never even seen?

Not that Parker had ever seen her, either, he reminded himself, the ridiculousness of the situation hitting him square between the eyes. How were three bachelors supposed to entertain some New York lady? With winter coming on, no less! She'd go out of her mind within days. Or they would.

When the train's wheels screeched angrily against the tracks as the behemoth labored to a stop, Roy crossed his arms and waited with as much patience as he could muster. At least meeting Mrs. Fitzsimmons as she stepped off the train would allow him the opportunity to get a good gander at the woman before Parker did. The moment tenderhearted Parker saw the old widow, he was bound to offer her his heart and all his worldly possessions right there in the middle of the depot. This way Roy could study her, and see if she looked trustworthy. If she didn't, maybe he could still warn his brother against her somehow.

He squinted up at the doors of the passenger cars. Two women dressed in black stepped down from the train—two widows, wouldn't you know it, which didn't make his job any easier. One was short and youngish looking, the other was tall and older—or at least he *thought* she was older. She was wearing a veiled hat, so her age wasn't easy to discern. He looked back at shorty again and quickly dismissed her. The tall regal woman who was wearing a very stylishly cut coat was undoubtedly Queen Eleanor who hobnobbed with Vanderbilts.

He ambled forward and tipped his hat curtly at the woman. "Mrs. Fitzsimmons?"

A smile touched the woman's wide mouth, but at the sound of the name, the blue eyes behind the veil fogged, then blinked in confusion. "I beg your pardon?"

Her voice was low and sonorous—a nice voice.

Too bad it sounded completely bewildered. Plus she was staring at him strangely, as if he were crazy.

"Parker!" a voice trilled behind him.

Something tugged at his sleeve, and Roy spun on his boot heel, coming face to face with the other, younger lady, who was wrapped in a heavy cloak, with a hat and scarf covering her head. Actually, her face was nowhere near his. She was so petite she barely reached his shoulder.

"It's me—Eleanor!"

He froze, feeling for a moment that the breath had been knocked out of him. *This* was the cultured widow? For some reason, he hadn't expected someone so young. Or so pretty! Tendrils of vibrant red hair peeked out at him beneath the black shawl, framing a face whose perfectly creamy skin was highlighted by a pert upturned nose and the liveliest, greenest pair of eyes he'd ever seen. And she was so small—although her delicate figure remained hidden beneath her heavy outer garments.

She beamed a dazzling smile at him that made his insides flop over uncomfortably. He didn't know what to say to her. He couldn't speak.

"Parker McMillan!" she exclaimed again, still grinning.

Roy stood in front of her, transfixed. Why, Eleanor Fitzsimmons was little more than a girl! Twenty, twenty-two at most. And there wasn't anything particularly aristocratic or aloof about her appearance, which surprised him. As she stood bending slightly forward into the wind, holding on to the crown of her hat to keep it lodged atop her head, her cheeks glowed a healthy red from the brisk wind. Who would have thought Parker's Mrs. Fitzsimmons would turn out to be the most bewitching creature he'd ever laid eyes on?

Her pink lips turned down into a frown. "You *are* Mr. McMillan, aren't you, sir?"

He shook his head. She had a different accent, a careful way of speaking that he supposed went with being rich and cultured. Kind of the way he always imagined English people might speak.

Her frown turned to confusion. "You're not?" She paled. "Oh, heavens! I must apologize..."

"I mean—well, yes I am," he stammered, giving himself a mental slap. "But not the McMillan you were probably expecting. I'm Roy McMillan."

"Parker's brother!"

When her face broke out into another sunny smile that seemed to light up the gloomy October afternoon, he grinned helplessly and nodded. "That's it."

"Parker wrote me about you."

"He did?" He didn't know why it pleased him so that she remembered. Maybe because it was so pleasurable just to stare into beautiful eyes greener than a meadow in springtime.

"Nothing's happened to him, I hope?"

"To who?"

"To your brother."

"Oh, no," Roy assured her. "He's just pulling the wagon around." Remembering his manners, he added quickly, "May I hold your bags while we wait for the rest of your things?"

She blinked up at him. "The rest of my things?"

"Yes, your trunk."

She tossed her head and emitted a gay little laugh. "Oh, I travel light! These two are all I brought with me."

Roy took hold of the two aged leather bags sagging at her feet, surprised at how little they weighed. He'd expected a rich lady to haul around half her worldly goods with her. Which just went to show, Mrs. Fitzsimmons was not only pretty, she had a little sense, too. Of course, she had been married already. Even if she hadn't been married for long, a little of her husband's natural male practicality seemed to have worn off on her.

A widow! What a shame.

Of course, maybe she hadn't really been in love with her husband. He'd heard that rich families sometimes married off their daughters to other wealthy people just to make a good match, like farmers trying to improve the quality of their livestock. He shuddered to think of anything so degrading happening to Mrs. Fitzsimmons. *Eleanor.* What an odd, fussy name for such a lively girl. He wondered if people really called her Eleanor, or something shorter. Nora, maybe, or—

"Shall we wait here for Parker?" she asked.

Roy shook his head, berating himself for being so absentminded, but looking at Eleanor, he felt a little addlebrained, as if he were catching cold. "He'll be here soon."

"Is it a long ride back to your farm?"

"Almost an hour's ride, if you take it slow." He spoke slowly, concentrating.

"Oh, let's—I shall enjoy every minute of it!" She took a breath as if she were inhaling warm springtime air instead of the cold wet stuff that felt as if it might turn one's lungs to a solid chunk of ice. "I just love looking at the countryside!"

Roy squinted out at the expanse of brown earth and grass around them. Facing away from town, the view was almost completely unbroken by trees. Born in this land, he'd long since ceased to marvel over it, but most people when first set down in the prairie grassland became almost seasick from the relentlessly flat terrain. They couldn't see the wonders hidden there—hills hidden by the uniform grass, waterways that would snake through the landscape almost unseen until a person was right on them. "You like it here?" Disbelief rang in his tone.

"If you'd been surrounded by buildings all your life, you would relish the open space." She took another deep breath, which seemed to darken the roses in her cheeks. "It's so refreshing, so clean!"

Air was pretty much air in his book, but swept away by her expression of joy and awe, he took a deep breath, too, and was astonished. It *was* refreshing!

"It's cold here, though," he warned her. "You've come at a bad time." He heard his sentence hang in the air, saw the look of mortification that passed over her face, and hastened to add, "A bad time of year, I meant. We have mighty cold winters—but of course we're pleased to have you."

She laughed. "Thank you! With such a kind host, I couldn't mind the weather."

Her answer tickled him. What's more, he believed her words. He believed her because her eyes sparkled with pleasure, and because even as the wind seemed to bluster across the prairie for the sole purpose of wrapping its icy fingers around them, Eleanor smiled with enjoyment. Unconsciously, he felt a silly, joyful grin pull at his own lips.

"Only..." Her eyes glinted merrily. "If that brother of yours doesn't come *fairly* soon, I might turn to block ice like the man hawks on Second Avenue."

Roy didn't understand Second Avenue *or* ice men, but her joke nevertheless made him throw back his head and roar. Which was the first time in months he'd laughed so hard. Now he was glad he'd waited. The feeling was like a dam bursting.

He wondered whether she was always this way. A little of her would be a damn sight better than Ike's flaccid humor. She was a lot easier on the eye, too.

Eleanor turned her head, and her smile broadened. "And this…" She gestured forward with a woolen-gloved hand. "This must be Parker!"

Parker walked forward and Roy felt his wide smile freeze on his face. How had Parker gotten that wagon around so fast? For some unknown reason, he wished his brother had taken longer. He wanted to pull Eleanor aside and talk to her some more, just the two of them. Laugh with her. He wanted…he wanted to have just a few more moments in which he alone was the object of her attention.

Which was silly, of course. He would have plenty of time to talk to the woman back at the farm. Probably too much time. More likely than not, the sight of her red cheeks and dancing green eyes would begin to wear thin after a few days.

But for now…

For now, he saw his brother approach and felt stricken to the core when he realized how handsome Parker was. How his blue eyes sparked with intelligence, and how his smile was so open and friendly. Almost like Eleanor's. And his overcoat was much nicer than the old farm coat Roy had put on when he left the house in such haste to meet the train. Roy's coat was the same one he wore to feed livestock, and it looked it.

When Parker and Eleanor greeted each other, it was as old friends would. Parker took both her small hands in his and inspected her from tip to toe. "Why, Mrs. Fitzsimmons! Look at you!"

She laughed gaily. "Mr. McMillan! You're even more handsome than I suspected!"

And then they turned and, arm-in-arm, headed toward the wagon, already chattering together like intimate friends. Both seeming to have forgotten Roy completely. Behind them, he trudged along with the bags, biting his lip to hold back a scowl. There was no cause for the sharp stab of jealousy he felt in his chest, just as there was no reason at all for the gloominess that suddenly sank over him like a raincloud.

But reason had nothing to do with the lost, forlorn way he suddenly felt. He probably looked just like Parker had last winter when he'd been forsaken by fickle Clara Trilby. And for all the world, he felt like *moaning!*

"You'll have to excuse my brother," Parker said. "He can be a little distant with people sometimes. Especially women."

Ellie was puzzled as she watched Roy disappear into a feed store Parker had just stopped in front of. *Distant?* That word certainly didn't describe the Roy McMillan who had met her at the station—although he had been a little quiet since they'd been in the wagon. "Is he shy?" she asked, remembering the difficulty he'd had finding his voice after she'd stepped off the train.

Parker considered. "Not shy so much as suspicious."

Oh, dear. For the first time since reaching Paradise, she felt a prick of uneasiness.

So far her trip west had been nothing but pleasurable, despite having left the only city, the only life, she'd ever known, and despite an exhausting, bone-rattling train ride. She'd been filled with hope and full of plans. Some might have been intimidated by the less-than-deluxe conditions, or the sameness of the landscape, but as Ellie sat upright on her stiff seat last night, only fitfully sleepy, she'd felt her anxieties slipping away just like all the material possessions she'd left behind. The open landscape, as flat in places as a tabletop, with its ocean of brown, gold, and amber waving grass punctuated with lonely towns and even lonelier farms, embraced her with its openness.

And Paradise was just the bustling little town Parker had described. It didn't quite live up to its namesake, but there was a lot here for her to like. The low wood buildings that lined both sides of a deeply rutted dirt road gave off their own sense of majesty and importance. And after travelling so far from the previous stop on the train, and especially from Omaha— the only town of real size she'd seen in Nebraska— she could well imagine how essential each and every enterprise here was to the people who lived nearby. In fact, the area gave her the feeling that the skills of as many people as possible were needed to keep the hard soil tamed and carry on the miracle of civilization on an unforgiving prairie. Maybe now she would feel essential, too—not, as she was in New York, a maid to be used and tossed aside when she became inconvenient.

That last thought reminded her that she was coming to Nebraska—and accepting the McMillans' hospitality—under false pretenses. She had a few secrets that would be best kept hidden for as long as possible if she intended to forge a new life for herself, and for her baby, here. There was no reason anyone should find out that her child was illegitimate. She wasn't going to allow him or her to pay for her sin.

But if Roy McMillan was the suspicious type…

"Your brother seemed perfectly harmless to me," she said with a cautious smile. "Besides, I cannot imagine why anyone would be suspicious of me. I'm…well, just what I seem."

Parker grinned back at her. ''Just a pretty young widow from Park Avenue?''

At that moment, a cold gust of wind dissolved her smile into a tooth-chattering grimace. Ellie shivered, both from the cold and from Parker's description of her, which didn't suit her at all, she was afraid. Perhaps, at twenty, she could still be called young, but pretty? Her swelling belly, which she took pains to hide beneath petticoats and wraps and her coat, made her feel about as appealing as Ahab's white whale. And of course, she was no more a widow than she was Queen of England, and as for Park Avenue, the only reason she'd ever been tolerated there was for her ability to appear unobtrusively with food trays.

Parker stared at her, concerned. ''You're pale— would you like to go inside and get warm?''

She shuddered, thinking of the man's suspicious brother, and how easily he would see through her if he looked in her eyes now. ''Oh, no—I am p-perfectly fine.''

''Is that why your teeth are chattering? You must think I'm a barbarian for not insisting we go in earlier. Here,'' he said, and before she knew what was what, he'd climbed off the wagon and was pulling her down, too.

They went into the store, Homolka's Feed and Seed, and were immediately the object of all eyes. Three men in shapeless coveralls and coats hunched around a small stove, while Roy spoke to a man standing by a back door. The building itself, which seemed more cavernous on the inside with its high beam roof and stacks and stacks of filled sacks of seed, intimidated Ellie for some reason. Smelling the strange, musty odor of the place, she knew immediately that she was in foreign territory—and from the way the men gaped openly at her, *she* was considered the foreigner.

Her feet were rooted to the floor until Parker gave her a gentle tug forward.

"Joe, Cal, Tom—this is Mrs. Fitzsimmons. She's visiting us all the way from New York."

Parker's introduction caused the men's eyes to bug even more, and they stared at her now as if she were something especially exotic.

"New York!" one of the exclaimed. "That's a long way."

Ellie smiled. "Yes. Yes, it is," she began anxiously. "It's been a long journey, but now that I'm finally here, I don't feel a bit tired. It's so interesting to see the place Mr. McMillan described to me so perfectly. It seems I know each building as well as..."

"Park Avenue?" Parker finished for her.

As she looked into his eyes, so kind and sincere, her smile broadened even as her conscience pricked her. Her descriptions of New York had been accurate...which was more than she could say for her descriptions of herself.

And yet Parker McMillan had been far too modest about his own appearance. He was tall and straight and proud, with a shock of blond hair atop his head that showed beneath the brim of his black hat. He had blue eyes that shone with kindness and intelligence. Though his frame was slighter, his eyes and hair lighter, he was almost the spitting image of his handsome brother...except that for some reason, Roy was the one who drew her eye.

And when she looked at Roy now, he was staring straight back at her with an intensity that made her fear he could see straight through her smiling enthusiasm down to the deceit that lay behind it. She shivered, shuffled closer to the stove, and concentrated on warming her hands.

She would have to be careful around Roy McMillan. Very careful indeed.

A lot had changed in Paradise, Isabel Dotrice decided, and for the better. Though heaven knows it couldn't have gotten worse from the last time she'd seen it! Back then there was a trading post and a feed store and a muddy trench that served as a street between the two. Now there were all sorts of establishments—a dentist, a drugstore, a lawyer's office, a doctor and a mercantile. A church steeple and the cupola of a schoolhouse were the highest points in town and quite impressive in their modest way. A handsome brick edifice that proclaimed itself a hotel sat plop in the middle of this bustling community, and there were even a few buildings just built, standing idle, awaiting new commerce. She was most amazed to see a wire for a telephone stretched above Main Street.

All in all, *quite* different, and much improved.

Isabel took as much of the frigid air into her lungs as she could stand and let it out, smiling as her veil billowed away from her face. So far her journey had been very promising. Could things possibly work out as well as she dared to hope?

She strolled along the surprisingly clean woodplank sidewalk and peered curiously into storefronts, drawing many stares. Nebraskans always were nosy about strangers, she remembered now. She smiled back at them and kept right on walking, and even tossed a wink at the dentist as he gaped at her while he was supposed to be extracting a man's tooth. The look on his face made her giggle to herself—heaven knows she wouldn't want to be the man's patient!—

but she was stopped in midchuckle as she came upon just what she'd been hoping for.

It was a small two-story wood building with a particularly appealing front, whitewashed and with a cheery red door. Perfect. She did love red! Peering in the window, she saw that the first floor was divided into a front and back room, which would be absolutely suited to her purposes. To the right, a small staircase—little more than a ladder, really—led to the upstairs. Of course the interior was rather dark, and painfully plain, but what was she here for if not to bring a little sparkle? Goodness knows these poor people needed a little brightness in their drab lives as they tried to cling to their patch of civilization on the endless prairie.

She strolled over to the dry goods store and walked in, enjoying the bell as it jangled her arrival. She would have to get one of those. Oh, there was so much to be done!

A bespectacled man looked up from the counter where he was measuring out a bolt of cloth for a customer. "Help you?" he asked tersely. He eyed her closely and, because she was a stranger, a little distrustfully.

She smiled. "I hope so. I was wondering whom I should speak with to inquire about renting the empty building next door."

The man's scissors stopped in mid cut, and the three other people in the room, all women, turned to gape at her.

Isabel paid them no mind, only straightened a little taller and smiled more. She noticed the younger woman, a pretty blonde, eyeing her outfit with interest. Isabel's cashmere coat was cut in the latest fashion, fitted to cover her wasp-waisted travelling dress. The Paris magazines apparently hadn't reached Nebraska for a few decades. From the looks of things she wouldn't be a bit surprised to discover these women were still blundering around in crinolines beneath their full, bulky skirts.

"Well now," the proprietor said in a drawl that seemed achingly slow. "I guess you'd mean Lew Offerman's place."

"The door is flaming red," Isabel said.

"Yes, that's Offerman's, all right."

She'd forgotten these country folk sometimes needed a mental nudge. "Where may I find Mr. Offerman at this time of day?"

"I saw him a little while ago going into the feed store."

"Splendid! Thank you!"

She turned to leave, but couldn't help stopping to view the hat display, though display was an overly complimentary term for the drab straw contraptions and poke bonnets which drowsed forgotten on a wooden rack in a corner. The sight made her mournful and determined all at once. Such a waste of material, such a lack of imagination, such a horror to think of one of them actually atop a human head. She'd arrived just in time, apparently!

At that moment, a wagon with two fine horses leading it passed the store, drawing all the attention away from her.

"Who's *that?*" the pretty blond girl cried, running up to the picture window and nearly plastering herself against it most immodestly.

The two older women joined her at the window and watched as the threesome Isabel had observed at the depot with such interest trotted out of town.

"There's a woman riding with the McMillan brothers!" the youngest brayed unhappily.

"I didn't recognize her, did you, Cora?"

The other woman, who looked suspiciously like the blonde's mother, pursed her lips at the disappearing wagon. "No, I didn't. Now who do you think she is, and why would she be driving out toward the Mc-Millan farm?" Her tone was disapproving, as if the McMillan brothers might be up to no good with this unknown woman. Or maybe they thought the woman would somehow be a corrupting influence on two grown men. "She didn't look like kin to me."

"Could she be a housekeeper?" the other woman asked.

The blond girl frowned. "Housekeeper! What would three bachelors want with one of those?"

The two older women exchanged a meaningful glance.

"It's *very* peculiar—but those McMillan men never did hold with convention. I thought the younger ones would be different."

"Hmph!" Cora exclaimed. "After the way Parker treated poor Clara? I should think not!"

Fussy cats! Isabel could maintain her silence no longer, even though she hadn't the slightest idea what exactly had happened to poor Clara, or even who poor Clara was. This was a point of honor. "Excuse me, but I believe the young woman is a visitor from out of state who just came in on the train."

Three pairs of eyes swivelled toward her; the people seemed startled that she would know anything about the stranger, being a stranger herself. Only the youngest was bold enough to ask, "Visiting who? Do you know?"

"Parker McMillan, I believe. Though she seemed quite friendly with both boys." Although they could hardly be called boys anymore. Isabel suppressed a melancholy sigh. Where *did* the years scamper off to?

The poor young blond thing paled, then raised her

hands and buried her head in them in a stunningly theatrical manner. "Oh, Mama—did you hear? Parker!"

Cora, the blonde's mother, didn't seem so much surprised by her daughter's untoward display as by Isabel's knowledge of the men in question. "For a stranger here yourself, you sound as if you know the McMillan brothers quite well."

Isabel laughed. "Well, naturally! They're my sons."

And then she turned and left the women standing in stunned silence as the merry jingle bell over the door jangled her departure.

Chapter Three

"So, Mrs. Fitzsimmons," Ike asked, "how handy are you with a butter churn?"

Roy's fork clattered noisily to his plate. He picked it up with an embarrassed shrug as the others seated around the supper table stared at him, then he threw an annoyed glance at Ike. It was bad enough that a woman of Mrs. Fitzsimmons's social echelon had to endure Ike's leathery pot roast and boiled-beyond-recognition vegetables for dinner, not to mention the usual paean to his mama's butter, did she also have to be interviewed as if she were a potential house-keeper?

"I'm ashamed to say that I've never made butter," Eleanor admitted. Her sweet, cultured voice made the very words seem laughable. "I'm afraid I'm rather useless in the kitchen."

Roy bristled at her apologetic tone. This was no way to treat a guest, especially one who was probably used to talking about books, art and whatever else rich people talked about. He glared at Ike. "Of course she's useless—she's a lady."

Parker guffawed, and Eleanor raised her napkin to her lips to hide a grin. Roy's face heated. "What I meant was, I'm sure New York ladies have better things to do with their time than stoop over butter churns all day.'' Though just exactly what those better things would be, he had no clue.

"Well...I do know quite a bit about *running* a household," Eleanor said. "But the particulars of how each little thing is done often elude me."

"There," Roy said, a little triumphantly. "She's used to having servants around her."

Eleanor flushed modestly as her cheeks dimpled in a smile. "Indeed I am."

"My mama had a hired girl to do the washing once," Ike said, returning to his favorite subject—a field already overcultivated, in Roy's opinion. "But the gal burnt a petticoat and that was the end of that. Mama was very particular. Only she and my sisters did things just the way she wanted."

"Sometimes it's best to do things oneself," Eleanor agreed politely, the very soul of graciousness. "Your mother sounds like a very intelligent, capable woman."

Ike beamed across the table at her. "I'll say."

Roy pursed his lips with impatience for the meal to be at an end and to be away from Ike's ceaseless jabbering, which was getting on his nerves more than usual this evening. And why wasn't Parker, who knew all about the highfalutin' things Eleanor might find interesting, adding anything to the conversation? He and Eleanor had been walking outside all afternoon, chattering like magpies, but now that there were other people around, Parker was as tight-lipped as a clam. Anyone looking at them would think Roy was the only one at the table with any breeding.

Besides Mrs. Fitzsimmons, that is. She had quality stamped all over her.

"What is it you do exactly, Mrs. Fitzsimmons?"

Roy asked, trying to show the others how to engage
a lady in polite conversation.

Her head tilted toward him, but she didn't quite
look him in the eye. "Oh, I have…little pursuits."

"That sounds far too modest."

She smiled guardedly. "I'm afraid I'm only a
woman of modest accomplishments." Quickly, she
turned back to Ike. "Did you have many sisters, Mr.
Gray?"

"Just two, ma'am. Both of them are married now."

"How nice," Eleanor trilled.

"My mama's departed this earth, I'm sad to say."

"But she lives on in your memory, obviously. And
in the memory of her wonderful butter."

Roy squirmed indignantly. She sounded as if she
wanted to talk about Ike's mother! Even though Roy
had attempted to rescue her from that tiresome subject, she'd barely spared him a glance, or a smile. His
resentful gaze lit on Ike, who was yawping and grinning as he lapped up the lady's attention.

He frowned, considering. Maybe it was just that
Ike was something unique to her—a rustic, she might
call him. Or maybe she was just going out of her way
not to appear snobbish. He admired her for that.

"What a wonderful dinner, Mr. Gray," she said,
placing her folded napkin next to her plate. Roy hurriedly did the same.

Roy jumped in. "I built up a real cozy fire in the
other room for you, Mrs. Fitzsimmons. I'm sure you'd
enjoy sitting there and relaxing after your dinner."

She looked at him oddly. "Shouldn't we clean up
the dishes?"

Roy quickly put her straight on that score. "No,
ma'am. We always take care of that ourselves." Besides, he doubted a woman like herself knew a sink
from a pie safe.

"Oh, but surely I could do *something*."

He shook his head firmly. "You're our guest."

"But—"

"Being bachelors, we're used to the work," he assured her.

Ike jumped in. "We always draw after dinner to decide who does the chore, see."

Parker produced the old worn deck and shuffled the cards, then shoved them toward Ike. Ike picked a card—the three of spades—then tossed in down on the table. "Dadburnit!"

Roy suppressed a grin, envisioning a pleasant evening ahead. True, he'd never cared so much for the company of women, but Eleanor was a sensible female, and very easy on the eye. And while at least one of the others was otherwise occupied, maybe he could get a word in edgewise with her.

Parker drew the five of clubs, lightening Roy's heart even more.

Roy reached over to the deck—and drew the two of diamonds.

At first he couldn't believe it. *He* was the low card? Tonight of all nights?

"That's hard cheese, Roy-boy," Ike taunted. "Think this might be the start of that bad streak you kept tellin' me you were supposed to have?"

"I wouldn't count on it," Roy bit out.

"You want help?" Ike asked.

"No."

Parker turned to Eleanor, sending her a pleasant smile and ignoring Roy altogether. "Shall we go sit by Roy's fire? I believe we've got a nice bottle of brandy if you'd care to have any."

She clapped her hands in delight and stood. "That sounds marvelous."

The three of them practically skipped out of the kitchen in one happy cluster.

Roy stewed. Parker and Ike, sitting by his fire, drinking his brandy...

He almost added, *with his woman.*

Good lord! He needed to get a grip on himself. Obviously, his hospitable urges were getting the best of him. What did he care about Eleanor Fitzsimmons and a stupid fire? They lit a fire every night. And he'd probably have ample opportunity to sit around with the woman, since she hadn't so much as whispered a word about her departure date.

He harrumphed indignantly, stood and started clearing plates. Perhaps making a bit more clattering than was necessary, he threw himself into the chore, trying to lose himself in the tedious tasks of pumping water, heating it, then soaping down the dishes. There certainly were a lot of them—he *would* get stuck doing them when they had a guest!

Thinking of Eleanor this way—as an imposition— put him back in his normal frame of mind, and made him feel better. It also kept his mind from remembering eyes so green they took his breath away, hair like a fiery sunset, and a sweet voice that broke into laughter at the drop of a hat.

"I suspect you'll be comfortable out here," Ike told Roy. "And to tell you the truth, I'll enjoy the company. Gets kinda lonely out here at times."

The two men stood in the freezing cold little bunkroom in the barn, which was cramped for one person and a downright squeeze for two. There was barely room enough for the two bunks, Ike's things, and the little washbasin stand in the corner. "It will be cozy," Roy said without enthusiasm, shivering as he tested the hard straw mattress on the bunk. He looked over at Ike, who was already stripped down to his union suit and settling into his bunk with no fuss at all, and felt a new respect for the man. Roy didn't want to take his coat off, never mind his shirt.

Why didn't Ike keep a stove out here?

"What's the matter, Roy? Got the can't-sleeps?"

Roy gathered his courage, braced himself for misery, and stripped off his shirt. The shock was like taking a dive into the Platte in January. He sucked in his breath and jumped into bed, feeling that it would be easier now than ever to see Mrs. Fitzsimmons less as a pretty face than an infernal nuisance. He thought longingly of his own bed, with its soft feather tick mattress and warm woolen blankets. He'd even gotten carried away and wrapped warmed bricks in towels and put them at the foot of her bed, an action that seemed the height of folly now.

In his own room in the house, he had layers of blankets and thick warm sheets. Sometimes he woke up in the middle of the night so hot he had to kick covers off his bed. His teeth chattered frantically at the memory of such luxury.

"Cold, ain't it?" Ike asked, chuckling. "These early cold snaps always come as a shock." But Ike's teeth weren't clackety-clacking like a runaway train, and with nothing more than a tattered quilt over him he looked as comfy as an old boot. "My mama always said a cold bedroom made for a strong constitution, though. Guess you've noticed I rarely come down sick myself."

Oh lord, not Ike's mama again! Not while he was trying to sleep....

Roy suppressed a groan, flopped onto his side, and tried to think about something else besides the cold and how smelly, hard, and lumpy the bed was. The first thing that leapt to mind was Mrs. Fitzsimmons. Eleanor. *She* was probably cozy and warm in his bed.

In his bed…. He envisioned Eleanor there, probably in some kind of lacy nightgown imported from France, maybe, long hair brushed out and spread across his pillow like a river of mysterious red. Or maybe she braided her hair at night, like his mama used to.

Roy gulped. Heaven help him, one night in the barn and he was turning into Ike!

Not that Eleanor was a bit like what little he knew of his mother. Pampered lady or not, Eleanor seemed like a lady with a little gumption, and spirit. And yet there was a vulnerable quality about her. Something in the way she tilted her head sometimes, as if expecting a reprimand. Maybe that was left over from when she was a girl. He wouldn't be surprised to find out that she'd been a kid with a mischievous streak— he could still detect it in the sparkle in those green eyes, or in her easy laugh, or the wry way she would answer one of their many questions. He bet she was a girl who found life full of fun and adventure.

A woman, he corrected silently. She might have eyes that sparkled with youth, but she had a woman's face and a body that hinted at womanly curves beneath her modest attire. That was another thing he liked about her. She didn't run around flaunting herself, like, say, that Clara Trilby. Good lord! *That* girl could take a few lessons in modesty from Eleanor. Maybe it was because she was a widow. Eleanor didn't strike him as a schemer, like so many women her age. He bet there wasn't an ounce of guile in her, though a woman that pretty could certainly use her looks to twist men around her little finger. And she wasn't only beautiful in the conventional way Clara Trilby was, either. Eleanor had spice to her looks.

"What'd you say, Roy?"

Roy bolted up to his elbows and looked over at Ike. "I didn't say anything."

"Well never mind. I thought I heard you moaning or something."

Roy grunted in displeasure. "Who wouldn't moan when it's so damn cold in here? How do we know we won't be solid chunks of ice by morning?"

Ike laughed. "Listen to you—I haven't heard you complain like this since the price of wheat went down. Why did you volunteer to give the woman your room if you didn't want to be put out?"

Good question. Roy huddled unhappily on his bunk, trying to rationalize his foolishness. "Because it wouldn't have been right for me to be sleeping alone in the house with that woman."

Plus, after meeting her, he'd been eager to be the one to make the sacrifice for her. Showing off, he supposed. That's what women did to a man—made him make all sorts of silly Sir Galahad gestures for her—and where did a fellow end up for his pains?

Left out in the cold, that's where.

"How's it any more proper for her to be alone in the house with Parker?"

Roy stiffened. He'd never thought of that. Not that Parker was a wolf or anything near it, but he'd been writing the woman an awfully long time. All this time, he had probably dreamed of her, longed for the opportunity to meet her, and built up a passion for her. Maybe even an uncontrollable passion!

Ike shook his head. "A man and a woman…a cozy house…a blustery night…" Ike chuckled. "Who knows?"

It was all Roy could do not to go tearing across the path to the kitchen door right that second.

Instead, he counted to five, *then* shot out of the bed.

Ike sat up, startled. "Where're you going?"

"To get another blanket!" Roy shrugged on his coat over his underwear, not bothering with his shirt. "I'll be back."

He stomped through the barn, hopping over drying piles of corn shucks and trying to get a little circulation back in his feet, then scuttled across the pathway to the house, trepidation mounting as he ran against the icy wind. God only knows what he was going to find going on in there!

Eleanor sank into the soft warm bed and let out a breathy sigh. Luxury at last! After a week of enduring Mary's cot, then the hard seats of the train, Roy McMillan's bed was pure bliss. Especially since someone had been so thoughtful as to leave a bed warmer at the foot of the mattress for her. Who had done it, she wondered. Parker?

It couldn't have been Roy. She shivered a little, then burrowed a little farther under the woolen blankets at the memory of the icy looks he had sent her throughout dinner, not to mention the hostile glances he'd shot Ike for talking to her. And it was certainly no coincidence that the man had very loudly volunteered to sleep out in the barn rather than spend a night under the same roof as her.

Parker had been right to warn her. Roy disliked women, and he seemed especially to dislike her.

Strange, though, how nice he'd seemed at the station! What could account for the difference? Had she said something to make him suspicious?

Despite the cold, her cheeks heated with the misery of a guilty conscience. The trouble was, Roy McMillan was so right to have his doubts about her! Here she was basking in McMillan hospitality, and not a word she'd told them about herself was true. She wasn't wealthy, or married. Worse still, she was a fallen woman, carrying a baby without a father. What would they say if they found out about that?

Oh, she'd thought it would be so simple to live a fiction. After all, she'd always *imagined* herself as a lady of leisure; how else could she have endured the drudgery of being a housemaid? And she'd read so much about rich people in books. But now that she was supposed to be really filling the role of Mrs. Eleanor Fitzsimmons, rich widow, imagination escaped her. She hadn't been able to answer Roy's probing questions about how she filled her day, so she'd evaded him by focusing all her attention on Ike. Had Roy noticed? Was he piecing together her falsehoods?

Her heart thundered in trepidation. *Found out, found out, found out,* its insistent beats shouted in her ear. If Roy could see through her, how long would it be until the others did, or until he told them that she was a fake? She could only hope it would be long enough for her to get her feet on the ground and decide what she could do here in Nebraska. Paradise was a bustling, industrious little town. Surely there was some occupation she could fill there.

But what if there wasn't? What if she had a baby to feed and care for, and no one in Paradise needed a sales clerk or a maid or a seamstress? What alternative did that leave her but the most dreaded, oldest profession there was?

She shuddered, remembering the many seedy back-of-barroom brothels near the train depots of various towns. Just looking at them had made her feel filthy. And her miserable experience with Percy Sternhagen, consisting of an unpleasantly frantic coupling in the upstairs linen closet, certainly did not make her eager to repeat the experience with other, rougher men.

How could those unfortunate women by the railroad tracks stand it? Was there some trick that would make the attentions of greedy, heavy-breathing louts less sickening? Could an exchange of money make the coupling less vile? Or maybe if the act were performed *on* a bedsheet, instead of simply being pressed against them in a cupboard....

But surely, *surely,* it would never come to that. She would certainly do any kind of degrading work before prostitution became an option. She could be a laundress or a cook. She frowned, trying to remember the last time she'd successfully cooked anything on her own more complicated than a tin of beans. But she could learn, couldn't she? If men here were accustomed to eating the kind of tasteless boiled and burned mess she'd sampled tonight, could she do any worse?

The thought of only having to meet that low standard cheered her. This wasn't a time for panic, she reminded herself. She was beginning a new life—just as she was carrying new life. She hugged her rounded belly under the covers, trying to will herself into believing her fiction. She was a widow. Percy Sternhagen—who she would refer to now as Percy Fitzsimmons—was dead. That, at least, was a state of affairs she could savor playing to the hilt! She could tell the McMillans that her dear departed husband had made some bad investments, and that she now had to earn her bread. People, believing she was a widow, would feel sorry for her when her baby arrived. No one would look down on her child because he or she had no father. The baby wouldn't be branded as illegitimate.

A loud rap sounded at the door, and Ellie shot up to sitting. "Yes?"

In an instant, Roy McMillan bolted into her room,

his glaring eyes focused sharply on her. Then he stared around the room hungrily, as if looking for something. When his gaze came back to her, alone in the bed, where she'd pulled the covers up to her chin, she stared at him in mute bewilderment. He was wearing boots and the same long overcoat he'd worn at the depot, but peeking out from underneath were only red leggings that appeared to be some sort of nightclothes.

"I came for another blanket," he blurted out.

Ellie blinked at him, uncertain how this could pertain to her. "And?"

"It's in a box on the shelf." His gaze was still fixed on her. "I won't trouble you but for a minute."

Even a minute alone with Roy McMillan was too much in her book. "Should I call Parker?"

"Why?" His dark brows raised suspiciously.

"To help you, naturally."

"Oh." He seemed almost disappointed with her answer. "When did Parker go to bed?"

She shrugged. "A while ago, I believe."

He grunted, still seeming vaguely unsatisfied. "He usually stays up later."

"Maybe I've upset people's schedules," she said. "Though I hope not. Are you comfortable out in the...what do you call it?"

"Barn," he said flatly.

Oh dear. Parker had called it a bunkhouse or something, but Roy's description conjured up the image of him and Mr. Gray bedding down in adjoining stalls, right next to the milk cows. It certainly didn't sound very comfortable. "I'm afraid I've put you out."

His lips flattened into a thin line. "Not at all."

He turned, looking up at the long carved shelf that ran along the length of the room over seven feet up. On it, neatly stacked, were old books, a few periodicals and boxes of different sizes. At the end, there was a large wooden box. Roy focused on it.

"May I help you?" she asked, jumping out of bed. "I'm sure I could reach it."

His gaze fastened on her gown, making her cheeks glow with heat. *Why* had she gotten out of bed? She'd just hopped-to on practiced impulse—still a maid.

Only now she was a maid in her nightclothes, and Roy McMillan's burning gaze was pinned on her. His eyes roved from the cheap eyelet trim of her simple muslin gown up each cloth button until they reached her breasts, where his attention stalled. She could well imagine why! She flushed with embarrassment, wishing she'd gone ahead and buttoned her gown right up to the top, even though it felt as if she might choke when she did that. He probably thought her immodesty was appalling. She only prayed the gathered folds of her nightgown hid her six months' swollen belly, as well as the tears in the muslin that she had neatly patched.

She lifted her chin proudly, trying to recover a somewhat regal bearing, even if her gown was torn.

His dark eyes met hers. "How the hell is a puny little thing like you going to help me?"

Puny? She hadn't been called *that* since grammar school! "I could stand on a chair." Responding instinctively to the challenge, she pointed to a cane-back chair in the corner and ran over to it. "This chair."

He shook his head. "Never mind. I can reach it."

"It's no bother," she said, scooting past him efficiently. The sooner she got that blasted box down, the sooner Roy would be out of her bedroom. His bedroom. She felt a little twinge of uneasiness to think that she would be sleeping in his bed, a fact that hadn't seemed to register until she saw him staring at her in it. That slightly different scent, fragrantly musky, which she'd noticed when her head was on the pillow—that was his. The sheets and blankets that covered and warmed her were the same ones that also performed the same service for him. The realization made sleeping in his bed seem almost inappropriately intimate now.

He grabbed the top of the chair, sending her spinning toward him. "This isn't necessary, Eleanor."

"Actually, I'm usually called Ellie."

Now why had she blurted that out? A fine lady would never tell a man to call her a silly name like Ellie! Besides, she'd never even invited Parker to use the diminutive, and she'd been writing to him for months. She sputtered to correct herself, lifting her chin proudly. "I mean, I would be so happy if you wouldn't stand on formality."

His full lips quirked up for just a moment. "Why thank you, *Ellie,* but even without the formalities, I believe I'm capable of getting a box off a shelf. You're a guest here, not a servant."

She flushed. "I know that!"

Clutching the chair back to her chest, she stepped to the side, watching him as he reached up to get the box off the shelf. Unfortunately, it was pushed far back enough, and the shelf was just high enough, that it was a little beyond Roy's reach. Also, he seemed to be self-conscious about keeping his coat closed.

"Maybe if *you* took the chair…?" Ellie suggested.

He flicked a red-faced glance back to her. "I can manage."

"Or if you stood on tiptoe, that would help."

He replied with a noise that was more a grunt than an answer. "I think I…*oooph!*…can just about—"

With just the tips of his longest fingers he managed to pull the box forward till he could get a grip on it—

but by that time the box was tipping precariously on the edge of the high shelf. Ellie let out a cry of alarm and ran forward with her chair. It was only male pride keeping him from accepting help from her, and that was silly!

She sprang onto the chair and held one end of the box. "I've got it," she told him. "If you'll just let me hand it down to you—"

Just then, the door in front of Ellie banged open, hitting the chair and frightening her out of her wits. "Oh!" She cried in surprise and sprang straight up in the air like a startled cat, but when she came back down it was definitely not with feline grace. One foot lost the chair altogether and the other barely glanced down on the edge, so that the chair tipped away from where Roy was standing.

"Ooooh!" she cried again, realizing she was in trouble. Her right arm still was trying to keep hold of the silly box, while the other whirled in loopy circles in a doomed battle for balance. Roy's eyes rounded in surprise when they registered that she was about to tip over. Now he had a dilemma. He could keep hold of the box overhead, or he could rescue her from a nasty fall.

Chivalry was by no means dead in Paradise, Nebraska. With self-sacrifice Ellie thought worthy of the best of Walter Scott, he let go of the box and with both hands grabbed at her. Ellie, however, was already in midfall, so that all he was able to grab was a hank of hair and some nightgown, causing Ellie to yelp both in pain and at the sharp *rip!* of her gown tearing. Fortunately, Parker—who had been the cause of the door banging open—stepped inside in time to catch Ellie before she fell.

But poor Roy! His letting go of the box had dire consequences, since it placed him directly under the heavy wood container as it came crashing down, first hitting his head and sending him reeling backward to the floor, then finishing its path of destruction by banging even more forcefully on the toe of his boot.

Sprawled on the bare floor next to the fallen chair, he released a howl of pain.

"Oh, sir, I'm so sorry! Are you all right?" Ellie sprang to kneel next to him. She didn't even need to see his annoyed glare to realize how foolish a question she'd asked. His poor head—a bump the size of a goose egg was already lumping on his temple beneath the line of his hair. And yet it didn't seem to be his head that was bothering him. Or even his male pride, this time.

"My toe," he gritted out, wincing.

Ellie looked down at his boot, wondering if anything could have penetrated the thick leather.

"What in heaven's name is going on here?" Parker asked, looking down at the scene with concern and just a touch of amusement. "Roy!" he scolded gently. "I thought I could trust you!"

Roy scowled defensively. "I was just getting a blanket!"

Parker's brows rose in interest. "What's the matter with the one in the cedar chest in the parlor?"

Roy grimaced as he attempted to stand. "I forgot—ouch!"

Ellie threw a worried glance at Parker. "We'll have to get a doctor."

"No doctors!"

Parker laughed. "Roy can't stand Dr. Webster coming out."

"The man's an alarmist," Roy said. "He'll look at my bruised toe and order me to stay in bed for three months."

"Well maybe you should." Ellie's conscience

pricked her. None of this would have happened if he'd stayed in his own bed to begin with. "And I insist you stay here."

He looked up at her with a frown. "And have you sleep out in that igloo with Ike?"

Parker chuckled. "*I'll* stay with Ike. Ellie can stay in my room."

Roy frowned. "Don't mind me," he said, stumping past them. "I'll be just fine."

But when she was back in Roy's bed, breathing in the whisper of his scent, she began to worry again. Was he all right?

Then there was the problem of the blanket sitting in the cedar chest in the parlor.... Why had Roy really come in here in the first place—to check on her?

More troublesome still, when would he begin to wonder why a fine New York lady had called him *sir* precisely as a servant would?

Chapter Four

"**B**roken."

Dr. Webster's declaration was met by a moan from Roy—not just because the broken toe in question throbbed like the devil, but because he could just guess what the old sawbones was going to say next.

"What you need is bed rest," the doctor advised. "Plenty of it. Stay off that foot for a month."

"A month!" Roy bellowed. Even by Webster's dire standards, that was outrageous. There was work to be done. And though he didn't want to admit it to himself, he didn't want to spend the next two months hobbling around like a fool in front of Ellie.

He glanced up at her hovering in the doorway, looking as guilty as if she'd purposely caused the trunk to land on his foot, and felt his face redden. He should never have come into her bedroom last night, and not just because he regretted being in the accident. On the contrary, what he most regretted was the memory of Ellie that floated in his memory—her in her soft nightgown, unbuttoned enough that he could see the pale skin of her full breasts. Of her long red hair, loose and flowing, its curly tendrils all but inviting the touch of a man's hand. Most of all, he couldn't forget the way her pink lips parted in surprise when he appeared suddenly in her doorway. His toe didn't ache nearly so much as he ached to kiss those lips of hers.

Dr. Webster stood and patted Roy on the shoulder. "Don't worry, Roy. You'll be better by the time of the school dance."

Parker smirked. "As if Roy cares about that!"

Roy bristled and took pains not to glance over at Ellie again for her reaction. What was Parker trying to do, make him out to be some kind of barbarian? "I'll be back at work next week, Doc." He glared at Parker. "I'll be dancing next week, too, if I've a mind to."

This time he couldn't help tossing a look over at Ellie, just to make sure she realized that he wasn't as uncivilized as his brother had intimated. She smiled her encouragement at him, which made her appear girlishly sweet, even if her clothes would be more appropriate for an old schoolmarm. Her bulky black dress had a high neck that seemed austere for such a young beautiful woman, to say the least, and to make her look just a little more uncomfortable, she wore a loose black pinafore over the outfit. Her hair was pulled back in a tidy chignon, denying him the vision of it in its full blazing glory. But her lips—she couldn't tuck those away. They were pink and full, lips that seemed to beg a man's attention.

Ellie had been apologizing nonstop since the accident, despite his assurances that he didn't blame her one bit for the incident. And he didn't. But he couldn't say he minded all the attention that she'd lavished on him since then.

Today he'd been awakened by her bringing him hot coffee and a freshly warmed foot warmer. And all morning until the doctor arrived, she'd hovered nearby like a protective shadow, watching over him, but then skittering away before he could engage her in conversation. She was ever-present and yet maddeningly elusive.

Parker smiled at the doctor and took his arm. "Don't worry, Doc, Ike and I will see to it that my brother doesn't take up the ballet any time soon."

Roy scowled as the doctor, chuckling, was escorted from the room.

When they were gone, Ellie came up to the side of the bed where he was sitting. "We forgot to ask the doctor if he had something to ease your pain."

Roy barked out a laugh. "All Doc Webster would have done was hand me some little white pills and said to take two with a slug of whiskey. It's the whiskey that does the work, but Doc got snookered by a patent medicine man about a decade back, and he's been trying to get rid of those white pills ever since."

"Oh." She smoothed back a few of the loose tendrils of hair framing her face. "Would you like some whiskey, then?"

"No, I'm fine."

"Tea?"

He shook his head. "You don't have to play nurse, you know. I'm sure a lady of your station doesn't do things like that."

She blushed. "Well…I did take care of my father in his last days."

"Your father is dead?"

She nodded. "He was the only family I had."

Roy frowned. "Besides your husband."

"Oh yes!" She bit her lip and clasped her hands till her knuckles were white. "Dear Percy! I'll never forget his departure."

Her eyes fluttered closed for a moment, and Roy felt low as a worm for reminding her of her late husband. *Percy*. He felt an unwarranted dislike for the man. How could a fellow up and die when he had such a beautiful woman in love with him, depending on him?

"What happened to him?" he couldn't help asking.

"To whom?"

"Your husband. He must have been very young."

She looked stricken, and he immediately wished he could take back his words. "He...he...drowned."

Poor thing. She could barely get the sentence out.

"In New York City?"

Her fingers twiddled nervously. "No—it was during a vacation. In South Carolina. It was so sudden, and shocking, of course. Poor Percy—he prided himself on his swimming prowess, but I suppose no man is a match for the Atlantic's tide. Now the ocean is his grave."

"They never found him? He just disappeared?"

She shook her head. "No. I waited weeks and weeks. Months. It was hopeless."

Ellie lifted a hand to her eye. Even if she was wasting an outpouring of emotion on a man who, in Roy's admittedly biased opinion, probably didn't deserve it, he could only admire the depth and honesty of her grief. It showed a steadfast nature he didn't usually associate with members of the weaker sex.

Instinctively, he reached out to touch her other hand, to give comfort.

At his touch, Ellie jumped back as if she'd been burned by a cattle prod. "I'm so sorry! I didn't mean to become so mired in self-pity."

"That's all right. Your feelings are perfectly understandable." Then, gritting his teeth, he added, "I'd like to hear more about Percy Fitzsimmons, if you want to talk about him."

Her eyes rounded. "Oh no. I won't bore you with that—not that he wasn't a fascinating man..."

"What was his line?"

She blinked. "I beg your pardon?"

"Line of work."

"Well...he was in business. He had a factory."

Roy laughed. "You don't sound too sure of what your husband was doing with his days."

She licked her lips nervously. "Well, you see, I'm a little confused as to...well, some financial things. It seems Percy made some unwise investments...."

"What in?"

Her face had that frantic confused aspect of a person not used to discussing money. "Um, silver, I believe."

"Silver!" Roy laughed. "And he *lost* money?"

She swallowed. "Well, there was something about a mine...."

That explained it. The idiot had probably thrown his life savings into a mine scam. He frowned. This revelation coupled with Percy Fitzsimmons's death sounded rather suspicious. "Have you ever wondered about the veracity of this drowning story?"

She practically jumped, and he reached out a hand to hold her. "What do you mean?" she asked indignantly. "That I would lie?"

He shook his head frantically. "No, I only meant..." He softened his voice. "Well, have you ever considered that your husband might have been a...suicide?"

Her eyes widened. "You'll have to excuse me. This is a more painful subject than I anticipated."

"I'm sorry, I didn't mean to distress you."

"No, of course not. I'll get you some tea."

She backed out of the room so quickly he didn't have time to apologize again. What a thoughtless oaf he was—tossing out a shocking idea like suicide when she was already in low spirits. He wanted to call her back, to explain that he could very well be wrong....

"Eleanor? Ellie!"

But when the door opened again a few moments later, Parker walked through it. "Well, you were right," he announced.

Roy shifted, trying to adjust to the change in tone. "'Course I was. Why the minute old Doc Webster hears a sniffle he's ready to call it pneumonia. I'll be up and running again by tomorrow, I'll bet."

Parker tilted his head. "I wasn't referring to Doc Webster, I was talking about Eleanor."

"Ellie?" Roy frowned. At first he hadn't thought the diminutive suited her, but now he found he liked the sound of it.

Parker nodded. "I'll have to admit that I didn't believe you. I thought you were just bitter toward all women. But the minute I saw her last night I knew. She *is* a scheming widow."

Roy was so astounded by the bald statement that it took a moment for him to be certain he'd heard his brother correctly. Indignation made his backbone ramrod straight. "A scheming widow!" he repeated, incredulous. Parker—sweet, trusting Parker—was saying this about their guest? The woman who, for all intents and purposes, he himself had invited into their home?

Parker's brows arched. "Why so upset? You were the one who first called her that."

"That was before I'd even seen her, and I only said she *might* be." Roy felt anger rising within him. "I haven't seen any evidence of her being a schemer."

Parker crossed his arms. "What about the baby?"

"The what?"

"The baby she's carrying that she failed to inform either of us about. Don't tell me you didn't notice last night when you saw her in her nightgown."

He'd noticed no such thing! Roy sputtered. "I—I noticed she was a little plump. Surely you're mistaken."

Parker shook his head. "When I caught her—while you were tumbling to the floor—her nightgown outlined her figure. I've never seen a woman who was plump only in her belly. She's carrying a child, Roy."

Roy could only stare speechlessly at his brother for a long moment. Ellie. Pregnant. Of course he hadn't noticed—he'd only noticed her beauty. But now that he thought of it, she had been wearing rather bulky clothing, and the pinafore pinned over her dress today might have had a purpose besides protecting her clothes from all that coffee and tea she'd been serving him.

No wonder she'd been so touchy. She was a woman carrying a deceased man's child—and Roy had insulted the memory of her child's father!

He sighed. "Poor Ellie."

Parker's eyes narrowed. "Roy, are you sure you're feeling all right?"

His brother obviously expected him to be indignant that Ellie hadn't told them of her condition. Which just goes to show Parker didn't know him as well as he thought he did. "Think of it, Parker. She's all alone in the world with a baby to raise. And she just told me that her husband had been hornswoggled in a mining scam. What is she going to do?"

"Hasn't it occurred to you that *that* might be the reason why she came here?"

"What might be?"

"Marriage. To one of us."

Roy went still.

Parker shrugged. "Even Ike wondered this morning whether Ellie might have travelled this way to find a father for her baby."

Roy barked out a laugh. "That's the most preposterous thing I've ever heard. For your information, Ellie just ran out of here distraught because I brought up the subject of her late husband. She's obviously too devoted to his memory to marry again any time soon. Besides, she didn't tell me she was destitute…not completely. And if she did choose to marry for money, why in tarnation would she pick you to hitch up with when she could probably have a Vanderbilt?"

Parker looked perplexed. "I'm not sure."

"You're just not using your potato if you think that woman has designs on one of us!"

"You're being generous giving Eleanor the benefit of a doubt, Roy."

Roy bristled. "Naturally I'd be pretty riled up if I thought the woman had come here with an ulterior motive, but I'm just not so sure that's the case. Why, there are all sorts of reasons she might have chosen not to tell us about this baby. Maybe she needed to get out of town and she was afraid we wouldn't want her if we knew she was near motherhood."

Parker pursed his lips skeptically. "Why would she have to flee town?"

"Maybe the surroundings there reminded her of her husband and she couldn't go on living there. There could be all sorts of reasons! Besides, even an oaf like me knows that fine society ladies don't talk about intimate subjects like pregnancy, probably not even among themselves. So why should she feel the need to sound off about it to us?"

Parker nodded slowly. "I wondered if that was the situation."

"Well of course it is."

His brother's blue eyes focused on him intently. "You surprise me, Roy."

Roy tried to shrug off his brother's piercing gaze. Forget Ellie's ulterior motives. He was afraid Parker thought there was a reason he was defending her...aside from his understandable desire to be a good host. Which of course was all there was to it.

"Well for that matter, I'm not sure I'd want some woman bursting into song about some other man's baby growing in her belly," he grumbled. "Would you? Not that I'm squeamish, mind you, only it just doesn't seem...seemly."

Parker laughed. "Why, Roy—I never knew you had such delicate sensibilities!"

His cheeks heated and he sent his brother a thin-lipped glare. "Fine—go ask the woman if she's got something in the oven, Parker. Mortify the supposed friend who travelled halfway across the country to visit you."

"You're right," Parker said. "Shocked as I am to admit it."

"I guess I know about as much about good manners as the next person. We shouldn't be inhospitable to a guest."

"All right then," Parker said. "I'll tell Ike that we should just ignore the whole subject...as long as it can be ignored."

"Of course. Now that she's here, the least we can do is make her feel welcome."

When Parker left, Roy lay back against the pillows. The questions swirling around in his head exhausted him. Ellie was going to have a child? When? Why would she choose to visit a place as far removed from her world as Nebraska when it was so close to her time?

Oh, he had more doubts than he'd let on to Parker. For one thing, contrary to what he'd told his brother, he truly wondered whether Ellie hadn't come here hoping to find a new father for her baby—a possibility that upset him far more than he would have ever admitted to his brother. And not just because he thought it would be underhanded of her, either. Not at all.

He was more disturbed by the thought that for a prospective daddy Ellie might have already decided on Parker.

The doctor came again later in the day, but as far as Ellie could tell, he didn't even intend to look in on Roy; instead, he and Parker and Ike sat on the front stoop for a while, braving the still-blustery wind for some privacy.

She wondered if they were discussing her. After all, her arrival at the home of three bachelors was bound to have caused talk in town. Why hadn't she thought of that before? Staying under the same roof with three men probably wasn't going to endear her to Paradise society when she finally decided to settle in on her own. She'd noticed a nice-looking hotel in town; then again, she couldn't afford to stay in it.

Which was too bad, because it would be a relief to get away from the tension she felt here. She'd thought today might be easier, but the problem of living a lie was harder. She could have sworn Parker and Ike were eyeing her curiously this morning—but that was probably just because they'd been discussing the scene in Roy's bedroom last night. Maybe there was even doubt in their minds about what she and Roy had been doing.

And then there was Roy himself. Roy, who she felt oddly compelled to help, since she had been the cause of his accident. The trouble was, every time she went near him, she felt quivery and nervous under his gaze. It was as if he could see right through her.

All those questions he'd asked about her fictitious husband! She'd thought she'd die of mortification. Why hadn't she anticipated someone would ask her about how her husband died? Having invented her status as a widow, she should have been ready for those questions. Unfortunately, when the inevitable inquiry had come, all she'd been able to do was stutter out a story. How was she going to keep track of all the falsehoods she'd built around herself?

When Ike came in, she followed him into the kitchen. "What is it, Ike? Has there been talk in town?"

Ike's wide-eyed expression indicated the affirmative. "Boy-howdy, has there! That town is abuzz with gossip."

"About me?" she asked, afraid of the answer.

Ike laughed. "Good lord, no. What would they say about you?"

She shrugged. "Nothing, I guess…except that I'm a stranger."

"Well the lady that's the talk of the town right now ain't no stranger, that's for dang sure. She's Roy and Parker's ma!"

Ellie stared at him as he took a drink of cold coffee from the pot left on the stove this morning. "I don't understand."

"Mrs. McMillan—Mrs. Dotrice, she is now—left Paradise when Roy and Parker were just boys. Seems she didn't take a shine to our Nebraska winters or something like that. Plus there wasn't much here back then but buffalos and Indians. Not to mention all the white settlers lived in dugouts underground, like prairie dogs. This wasn't such a bustling place back then as it is now."

Ellie wondered what Ike would make of Mulberry Street in Manhattan, where new immigrants were packed into tenements like pickles in a barrel. "And their mother's been gone all this time?"

"Yes, ma'am. Hasn't seen her sons in upwards of twenty years. And not only that, she's been remarried and widowed again to a man in Philadelphia, Doc says. Parker's going back to town this evening to see her."

"What about Roy?"

Ike's face was an unreadable mask. "Parker doesn't think Roy's in any condition to see his ma."

It's true the trip would probably be painful for him, but didn't he deserve to visit with his only living parent as much as Parker? She frowned. "That doesn't seem right."

"I wouldn't worry my head about it none, Ellie. The McMillan boys have their own ways, and I've decided it's best just to say 'to each his own.'"

She crossed her arms, vaguely dissatisfied with that answer. "Still, it seems strange. Poor Roy."

Ike laughed. "He sure doesn't like to be sick. That's a fact."

Guilt swallowed her. "I feel so terrible about the accident. I've been trying all day to make amends, but…"

The farmhand shook his head. "Don't you worry. Nobody's blaming you for what happened."

She let out a sigh.

"You're just gettin' restless here, I'll bet. Tell you what. Tomorrow I've got to go into town. So if'n you want to come along and take in the sights, it would be pure pleasure for me to have you along."

Ellie was grateful for the invitation. She needed to

find out what kind of opportunity there would be in town for a widow with a baby. "Yes, I think I will go with you. Thank you for offering."

Ike blushed with satisfaction that she'd accepted his offer, which made her think perhaps she was just being overly suspicious when she'd feared Parker and Ike had been eyeing her strangely. If they had been looking at her in a way that was peculiar, perhaps it was because they weren't accustomed to having a woman in the house. That was a logical explanation, wasn't it?

Feeling better, she decided she needed to make herself useful. She wasn't used to being idle.

But of course, she didn't want to make herself *too* useful. That's how things had gone so impossibly awry the night before—her inability not to bustle about like a maid. But surely she could manage a few chores without raising any eyebrows.

She looked at the fresh-scrubbed kitchen cleaned by Parker just that morning and sighed. No work to be done here. When she went out into the parlor, she was further disturbed by the lack of untidiness there, too. She sighed, wondering what to do next, and decided it had been too long since she had checked on Roy—a prospect that made her heart skip irregularly.

Fear. That's what caused that odd racing sensation in her pulse at the thought of seeing Roy. Parker had warned her that Roy was suspicious of women, and the man had certainly proved himself to be more meddlesome than his younger brother. His appearance in her room last night was indication enough of his distrust of her.

Then again, there was something else in the way that he looked at her, especially when he didn't think she was watching him, that also made her wary. It was that look of masculine curiosity she'd been on the receiving end of on more than one occasion. Foremost in her mind among those times was the moment she'd first caught slick, handsome Percy Sternhagen's eye.

She didn't need any more attention of that nature from men in this lifetime!

And yet there was something about Roy that seemed very different from Percy. She couldn't put her finger on it. Certainly his probing blue eyes made her jittery in the same way—noodle-kneed and breathless.

But it was a small house and she couldn't avoid him forever. She went back to the kitchen, heated some coffee, and fixed a tray. When she rapped on his door, which had of course been Parker's door before she had arrived and sent the whole house topsy-turvy, her knock was met by his gruff voice.

As she entered the room, Roy, standing by his bed, met her with an expression that didn't ooze happiness at seeing her again. In fact, after a quick glance, he seemed to try to be avoiding looking at her at all.

"I'm not an invalid, you know," he grumbled.

She smiled in spite of his grumpy attitude. Better by far to be around a cranky man than a randy one. "The doctor said you're to stay in bed for a bit. I don't want you to dehydrate."

"Slim chance that could happen with you infusing me with liquids every hour."

She set the tray down and frowned. "You're welcome."

His pout made him look almost like a little boy. "I mean, thank you."

She laughed, and it seemed to her that when she did, a glimmer of attraction flared in his blue eyes. Something fluttered deep inside her, giving her the urge to giggle or prance like a foolish schoolgirl.

She fisted her hands and asked, "Is there anything else I can get for you?"

He grinned, and immediately she felt her mistake. Would she ever stop acting like a domestic? For years she had dreamed of escaping servitude, and now she couldn't seem to stop speaking like an upstairs maid.

"I'm the one who should be bringing you coffee. You're a guest, remember?"

"Oh." She shrugged. "So much has happened... I'm afraid I've been more of an irritant than a visitor."

He stared at her a long while, until she felt her cheeks blushing under his scrutiny. She should never have come into this room....

"Do you know what surprises me most about you, Ellie?"

Her gaze couldn't seem to pull away from his blue eyes. Funny, that eyes so like Parker's could affect her in a completely different way. "No." Her voice came out weak, breathy.

"You're so much the opposite of the grand lady I expected."

Her blush deepened still, and belatedly she did try to draw herself up as if she were that grand lady he'd expected. If only she weren't so small!

He laughed and picked up the coffee cup she'd brought him. "Don't get me wrong—I'm not disappointed. In fact, I was sort of dreading having a snooty old dame around the house. You aren't like that at all."

"Thank you." She attempted to walk past him, but he caught her arm and she spun, ending up closer to him than ever. Close enough that she could feel the warmth radiating from his chest, see his afternoon growth of beard along his strong jaw. Close enough that she could imagine how it would feel if he bent down and touched his lips to hers.

She closed her eyes for a moment, steeling herself against such terrible thoughts. Hadn't her experience in the linen closet with Percy taught her anything?

"I should go." But when she backed up, her knees hit the back of Roy's bed.

He steadied her from tripping with his one hand, and she realized suddenly how strong he was. Though he was just slightly taller than Percy, hard work—something Percy had never become acquainted with—had made his body strong, almost formidable.

"Why?"

She swallowed past the sandy dryness in her throat. "I shouldn't be in your…" Somehow, the word *bedroom* died in her throat, and so she just skipped over it. "Because, look, you're on your feet, when you should be lying in…"

He grinned. "Bed."

She nodded; perspiration beaded around her face. Her brow felt fiery hot, despite the fact that it was quite chilly in the house. He lifted a hand to touch a tendril of her hair—a gesture she remembered Percy making.

At that startling thought, she jumped back, accidentally hitting his arm with her hand. Coffee flew from his cup across his bedcovers. "Oh!" she cried, watching the liquid radiate a stain across the worn linens. "I'm so sorry!"

Roy frowned. "Never mind."

She backed quickly away, toward the door, toward escape. What had he been doing, touching her like that? Putting his hand to her hair wasn't just a friendly gesture! Had he been sincerely moved to do so, or was this just a more elaborate attempt to unmask her? Was there something about her that invited men to behave forwardly with her—or was he merely trying to see if she was the kind of woman who could be toyed with?

In other words, not a lady.

She redoubled her efforts to be a lady—the kind he was so surprised she didn't resemble—and drew herself up proudly, bugging her eyes much in the manner of her old employer, Louisa Sternhagen. No one would have ever caressed *her* hair!

"I'll get fresh linens for you," she said.

He looked annoyed. With himself, or with her?

Before she could discover the answer, she fled the room, returning minutes later with fresh bedcovers. "I hope these will do," she said, suddenly remembering that she was being maidish again. Louisa Sternhagen had probably never made a bed in her life. At that thought, she blinked innocently at Roy. "Do you know what to do with these?"

He was still scowling. "You mean you don't?"

She almost laughed. How wonderful it would be if she didn't! "Well...not exactly."

His lips twisted into a wry grin. "I guess you wouldn't. Well don't worry. I'll do it."

She smiled back at him as if there couldn't be too much starch in her drawers. "I'm sooo sorry, Roy. I seem always to be making a nuisance of myself."

"That's all right." But he didn't look like it was. His thwarted caress didn't appear to sit well with him.

"I know!" she exclaimed, clapping her hands together. "Tomorrow Ike's taking me into town. I'm going to bring you back a surprise."

He looked at her doubtfully. "What for?"

She laughed. "For fun, because you're sick, and because I'm such a bumbler, causing you to break your toe and have coffee in your sheets."

It would certainly make more sense to simply assuage her guilt for Roy's troubles with a present rather than trying to wait on him, which wasn't helping him or helping her maintain her ladylike facade. But if she gave him a small gift, perhaps she would appear gracious and they could let the whole matter drop. And she might be able to stop dreaming of being locked in a linen closet with Roy.

What could she get him, she wondered? What would she find in Paradise to offer him?

He seemed to be wondering the same thing. That glint was back in his eyes again. "I haven't received a surprise present since I was a boy."

She smiled, and this time managed to stay a safe distance away from him as she headed for the door. "Then I'll have to make sure it's an especially nice surprise, won't I?"

Chapter Five

Ike dropped Ellie off at the mercantile in Paradise without a word of warning as to the attention she might receive. Now as she browsed through the store, curious gazes tracked her movements as closely as a cat tracking the movements of a mouse.

Apparently her arrival at the McMillan house had become widely known and raised as much speculation as she had feared. Having so many eyes focused on her made her apprehensive. In New York, strangers were the rule, not the exception. She hadn't really deliberated on the steps required to insert herself into a smaller community; the steady stares made her realize, however, suddenly and with force, that her dreams of plopping herself into the middle of Paradise without any fuss were, like all her dreams, overly fanciful.

She sauntered along the displays as casually as she could, concentrating on the wares before her. Staring at the vast assortment of goods, however, just made her come to the depressing realization that even the simplest trinket was beyond her means. What kind of surprise could she buy Roy? In playing the part of a grand lady, she'd forgotten she still had a pauper's pocketbook. She had so little money, and what little she had she couldn't afford to waste.

She needed to find a direction; a job. But where in this town would she find a place for herself? As she and Ike had driven through town, she had seen no establishment that might need workers, except for the hotel, and the prospect of working there made her heart sag with dread. In her heart of hearts she had hoped to finally escape domestic servitude, but it appeared that she was even going to descend a rung on the ladder. All the years she'd worked in private homes, she'd heard derisive whispers from other servants about women who worked in hotels. According to some, it was akin to working in a brothel.

But if a position as a hotel maid was all that was open to her here, she would simply have to harden her resolve and set to it. A glare from a young blond woman behind the notions counter speeded Ellie's exit from the store, and she hurried down the sidewalk, her head bent into the cold wind, in the direction of the hotel.

Her heart felt as heavy as a solid chunk of iron. A maid. *That* would be a surprise for Roy—a surprise to all of them. How was she going to explain this sudden change in her circumstances? Even after the hint of her distressed financial circumstances she'd given Roy, the descent from fine lady to chambermaid was going to be a little difficult for her to explain without revealing that she had been a liar from the moment she first put pen to paper to correspond with Parker.

Oh, why hadn't she simply confessed her situation when she stepped off the train? Everything would have been so much simpler!

By eastern standards, the Paradise Hotel was no Waldorf-Astoria, but Ellie was impressed as she looked up at the two-story Italianate structure. Its red brick stood out from the rest of the town, which was mostly composed of wood buildings. She crossed the threshold anxiously, and found herself staring around an oak-panelled lobby in the center of which hung a large, elegant chandelier. Comfortable couches covered in plush red velvet stood next to marble-topped tables, and a large mahogany grandfather clock chimed the hour in the corner. Paradise, indeed!

For the first time, Ellie felt a little excitement at the prospect of working here. Having such fine surroundings would be a comfort, at least.

She walked up to the front desk, where a middle-aged man sat reading a newspaper—though he couldn't have been too absorbed, because he quickly put the paper aside when she walked up.

"Help you?" he asked in a friendly voice. "Are you staying in town?"

"N-no..." She felt suddenly awkward. "I'm staying with friends."

He squinted at her through his spectacles more critically. "I see. You're the McMillan's visitor."

She nodded. "Actually, I came here to inquire after a position."

He arched an eyebrow.

"A job," she elaborated.

Twisting his lips, the man reached forward, slapped his palm against a bell whose abrupt jangle nearly scared Ellie out of her wits, then returned to his newspaper. "Wait right there," he said without looking back up at her.

Ellie stood awkwardly in front of the counter, waiting for she knew not what. Then, suddenly, a tall, dark-haired woman wearing a severe black silk dress appeared before her. The woman had small eyes and a long nose, and her expression was pinched.

The man gestured toward Ellie, and the woman in black looked her up and down with such disdain that Ellie wondered how in heaven's name she was going to get through the ordeal of speaking to this woman. "Yes?"

She had expected a few pleasantries, but since she saw there would be no beating around the bush at all, she replied simply, "I was looking for a job. I was wondering if you might need a serving girl or a maid."

Lips that were already downturned puckered at her in further displeasure. "I'm sorry."

Ellie took a deep breath, sorely wishing that she were a foot taller so that this steely matron couldn't look down her pointy nose at her. "But mightn't you need more help sometime in the future?"

"I can't predict the future," the clipped voice replied.

There was one good thing about being so wholeheartedly dismissed, Ellie thought as she made her way back out onto the sidewalk. At least she hadn't had to confess to being pregnant, which she surely would have if the hotel manager had shown the slightest interest in hiring her.

But that was a cold comfort, and one that still left her with a mighty problem. How was she to earn her bread and support her child?

She was walking back to the mercantile to meet Ike when she was suddenly stopped by a friendly voice. "Oh! I was hoping to run into you!"

Startled, Ellie looked up and found herself gazing into a pair of familiar blue eyes. Only, the woman before her was completely unknown to her. "I beg your pardon?"

The woman's lips turned up in a whimsical smile.

"Yes, I forgot you wouldn't know me at all. I'm Isabel Dotrice."

This simple statement apparently was meant to clear up all confusion, but Ellie gaped at her in continued ignorance.

The woman laughed. "Roy and Parker's mother."

"Oh!" Ellie peered into the older woman's beautiful face with renewed interest. No wonder the eyes had seemed so familiar! They were Roy and Parker's exactly, as were her height and proud bearing. Her figure was slender and elegant, her dress tailored like something out of a French ladies' magazine. Isabel had perfectly straight white teeth that she flashed in a beaming smile, beautiful red cheeks and dark brown hair with just a hint of gray peeping out from under her stylish hat. Ellie might have thought she was in a dream, so incongruous was Roy's mother's graceful appearance on the dusty windswept street. It was like meeting a swan in a chicken coop.

"I saw you at the train depot my first day here," Isabel explained, easing into conversation as easily as if they were old friends instead of complete strangers. "Then, through the window of the mercantile, I saw you again. My dear, what a fuss you created!"

Ellie remembered Ike telling her that Isabel herself had created quite a bit of gossip; she wondered if the woman knew that. "I just came from the store, where everyone was staring. Apparently the fuss hasn't died down a bit." She frowned. "And just now, at the hotel, I met the strangest woman."

Isabel leaned closer and lowered her voice. "A pinched old crow of a woman?"

Ellie nodded. "Yes, exactly!"

Isabel laughed. "That's Tilda Archer. Don't pay her any mind. She's Munsie Warner's married sister—oh, but you wouldn't know who Munsie is, ei-

ther.'' Laughter bubbled from her lips. ''Well, for that
matter, I barely know them myself. Only the two sisters have been here forever and are both very stern
types. Tilda made the mistake of marrying and forced
her husband to build the hotel to keep him occupied.
But mostly it keeps her occupied, I believe. I know
she disapproves of me because I'm a divorcée.''

Ellie nodded, suddenly understanding. If word had
gotten out that she was a stranger staying at the Mc-
Millan farm…no telling what a town moralist might
make of that situation!

Isabel laughed again. ''Well it's a small world
here—these poor people have little enough to talk
about. Indeed, I count myself among the curious
horde now, too, because you've been on my mind
often since I've taken up citizenship in Paradise.''

''Oh, goodness, I don't see why—''

''I thought perhaps you might be engaged to one
of my sons,'' Isabel interrupted brusquely, ''but last
night Parker informed me that wasn't the case.''

''N-no,'' she stammered, blushing furiously. ''Of
course not!''

The older woman pursed her lips pleasantly. ''Pity.
Of course, a woman can't be in any hurry to be a
grandmother, but I thought you would do very well
for one of my boys.''

Ellie was astonished. The woman hardly knew her!
And did her comment about grandmotherhood indicate she knew about Ellie's condition? She was flustered almost beyond speech.

How could the woman possibly know what kind of
woman would ''do'' for either Roy or Parker, especially since she hadn't even spoken to Roy since her
return from an absence of over twenty years?

Ellie's mind fastened on this last fact for a moment,

and when she saw Ike's wagon driving toward the mercantile, she suddenly had an idea.

Others might say that Roy was in no condition for a visit from his mother, but wouldn't the best judge of his readiness be Roy himself?

"Are you ready for your surprise?"

Roy sat in the rocking chair by the fire in Parker's little room and looked up with pleasure when Ellie peeked in the doorway. Her cheeks were flushed from the cold, and she hadn't stopped long enough even to remove her scarf. For some ridiculous reason, it pleased him that she would be in such a hurry to deliver a surprise to him. Or that she had remembered her promise at all.

Heaven knows he himself had thought of little else since hearing Ike's wagon leave after breakfast. He sat up, smiled, and nodded.

"Close your eyes."

Releasing a long-suffering sigh, he did as told. It was silly how excited he felt; like a kid on Christmas morning.

For a moment the only sound in the room was the sound of light footsteps and the swish of skirts. Had Ellie gotten herself a new dress? That would certainly be a welcome surprise in light of those drab outfits she'd been wearing!

Suddenly, he caught a whiff of violets in the air— an extraordinarily familiar smell. Roy's breath hitched; his heart was racing before he could realize why. Hair on the back of his neck stood on end, heat flooded him, and his eyes flew open.

"Good lord!"

The words rushed out of his mouth. He could hardly believe his eyes. But it was *her;* there was no doubt in his mind about that. Seeing her was discon-

certing, as if she had just strolled casually out of the
past. His mother: older, perhaps, but in a way even
more beautiful than the boyish ideal he'd kept in his
memory over the years. His mother: smiling at him
as gently, as fondly, as if he were still a little boy
toddling about their cavelike old soddy.

She clasped her hands together, her brow suddenly
puckering in worry. "Roy, you hurt yourself! Are
they taking good care of you now?"

The voice was so startling—and yet suddenly he
realized that he'd seen this woman very recently.
When? "Who do you mean by *they?*" he asked, unable to keep the petulance out of his tone. "*We've*
both been taking care of ourselves for a good long
while."

She sent him a quizzical glance, jolting his memory.

"The railroad station!" he exclaimed.

She nodded and stepped closer; his scowl apparently stopped her in midstride, however. "Yes, that
was me—and now I detect you're mad at me for not
saying something then. Don't be, Roy. How could I
introduce myself when you were so obviously keen
on finding someone else?"

She tossed a glance back at Ellie standing silently
in the doorway. Roy redirected his scowl at her now.
This was her surprise? An awkward meeting with a
woman he'd rather not have come in contact with for
the rest of his life?

Catching his angry gaze, Ellie shrank back a step.

His mother made a *tsk*ing sound. "Roy, you always
were a mopey lad. That hasn't changed, I see."

His head was spinning. She dared to sashay into
his life after two decades' absence and call him a
mopey lad? Had she abandoned her children at tender
ages only to appear twenty years later expecting a gay

reunion? She'd left himself and Parker motherless and later to be raised by bachelor uncles after their bitter heartbroken wreck of a father died, and now she worried that he would be angry because she didn't say hello to him at the station? There were so many more important things to resent this woman for, the slight at the railroad station was a mere drop in the bucket!

"It's a wonder you've got nerve enough to speak to me at all," he gritted out.

At his venomous tone, she blinked. "You're angry, aren't you?"

Roy thought for a moment. The woman's blithe tone indicated she hadn't the slightest idea what she'd done, how her leaving had affected all of them. He wanted to choose his words carefully so she would realize that if she'd come here seeking an easy absolution, she was sorely mistaken. "The word *angry* couldn't possibly contain what I feel concerning what you did."

She nodded, absorbing his words, then her lips quirked up in memory. "You were always a serious boy, Roy. Such a grave outlook is rare in children, I think."

"Maybe I was so serious because I learned at an early age how untrustworthy people could be—especially women."

She shook her head. "Perhaps, but you were a solemn little boy long before I left you with your father. So somber, and yet no one could help loving you as much as if you were a laughing cherubic little thing!"

Her unflappability stunned him. If he hurled accusations, called her duplicitous and uncaring, vented all the rage in his heart at her, would it matter, or would all that rage slide off her like cracked egg oozing off a slick surface? What kind of metal was her heart made of that the strongest, hottest words couldn't make a dent in it?

"I can see you're crippled with regret," he bit out sarcastically.

"I certainly will be if we can't be friends, Roy. You may think I forgot you, but I never did. Your uncle Ed surely told you that."

Uncle Ed? His last bachelor uncle, who still lived out on the old McMillan homestead, had never mentioned his mother to him.

A cynical snort shook through him. *"Friends!"* he spat. "What could that word possibly mean to a woman like you?"

She cocked her head at him, making him notice the jaunty plume decorating the red velvet hat perched atop her head. "A great deal more than you realize, obviously."

Her patient smile irritated him. Had the woman no shame? He looked over to the doorway, seeking confirmation that he was dealing with an impossible woman, searching for a reason to think that all women weren't so duplicitous and callous, but Ellie had disappeared.

"Oh, Parker, I've made a horrible mistake!"

Parker grinned, poking the fire in the parlor aimlessly. "I was wondering how long it would take for you to figure that out."

Mortification was too kind a word for what she felt. "I thought you all felt that Roy was merely too sick to see his mother, not that he hated her!"

Parker looked questioningly at her. "Do you think he does?"

Could there be any doubt? "Why didn't someone say something?" Apparently Ike had been too amazed to point out she was making a huge blunder by inviting Isabel to the farm. "If I had only known…"

Parker shrugged. "What could I do? She was already here, and she seemed determined to see Roy." In that one unflappable gesture, Ellie could see that despite the years of separation, he was still his mother's son.

Hotheaded Roy, however, must have been cut from an entirely different bolt of cloth. "If you could have seen them together—it would have broken your heart!"

His dark blond brows raised in interest. "Don't tell me they had a tearful reunion."

"Just the opposite!" she exclaimed. "Roy was so brittle, and as for your mother—well! She didn't express a drop of remorse about having left you all. I could have cried. Roy was so unforgiving, and yet she didn't seem inclined to say one thing that would sway him, or express the tiniest morsel of regret."

He nodded, but looked a little puzzled. "What could she say?"

"She could tell him she was sorry!"

"And that would make up for two decades' absence?"

Ellie felt as if she were battering her head against a stone wall. "It might have been a start." Roy clearly needed that humbling expression of regret from her, and she didn't seem willing to give it. Ellie felt so for Roy, the whole situation made her want to scream.

Parker gazed at her patiently. "I think I'll see to tea for the guest," he said, turning toward the kitchen.

The coldness in the house racked Ellie's bones, and she moved closer to the hearth. Yet why should she be so involved in the lives of these people? Their familial relations should have meant nothing to her.

She, too, was raised motherless—because of death, not abandonment—but to her, that fact just made her love her father all the more dearly. As always, thoughts of her father warmed her. He'd given her so much; humor, a love of knowledge, endless kindness. Even if theirs was only a family of two, she was lucky to have belonged to it.

Footsteps approached from Roy's bedroom.

"Well, that's that!"

At the sound of Isabel's voice and the sight of the placid lift of her shoulders, Ellie thought for a moment that she would give the woman the tongue-lashing Roy had managed to restrain himself from giving her. But then she looked into Isabel's eyes, dark blue orbs shiny with sorrow, and she sensed that Isabel felt the sting of her son's iciness more than she had let on.

It wasn't only Roy she had hurt by bringing Isabel here.

"I'm so sorry!" she exclaimed, barely holding back tears as emotion flooded her once more.

"Don't be," Isabel said, smiling as she placed a hand upon her arm. Funny how she was so demonstrative and easy with a comparative stranger when she couldn't communicate with her own son. "That meeting had to happen, you know. And now, perhaps, things will go easier next time."

Next time! From the glower in Roy's eyes, Ellie couldn't imagine there being a next time.

Isabel smiled. "I think it's sweet that you're so worried about Roy, which is just why I hoped you were his intended. He might pretend to be a gruff old bear, but everyone needs an ally, I think." She smiled. "I had one once, and it helped more than I can say."

Ellie was once again baffled by the woman's musings. Who could she possibly be referring to—her first husband? Her second? God forbid, someone else? She sensed that whoever it was was a man. Isabel looked like a woman who would attract men like a flame would entice fluttering, misguided moths.

In fact, even Ellie felt compelled to like her. Her actions might seem callous, but when one looked into Isabel's eyes, it was hard to believe there wasn't good in her. Anyway, she was Roy's mother. Ellie would have done anything to have her father or mother brought back to her—why couldn't Roy be more forgiving?

"Perhaps Roy will come around, sooner or later," Ellie said. "He's just a bit…"

"Hard? Stubborn?" Isabel laughed. "Lord, yes. So was his father!"

This was the first description Ellie had heard of Roy and Parker's father. "He was like Roy?"

"Oh, my. There wasn't a bit of give in him. It's obvious Roy takes after him somewhat—but only somewhat, I hope." For the first time, she saw Isabel make a grave face. "That's why I had hoped he would fall in love early. With you, for instance."

Ellie sputtered incoherently before even managing to get the simplest word out. "Me?"

"Wouldn't that work best for everyone?" Isabel blinked. "Roy desperately needs someone to love, and you—if you don't mind my speaking frankly, Ellie—you obviously are in dire need of a husband with that baby on the way."

If embarrassment had a name, it was Eleanor Fitzsimmons. She'd feared that Isabel had known she was pregnant, but now that her suspicion was confirmed, she wished she could sink straight through the floor.

Isabel didn't seem to discern her discomfort with the whole subject. "The first moment I saw you, I thought you would provide just that soft touch Roy's always needed. And why shouldn't you marry Roy? He could provide well for you and your child—give you financial stability for the first time in your life.''

How did she know so much about Roy? About herself?

Ellie was stunned. ''But…'' Any inclination to draw up, play Park Avenue matron, and deny the statement, completely eluded her. Instead, she almost sagged with relief and spent ten minutes spilling her story to Isabel. The words just tumbled out of her. She didn't know why. Perhaps because she'd needed someone to talk to for so long—and there was something about Isabel that made Ellie believe that she would understand.

Isabel listened sympathetically, and nodded when she finished. ''Yes, I thought your background would be something like that.''

''How did you know?''

Isabel chuckled softly. ''My dear, that dress! Certainly, it's a cut above some of the rags these poor women around here wear, and the puffed sleeves are rather stylish, actually. But I could guess by the color and the simplicity that it was a maid's uniform, slightly disguised.''

''Oh, dear.'' And this was her *best* dress!

''Widows I have known,'' Isabel informed her, ''especially young ones, usually try to look their best. After the shock has worn off, of course. After the first month they'll come by my shop for a jaunty black outfit.''

''Is that what you are, a dressmaker?''

''And milliner. I intend to open a shop in Paradise.'' She looked critically at Ellie's bonnet. ''You might consider becoming one of my first customers.''

Ellie smiled. ''Would you consider hiring me as your first employee?''

Isabel shifted, her expression all business now. ''Do you have any experience making hats?''

Ellie shook her head. ''No, but I'm a fast learner.''

''Are you quick with a needle?''

Ellie swallowed, remembering all the crooked hems, loose buttons, and uneven cuffs she'd left trailing in her wake. ''Quick, yes.''

Her potential employer cocked her head. ''Have you ever worked as a seamstress?''

''No…''

''But you did mending for your previous employer, surely.''

Among the throngs of women working at the Sternhagen house, there had been many skilled seamstresses. ''Once or twice perhaps,'' she confessed, fearing opportunity was slipping away from her. ''But I've always mended for myself, as well as for my father while he was alive.''

Her poor father, trundling off to work with his clothes bunching at the seams!

Isabel smiled as kindly as she could. ''It's not very nice work anyway,'' she said in consolation. ''Think how much happier you'd be married to Roy.'' She shrugged. ''Or Parker.''

''Oh, but—''

Isabel patted her on the shoulder. ''You already have my blessing.''

''Yes, but—''

''And surely you want your baby to have a name?''

Ellie shuddered. ''You can't mean that I should set out to…well, to trick them!''

Isabel smiled, then straightened her trim coat jacket. ''In any case, marry one of them. Isn't that the logical thing for a woman in your position to do?''

Then, as if the subject had been thoroughly discussed and settled to her satisfaction, she turned to the kitchen. "Goodbye, Parker!"

By the time Parker could dash to the doorway, Isabel was gone, leaving only the cool wind from the opening and closing of the front door to let them know she'd been there, rather like a ghost would.

Parker glanced at Ellie, astonished. "I should give her a ride back to town."

Ellie nodded numbly. Isabel knew. How long before she told her sons all about their guest?

Or would she? Ellie wondered as she saw Parker scramble for his coat and speed out the door to catch up with his mother. Isabel wanted her to marry one of her sons. She wouldn't do anything to jeopardize what little chance there was of that actually happening.

Isabel was right in many respects. It was going to be terrible to have the baby by herself—and worse on the child than on herself. She'd thought perhaps the west might be more accepting of these things, but from the stares she'd received today, she realized that she'd moved to a smaller, more insular world where illegitimacy might be even more of a stigma. True, she had her false identity as a widow to hide behind—but if Isabel could see through that facade so quickly, wouldn't others as well?

But to marry just for the sake of necessity—she rebelled at the unromantic notion. She'd always assumed she would marry for love, like in books. Jane Eyre wouldn't have married Rochester for convenience.

Then again, Jane had steered clear of linen closets.

But it would never work! Even if her overly romantic nature didn't forbid marrying for the sake of convenience, what chance did she have of success?

The only man she had tried to win had fled the length of six states to avoid further contact with her. History hadn't shown her to be a precious marital commodity.

Or even a precious domestic commodity. She'd known of cases, of course, where servants were so valued for their skills that lapses in character could be forgiven. Wainright, the Sternhagen's irreplaceable butler, had also been at times the chief consumer of the Sternhagens' wine cellar. During lapses he kept his job by dint of the fact that he had been with Mr. Sternhagen since before his marriage, and therefore knew exactly what temperature the master liked his bath, what time he expected his nightly toddy, and to whom to say that Mr. Sternhagen was not at home.

That's what she needed to do. She needed to make herself irreplaceable.

"Ellie!"

Roy's call was almost a roar.

She hurried toward his bedroom.

"Yes?" she asked breathlessly at his threshold. "Is there anything I can do for you, Roy?"

His arms were crossed and he looked as angry as a bear. "You can drop the surprises from now on."

"I'm so sorry, Roy. I had no idea!"

"Neither did I!" He harrumphed, scrunching down into his chair as he brooded. "Did you hear what she said? Did you hear even the tiniest apology?"

She shook her head sadly. Now that she was back with Roy, it seemed impossible not to take his side in the matter. Yet she couldn't forget that prick of sympathy she'd felt for Isabel when they'd spoken in private. Nor could she forget the things Isabel had said to her.

Marry Roy, indeed! Right now Roy looked as if he never wanted to see another woman as long as he lived.

And yet he *had* called her into his room. He hadn't asked for Parker, or Ike…. Did Isabel sense something Ellie was too shortsighted to see herself?

"Well, of course it wasn't your fault, Ellie," Roy said. "You didn't know how things stood. It was Parker who should have told me she was in town."

"I'm sure he would have…eventually."

He laughed. "A fat lot of good that would have done me if I had run smack into her in town one day. I suppose I should thank you for not keeping me in ignorance."

She was thunderstruck. *Thank her?* He should have wanted to throttle her!

She tilted her head, regarding him more closely. Maybe Isabel wasn't so far off the mark. Maybe Roy and she…

She blinked, astonished at her thoughts. Oh, no! Roy was a crusty old bachelor, through and through.

But luckily for her, even crusty old bachelors needed housekeepers!

Chapter Six

Clara Trilby pretended to be tidying buttons while Doc Webster gave a detailed description to her parents of what exactly he'd seen at the McMillan farm.

"Oh, I suspect it's all innocent as can be, all right," the old doctor said, then added ominously, "for now. If you ask me, that New York widder woman's got one thing and one thing only on her mind—marrying one of those McMillan boys. Why she had to come all the way out here to catch a husband is beyond me. Except I heard she and Parker were writing heaps of letters to each other. Love letters, no doubt."

Clara's heart stopped. Love letters? *Oh, Parker!* It was too, too awful!

"And no doubt the McMillans would like to get their hands on all the money she's supposed to have," the doctor finished.

This was more distressing news to Clara. How could she compete with a New York woman—some rich vixen who'd already hooked one man and now had her sights set on Parker!

"Rich?" Cora's voice was full of disdain. "Rich in blarney, maybe! Munsie Warner was here earlier this morning and said that her sister told her that the Fitzsimmons woman had gone by the hotel looking for a job! Naturally Tilda turned her down cold. Said she didn't want any girl working in her hotel who was bold enough to take up residence with two bachelors and no chaperone!''

"Rich or poor, there'll be a wedding in that house by January, mark my words," Dr. Webster said. "Three bachelors, and a girl that pretty...?"

Clara feared she might pass out.

It just wasn't fair. Everyone knew Clara and Parker were going to be married!

Eventually...

Well. Maybe she herself was the only one who really knew it, but it was true nonetheless. That little tiff she'd had with Parker was just a slight snag in their relationship, and the fact that he hadn't spoken two words to her in nine months...well, every couple had little disagreements now and then. It was just natural. And theirs had been over such a silly thing!

She could just picture the scene now. Last November on a fine sunny Saturday they had gone on a romantic afternoon picnic together and were leaned up against a golden haystack, looking out at a little colony of prairie dogs nearby, standing at attention outside their homes. Parker had his arm around her, and she felt especially hopeful that something was going to happen between them, that they might become engaged. She was in love with Parker...and besides, her mother was getting very impatient with her to marry Leon O'Mara, the dentist, who she couldn't abide.

Feeling Parker's warmth next to her, she was flooded with hope. "Oh, Parker, don't you think those prairie dogs look so happy together, so...domestic?"

A girl had to hint every now and then, after all.

He'd nodded, making her heart patter against her

corset. "Sure do...sort of reminds me of Roy, Ike and me."

That had brought a troubled frown to Clara's face! "But you must get weary of having just Ike and Roy for company," she said. "I mean, you must enjoy talking to someone else or you wouldn't come visit me all the time. In fact, I have big plans for tomorrow. I was going to make fried chicken and—"

He cut her off. "I can't come to town tomorrow."

Parker went on to say that he didn't want to see her the next day because he had some work to do, and then he wanted to finish reading a book. *A book.* Just the memory of it made her blood boil afresh. The man had actually chosen a book over her! So she had told him that if he liked books better than her he might start trying to dance with a book and have a book make fried chicken for his picnics, because from now on she wasn't going to have anything to do with him.

What's more, she told Parker that if he was going to come all the way to see her just to say foolish things like he preferred books to her, he could just stop coming for visits altogether. In fact, she would be perfectly happy if he never spoke to her again!

And he hadn't.

And now he had a new woman hanging about him in his very house—a rich New York City woman, or else a grasping marriage-minded New York City woman, who, in either case, no doubt knew everything about everything.

"A redhead!" Mrs. Trilby exclaimed in disdain. "My good mother always says you shouldn't trust them." She threw a glance over at her daughter. "For heaven's sake, Clara—stand up straight or you'll bring down that whole button display. I swear you're sagging like a wilted sunflower."

Clara made a halfhearted effort to do as she was told. Her mother always wanted her to look her best because Leon O'Mara made daily stops at the store. Leon was nice enough, but he wasn't handsome like Parker. In fact, he was five and a half feet tall and looked like the slightest breeze would blow him over. He never talked about anything besides the weather and people's teeth. But she'd made the mistake of being nice to him once after Parker had abandoned her and she was just desperate for something eligible and male to talk to, and now Leon was as hard to shake as a cocklebur in her skirt hem.

Her mother clucked her tongue. "Of course I always did say Parker McMillan was a weak-willed sort of character. It's no surprise to me that he's let himself be twisted round the finger of some skinflint wily redhead."

Clara moaned.

Her mother looked at her sharply. "Good heavens, child, what's the matter with you!"

Clara was about to choke out a defense of Parker McMillan, when suddenly her mother's face brightened unnaturally. The bell at the store's entrance tinkled, and the older woman practically did a minuet as she hurried toward the door.

"Why, Mr. O'Mara! I was wondering when you'd drop by."

Clara spun on her heel and bolted behind the counter, where she bent to fiddle with her shoe.

Mrs. Trilby bustled over to Clara, grabbed her by the arm, and pulled her up to standing. "Look, Leon, here's Clara."

Clara smiled limply.

To her distress, Leon's eyes lit up when he looked at her, and he scurried forward, an anxious grin on his face. "Oh, good. I wanted to ask you to the dance, Clara," he blurted out unceremoniously.

Clara froze. "What dance?"

He frowned. "The autumn school dance, of course. This year it's to raise money for a library."

Lovely. More books!

"But Leon, that's over a month away!"

"I thought I'd better grab this opportunity. I wanted to ask you last year, but last year it seemed Parker McMillan had you reserved forever."

Oh, the wretchedness of having Leon O'Mara talking about Parker's abandoning her, right here in front of the doctor and her parents! Especially when her parents were so much more anxious for her to marry Leon than they had ever been about Parker. They were all colluding against her!

Gasping, Clara paled, turned on her heel, and bolted from the room. Oh, she knew it was rude, but she simply couldn't face talking to that man another minute—or worse, having her mother coerce her into going to the dance with him.

She simply had to do something to get Parker back, and avoid the terrible fate of becoming Clara O'Mara!

Overnight, it seemed to Roy, Ellie took over the house.

He wasn't quite sure how it happened. Or exactly when, even. Suddenly, however, he noted things getting done that one of the three men had heretofore had to do themselves. Eggs were gathered. Cows were milked twice a day. The house was kept spotless without any of them having to lift a feather duster.

A lot of this activity took place under Ike's tutelage, although the farmhand liked to brag on his pupil, saying that for a fine lady she took to housework like a duck took to water. Soon she was also cooking, baking up mouth-watering cornmeal batter bread in the morning, and biscuits and flapjacks. During the long days when they harvested sorghum, she managed the evening meals, too, albeit a little less successfully. Ike, so much needed in the fields, wasn't there to instruct her during the day. But as they often pointed out, nothing could taste worse than what they were used to cooking for themselves.

Ellie's new accomplishments made Roy uncomfortable on several fronts. He didn't like the idea of a fine lady visiting them being put to manual labor. It wasn't right, and he told Parker so. But even after they confronted her with the fact that she was a guest in their house and it reflected poorly on them to have her slaving away all day, she merely chirped that she enjoyed pitching in while she was there. She wanted to learn all she could about prairie life, she said.

But why? Roy wondered. Could it be that she had secret plans to become a prairie wife? That possibility made him anxious; he began watching Ellie and Parker together very closely. And watching them with something that felt suspiciously like jealousy.

The jealousy was silly, he knew—another result of his mother's brief visit. While she'd been here, after Ellie had left them alone in the room, Isabel had told him that she thought Parker and Ellie made a nice couple. A couple! She'd even gone on to say that Ellie would make a good *wife* for Parker.

The woman had the nerve to come waltzing back into their lives without so much as a howdy-do, then had the additional gall to start assigning them spouses!

Even now he had trouble containing his lingering ire. Not that he had any cause to be worked up over any imaginary union between Parker and Ellie. Because that's all it was—a figment of Isabel's imagination. Why, anybody with half a brain could see that Ellie and Parker were just friendly. He'd seen none of the warmth between Ellie and Parker as he'd witnessed between, say, Ike and Ellie. Yes, she was much friendlier toward Ike. And as a matter of fact, he had to admit—objectively, of course—that Ellie was even much friendlier toward himself. Naturally, having absented herself from their lives since he and Parker were barely out of diapers, Isabel wouldn't have noticed *that*.

Parker and Ellie!

Not that he was interested in giving up the bachelor life himself. Not at all. In fact, that was another reason Ellie's sudden interest in housekeeping rubbed his fur the wrong way. Instead of batching it happily, the three men were now becoming dependent on Ellie's help. Especially now, when Roy's damn toe still smarted like the dickens and he couldn't do half the work he was usually capable of, Ellie's work seemed like a gift, a godsend.

And that, too, made him uneasy. He couldn't help thinking that a woman's gift was usually of the Trojan-horse kind, and what looked too good to be true at first blush would actually turn out to be not such a bargain after all.

Yet this was Ellie...Ellie who he liked beyond all expectations. Whose laughter could bring a smile to his lips even when he was in one of his broody moods. Who had a household of grown men suddenly spending Saturday nights showing her how to pull taffy. He came home from the fields at night with a quick step, which quickened a little more when he discovered the chores that he'd so dreaded at the end of the day had been magically done. Horse stalls were filled with fresh hay. Pigs were slopped and watered. Chickens were fed their thick, sticky cornmeal.

The times he didn't look on her being here as a dangerous affliction, he thought of Ellie as something as a miracle. Despite his uneasiness, his heart beat lighter, faster. His limp had a skip in it when he least expected it. He hummed tunes he couldn't even remember hearing before.

And for the first time, he felt dangerously close to making a fool of himself over a woman.

They could only wait a few days after harvesting the sorghum to mill it into molasses, or the juice inside the stalks would go sour. So the miller, Tom Bartlett, was sent for, and two whole days were set aside for making enough of the dark syrup to sustain them through the next year.

The morning Bartlett arrived seemed positively festive to Ellie. Their daily routine would be disrupted completely, and for a few days, the men would be around the house, tending to this special chore. A city girl, she'd never known that such a simple thing as molasses could involve such intense labor. But she was beginning to understand that most of the things she'd bought in stores and had always taken for granted were actually the products of considerable toil.

The men had already spent several days stripping down the sorghum stalks; the discarded leaves stood in piles to be used later for animal bedding. The dark seed clusters had been lopped off and saved, too, the only part of the plant that would be used for feed, Ike had informed her.

Now the harvested stalks were being hauled to the front of the barn, where the mill was set up. The contraption, which was powered by an orbiting horse attached to a circular sweep, ground the cane stalks between several rollers and drained the resulting juice through a muslin strainer into a barrel. Ike and Parker tended to these tasks, including spreading the pressed, discarded stalks out to dry. Nothing would be wasted.

On the other side of the yard, outside the kitchen door, a boiler had been set up to cook the molasses, and Roy, still nursing his toe, had accepted the task of keeping the fire going and cooking the syrup.

"I could handle this," Ellie assured him, "if you just instructed me what to do."

At her suggestion, Roy shook his head adamantly. "It'll be easier for me to do it myself."

"I could learn."

When he looked up at her, his light brown hair blowing in the breeze warmed by the smokey fire, she felt a powerful pull toward those blue eyes of his. He'd been watching her often these past few days...why, she couldn't say. Half the time she felt something like a tug of attraction from him; other times, he seemed to view her much the way General Lee must have viewed General Grant. As if she were his natural enemy. The Yankee invader.

This wouldn't have been so terrible had she not found herself so attracted to him. She had tried to avoid acknowledging the strangely familiar feelings that welled inside her whenever Roy was nearby. She'd tried to keep her thoughts focussed on learning so much she would be irreplaceable to a household—maybe even this one.

But more often than not, those blue eyes defeated her, and she found herself drifting into a girlish, dreamy reverie in which Roy was Heathcliff to her Cathy, a dashing Ivanhoe to her Jewess healer, or Byron's Corsair to her lady in distress. Silly thoughts, unworthy of a woman mired in the reality of needing to prepare to support a child on her own. And yet the fantasies came anyway, no matter how hard she tried to concentrate on scrubbing and cooking and unfamiliar farm chores.

How much easier it would have been to keep her head on straight if Roy were older, with unsightly warts. Or if he looked at her with disdain *all* the time instead of only half!

"You've been learning a lot lately." His low voice suddenly sounded as sweet as the liquid bubbling in the boiler pan.

She tucked her shawl around her shoulders, attributing the little shiver that moved through her to the cool nip in the air. "I'm trying."

He grinned, then leaned down to toss another log into the fire. "Why, I wonder."

"I don't like to be useless when there are things to be done."

"And did you come all the way out to Nebraska to make yourself useful?"

"No," she answered truthfully. His questions made her uneasy. "I needed to get away...from the past."

He nodded, then, surprisingly, grinned. "And now our fine New York visitor is learning all about where molasses comes from."

He had the darnedest way of terrifying her with his suspicions, then reassuring her with that easy grin of his. She couldn't trust her instincts around him, and yet staying away from him proved impossible. In the mornings, he always seemed to be hovering somewhere near. In the evenings, he was always the first man back from the fields. He watched her like a hawk, but when she smiled at him, his expression would turn gentle.

No matter how much she tried putting the idea out of her mind, Isabel's words came back to her. *I hoped that you would do for Roy....* Foolish idea. Silly!

Right now the most she could hope for was to be Roy's housekeeper.

He skimmed foam off the top of the molasses with a wire attached to an old broom handle.

"I've enjoyed learning all these new things," she said truthfully as she watched him. Then she laughed. "It's you I feel sorry for."

He raised his golden-brown brows at her inquisitively. "Me, why?"

"Because you've had to put up with my failures. In a few short weeks I've ironed holes through your clothes, I've charred more food on that temperamental iron monster in the kitchen than I care to think about, food you've been kind enough to eat anyway, and I've angered the cows so with my inept milking skills that you're lucky Beulah and Lacy don't declare a worker's strike."

Roy laughed. "Don't go putting ideas into their heads. You spoil them like lapdogs already."

That was another thing she loved—all the animal life around her. Chickens, hogs, barn cats, mules, horses and milk cows. The industry to keep them all fed and milked and happy was enormous, but enormously enriching. She tried not to develop too much affection for the chickens and hogs, which she knew were doomed to be slaughtered, but Beulah and Lacy she felt free to treat like royalty. "Let me have my fun, Roy. I've always wanted a pet."

He frowned. "You've never had a dog?"

He made it sound as if she'd been thoroughly deprived. "No. I was always fond of my father's horses, of course…"

"You had a stable in the city?"

"Oh yes, a large one." She didn't add that she lived above it.

She looked down at the bubbling, darkening mass

for a moment. "There's no dog here," she pointed out. "Did you ever have one?"

He nodded sadly. "Pearly. She died a few years ago, and neither Parker nor myself had the heart to find a replacement."

She was surprised by Roy's somber tone, and began to wonder whether he hadn't been the brother most loath to find another dog to take Pearly's place. *Not a bit of give in him*….his mother had described Roy. But she didn't find him so unyielding. In fact, she found his attachment to his old animal friend very endearing.

He dipped a wooden spoon into the boiler pan and then held it out in the air to let it cool. He tested it with his finger, then licked the molasses off. "Mmm, nearly done." He held out the spoon to Ellie. "Want to give it a try?"

She came forward, eager to sample the fruits of the day's labor. He handed the spoon to her, and she followed his example, licking a little of the sweet still-warm liquid off her index finger. "That's good!"

He grinned. "You sound surprised."

"I am. I never expected it would taste so like…molasses."

"Why? The stuff you've been cooking with and pouring on biscuits in the morning was made here last year."

"Yes, but I wasn't there to see it start its life as a stalk in a field. You have to admit it's sort of a miracle."

Instead of answering her right away, he stared down at her, his eyes doing his speaking for him. There was laughter in them, and tenderness, even. She grinned up at him, and handed his spoon back to him.

Instead of taking it, however, his hand clasped down on her wrist, and he took a step forward. "I never was a big believer in miracles," he said, his husky voice raising gooseflesh on her arms. "But since you showed up here, all sorts of amazing ideas keep popping into my head."

A light brown lock of hair fell over his forehead as he looked down at her, and her mouth went dry as she suddenly realized how handsome he was. And how strong. He was standing close enough for her to gauge fully the power in his work-hardened muscles; he was also close enough for her to smell his particular masculine scent—the same scent he'd left imprinted on the pillows she slept on at night.

Ellie's pulse sped. She caught a glint in his eyes that she hadn't seen a man look at her with since Percy Sternhagen.

That thought, and the realization that Roy's gaze had strayed to her lips, made her mouth drop open with a gasp. Surely he wouldn't try to kiss her here, out in the open, where anyone could see them. Oh, dear! She didn't even want attentions of that nature—especially from a man she was hoping might be her employer someday soon!

A muffled cry of alarm escaped her lips and she jumped backward, dropping the wooden spoon into the dirt between them.

"Oh, no!" she said. "I'm so clumsy. I'll just run in and get another one—"

He held her fast for a moment. "Wait, Ellie."

She shook her head. "I'll be back in just a moment!"

"Hang the spoon—"

She finally managed to tug away and fled inside, praying that by the time she had to go back out, clearer heads would prevail.

Chapter Seven

For the rest of the molasses-making, clearer heads did prevail. And even for a day beyond. All the while, Ellie grappled with the problem of trying to impress Roy and ingratiate herself to him without appearing to flirt with him. She had heard that the way to a man's heart was through his stomach, and she was attempting that method, hoping that in this case his heart would eventually be sympathetic to the plight of a woman who needed to support a child.

Parker, she was fairly certain, would be agreeable to hiring her. Kind-hearted Ike, if he'd had a say in the matter, would have hired her himself weeks ago. But Roy…she still wasn't sure of him.

She'd gone out of her way to be nice to him, but keep him at a respectful distance. She'd never known a man who could put such foolish desires in her head with just a touch or a look, but there was something about Roy that made her forget her better judgment. And her better judgment told her that the last thing she needed was to succumb again to the charms of a man with the power to use her and toss her aside.

She turned, and as if conjured by her own fantasies, Roy appeared in the kitchen's doorway. She nearly dropped a sheet of cookies she'd been preparing to put in the oven.

"Are you all right?" she asked, fearing his foot might still be bothering him, or worse, that he had reinjured it.

"Of course."

Then why was he here? It was early afternoon yet. Besides, he looked uncomfortable. He held his hands awkwardly behind his back.

"Are you sure nothing's wrong?"

He stepped forward, a peculiar grin on his lips. "I wanted to be alone with you when I gave you your present."

She tossed her cookie sheet in the oven and wiped her hands on her apron. Present? So that's what this was all about. She suddenly felt giddy with anticipation. "What—?"

Just then, she heard a plaintive mewing and her heart fairly stopped in disbelief. Seeing that his surprise had been spoiled, that the cat was out of the bag, so to speak, Roy brought his hand forward.

Cupped in Roy's enormous palm was a tiny orange tabby kitten with round golden eyes. The little ball of fuzz blinked up at her and released a loud meow. Involuntarily, Ellie let out a high-pitched squeal of delight and ran forward to pet it. "Oh, Roy, how sweet! Where did you find it?"

"It belongs to the barn cat. She has several kits, but this is the only friendly one. The rest are skittery, like her."

Ellie grinned as he handed the little ball of fur over to her. The kitten immediately began to climb her dress up to her shoulder. She laughed. "She wants to be a parrot!"

"Maybe you should call her Polly."

She shook her head, but a few springy red curls

captured the kitten's attention and he began to bat at her hair. "You aren't really giving her to me, are you?" No one had ever done anything so thoughtful, so foolish. She couldn't have a cat. She didn't even have a home! And yet when she looked into those golden trusting eyes, she felt a fierce possessiveness for the little creature in her care.

And when she looked into Roy's warm blue eyes, their delight in her pleasure so baldly evident, she felt her legs go limp beneath her. She lowered to the floor to play with the kitten.

He chuckled. "You said you'd never had a pet. I had to remedy that."

"That's very thoughtful of you. But where will I keep it?"

"How about right here?"

She looked up at him sharply and felt her pulse begin to race. Sending the kitten scampering after a leaf Roy had brought in on his boots, Ellie stood and turned her attention back to the cookies. To her work. "If I don't watch out, these cookies will burn. I keep losing my concentration...."

He walked over to inspect the ones she'd just removed from the oven. "Oatmeal. My favorite."

"I know." The words came out, and she felt as if her face were on fire. "I mean...that's what Ike told me."

Roy grinned knowingly. "Lately, it's been hard for me to concentrate on my work, too. I keep getting sidetracked by my own thoughts."

At first her mouth felt too dry to speak. This close, his physique was very impressive, and the smell of work and the outdoors penetrated the cozy baking aroma in the air. "I often catch myself daydreaming," she said, a little haltingly. "I don't suppose there's any harm in it."

His brows raised high on his forehead. ''Isn't there?'' He grabbed her hand, sending a bolt of lightning through her. ''What if what you're dreaming about is kissing a woman you've no right to be thinking about?''

Her heart beat as quickly as a bird's as he gripped her arm and reeled her in toward him. In the surprise of the moment, she didn't think to resist; her own daydreams had been so focused on a moment such as this, both dreading it and dreaming about it, that she could hardly wait to feel the pressure of his lips against hers, to have his arms wrapped around her.

''Ellie, I know you're grieving…''

She blinked up at him. Grieving? He was so close she could feel the warmth emanating from his chest; they were just a hair away from an embrace, which is all her cloudy thoughts could concentrate on.

''Say any word and I'll stop this right now.'' The raw, husky whisper of his voice sent a shiver through her.

She wasn't certain whether he pulled her toward him or she simply sagged into his arms, but within a hair of a second the desired moment of her daydreams was being fulfilled. Roy's lips met hers, sending a wave of warmth through her. For an instant, she was terrified when she felt his bulk pressing against her and the strength of his arms, his chest, his legs' pressure against hers. The man was all brawn. And yet his lips, his hands, were gentle. He coaxed her lips with his tongue, seeking entrance.

As she opened her mouth to him, she felt as if her whole body came alive. She shimmied closer and snaked her arms around his neck, itself a mass of corded flesh. His thick bristly looking hair felt surprisingly soft as she threaded her fingers through it, pulling him closer to her. She was shocked at her own boldness, and at the force of this mere kiss. In a book it would have taken place on a stormswept sea, or the rocky moors, or in a dark moonlit setting, the air thick with the scent of night-blooming flowers. They were standing in the middle of a kitchen, the domestic air scented with nothing more romantic than baking cookies, and yet Roy's kiss transported her to all of those exotic places.

His large strong hands managed to both hold her fast and caress tenderly—her arms, her back, her hips. Her breath came faster, her head spinning with the sensations he stirred in her, and she suddenly recognized the heat building in her.

Desire. It swirled inside her, tempting and taunting, an old enemy she longed to embrace. *But this was different,* her mind told her, dismissing all the qualms she'd had for the past weeks. What she'd experienced with Percy Sternhagen was rushed and ugly; paradoxically, the best thing to come out of her encounter with him was the child within her. That baby might have driven her from her old life, but it had brought her here. To Paradise. To Roy.

His hand, which had been nestled on her hip, moved around slowly, and the very core of her womanhood seemed to turn liquid. She moaned, then felt his hand stop and massage her just below the waist of her dress. Just where her tummy protruded most.

The baby gave a little kick beneath his touch and she gasped, pulling back from him, but another arm against her back pinned her to him. She looked up into blue eyes burning so darkly she thought she could hardly bear it.

"You know," she said, wishing suddenly that he would stop, that he wouldn't touch her there. Her face was flaming, she was sure of that. She felt she was going to die of embarrassment.

"I've known for some time," he said, his voice still low, still husky.

Still seductive. She fought against a shiver moving through her and forced herself to meet his eye. "Ike and Parker?"

His lips turned down in a frown. "They know too."

She couldn't believe it! All of these weeks—probably from the very first—they'd known and hadn't let on. Confused, she twisted to free herself; Roy held her arm.

"What's wrong, Ellie? Don't you enjoy this?"

All her runaway emotions froze inside her. A shudder seemed to wrack her body as memories of Percy came back to her. *He'd* wanted to know if she'd enjoyed it, too; she hadn't, but she'd pretended to because she fancied herself in love with him. It didn't matter. He'd still cast her off like so much rubbish.

Now she was far from Percy, yet she still felt like an upstairs maid. Is that how Roy saw her? A thing to be enjoyed? Or maybe he thought her supposed lofty position would free him from any obligation. She'd always heard that widows were easy targets for male attentions. Instead of the flattery Percy had used, maybe Roy thought he could seduce her with little furry creatures.

But it didn't matter. She didn't have time to discern whether Roy's kisses were real expressions of affection or simply male play. Her attraction to Roy had nothing to do with her need to provide for her baby. If she was tossed out on her ear again…

Where could she go next?

She wrenched away from him. "I'm sorry—I can't—"

She shook her head, wanting to believe the dark-

ness in his eyes was genuine caring for her, not just
the annoyance of having his desires thwarted.

"I must go," she said, spinning on her heel. Then,
feeling foolish, awkward, and ashamed, she turned
back to him. She wanted to ask him never to take her
into his arms again, but the words wouldn't come.
Instead, she blurted out, "Please make sure the cookies don't burn!"

Followed by her furry new dependent, she ran out
to the chicken house to catch her breath and wonder
just why she always wound up living around men she
cared for, but shouldn't.

The woman was making him forget the McMillan
bachelor credo.

That fact alone was frightening. That Ellie reacted
to his kiss much as a lady might react to finding a
fuzzy black tarantula in her teacup only added to his
chagrin.

Roy walked gingerly down the windy Paradise
sidewalk, his footsteps taking him almost instinctively
toward the Lalapalooza. Never mind that it was ten
o'clock in the morning and he had no thirst for anything stronger than hot coffee. Never mind that it was
too early for any of his cronies to be there and up for
a companionable card game. Just breathing the heavy
air of stale cigar smoke and spilled whiskey was sure
to snap him out of the odd mood that had been plagu-
ing him lately. Also, there was a pretty young thing
working there, Flouncy, who had a figure certain to
make him forget all about Mrs. Eleanor Fitzsimmons.

He nearly laughed. In fact, he gave himself permission to go ahead and whoop real good. He, Roy
McMillan, chasing after an unwilling pregnant
widow? Wooing her with cuddly kittens and stolen
kisses in the kitchen? The notion was preposterous!

Let Parker have her, and good luck to him. As he always said, women were nothing but trouble. If he needed any evidence of how troublesome they were, he need go no further than the Paradise hotel, where his mother was staying. She hadn't belonged in Paradise, but his father had married her anyway—and look what had happened! She'd run out on them. Who was to say Ellie wasn't cut from the very same fickle cloth?

As if beckoned by the very word *cloth*, a bright bolt of fabric caught his eye. It was in the front window of Trilby's Mercantile, and he gravitated toward it as if drawn by a magnet. The heavy wool was woven in a colorful plaid of green and blue; the brightness caught his eye, and he couldn't help thinking how beautiful Eleanor's hair would look against it— maybe done up in a scarf or a hat. Her scarf was such a drab gray, it depressed him just to think about it.

His footsteps turned toward the mercantile's entrance, and when the bell jangled his arrival, he suddenly felt an excitement upon entering the establishment that he hadn't felt since he was a boy buying sticky peppermint candy. His eyes feasted on the store's contents as if they'd never seen the place before—so many different things, so much to buy! He headed toward the bolts of cloth only to be sidetracked by ribbons. Ellie didn't have any pretty hair ribbons.

And then there were also a few ready-made items, like stockings, that Ellie could surely use. She would need some warm stockings for the fierce winter ahead, and maybe a sturdier pair of boots, too. Trilby also had a pair of green velvet slippers that might come in handy for her, too....

Though he stood transfixed by the slippers, something stirred in the corner of his eye. He suddenly felt the strange sensation he'd experienced once when he'd looked up from working in a wheat field and seen a tornado bearing down on him; only this was no tornado, but Clara Trilby flying at him in a whirlwind of blond curls and frilly dress and heavy sobs. Too late, he stepped back. Clara launched herself at him and landed on his chest with a force that nearly knocked the stuffing out of him.

"Oh, Roy, oh, Roy!" she cried. "Isn't it just terrible? Isn't it simply tragic?"

He gasped for air. For a moment he thought he was wheezing; but that was Clara. Tears rolled down her cheeks and she could barely take in an even breath, she was so upset.

"What are you talking about?" he asked.

"That woman who's got her hooks into Parker!"

Roy froze—or he would have if Clara's sobs hadn't been shaking him. Good heavens, Clara Trilby was annoying! He'd almost forgotten how much he disliked her, and now she was clinging to him like a slug on a rain barrel. "Ellie?"

The name brought a fresh wail from his slug. "Oh, that awful woman! What on earth could Parker see in her? She's so *old!*"

Roy was so confused he could barely take it all in. "She's twenty."

Clara looked up at him with distrustful blue eyes, her lips in a pout. "Well, she looks older from a distance. And she's a widow!" Clara stomped her foot. "Why would Parker want a widow when he could have…well, someone young and unspoiled?"

Roy bit his lip to keep from barking out a laugh. *Young* Clara might be; *unspoiled,* however, was not the word he would have picked to describe her. In fact, she might be the single most pampered woman in Nebraska. Of course she might have used the word *unspoiled* in reference to her state of pristine virginity; he couldn't speak to that issue, thank heavens.

But he did feel an instinctive anger kicking in to hear Ellie maligned—not to mention coupled inseparably with his brother. "You've got it all wrong, Clara. There's nothing definite between Ellie and Parker."

For a moment a flicker of hope lit her eyes; but it was extinguished just as quickly. "But there will be, won't there? They're out there together in that little house of yours. That's what the doctor said. He said the two of them seemed real *companionable.*"

Did they?

She clucked her tongue, and was unable to keep a fresh tear from dripping down her cheeks and spilling onto his coat. "That's just what Parker always said he wanted—a *companion.*" She spoke the word as if it were a curse. "And now he's got one in his very own house! It's not fair!"

Roy's mind was racing, trying to remember just how companionable they were. Of course they talked together, and read, and played chess, and...

He gulped. Good lord—they *were* companionable!

Parker always said he wanted a companion? What an idiotic thing to look for in a woman!

Clara nodded miserably. "I'm sure Parker's going to marry her." Her chin wrinkled and quivered as she said the terrible words.

"That's preposterous!"

Unthinkable, even!

Clara looked up at him, blinking hopefully. "Am I wrong, Roy? Oh, please tell me I am!"

He frowned down at her. "You might be if you decide to do something about it."

"I'd do anything! Do you mean that Parker still cares for me?"

He tried to weigh his words carefully. "I believe he might still have a...yen."

She was jumping with excitement; unfortunately, she jumped right onto his sore toe.

"YEEEEOOOOOOOOWWW!"

Clara's hand lifted to her bow lips. "I'm sorry—did I hurt you?"

Roy hopped frantically backward—away from the blond menace—and at one point caught a glimpse of his purple face in a mirror. He grimaced in agony. "Oh no," he gritted out. "You just crushed my *already broken toe.*"

What an awful creature! Whatever could Parker have seen in her?

Clara fluttered forward, grabbing his arm. He had to keep from flinching away. She was fickle; she was vain and spoiled; she was in every way a complete ninny. But this female of his nightmares was also his one weapon against a romance between Ellie and Parker.

"Oooh, poor Roy," she cooed. "I'm so sorry. Would you like to sit down?"

He bit down on his lip—transferring a little of the pain from his toe northward—and leaned against the candy counter. He didn't know where the older Trilbys were, but he was grateful for this time alone with Clara, something he never thought he would be.

"Listen to me," he said. "Do you still have feelings for Parker? Genuine feelings for him?"

The question was absurd, of course. He couldn't imagine this woman loving his brother any more than she would love a new dress or pair of earbobs—but he had to at least make the effort to convince himself he wasn't acting completely out of self-interest.

She clasped her hands together. "Oh, yes! I love him!"

He had to keep from rolling his eyes. And yet he did feel a little sympathy for her. In fact, he was beginning to sympathize with all the hard-luck heartbroken sucker stories Ike was always dredging up on cold winter nights. He just hoped he wasn't about to become one himself.

"All right then. I've got a plan."

Her blue eyes widened, and she clapped her hands together. "Oh, Roy, how wonderful. I always knew you were more clever than everyone said you were!"

He twisted his lips, wondering one last time whether he could stand this woman as a relative. What if they had to live in the same house together? Were there especially stiff penalties for killing one's sister-in-law in the heat of anger?

Deciding it was a risk he would just have to take, he nodded ruefully. "Save your flattery for Parker."

Her eyes glistened. "When can I see him? Soon?"

"Is tomorrow soon enough for you?"

He was expecting her to squeal with joy; instead, she howled in outrage. "Tomorrow? I couldn't possibly!"

He was nearly dumbfounded. "Why on earth not? You just said you wanted to see him soon."

"But not *tomorrow!* I'm making a new dress and there's no hope of having it done by tomorrow. I've ordered the lace especially, and it won't be here till next week at the earliest."

Of all the cockeyed reasoning! Roy crossed his arm and shot her a warning glance. "And what if Parker and Eleanor elope before your lace gets here?"

She lifted her chin. "I do suppose I have some nice things Parker hasn't seen on me before."

"Good. Gussy yourself up and be sure to be at Whitman's Pond tomorrow at noon."

She frowned. "Whitman's Pond? That's in the middle of nowhere!"

"But, it's secluded. Private. You might even say, romantic," he told her.

Her lips slowly twisted into a grin. "Oh, Roy— you *are* smart!"

She hurled herself at him once again, and he squirmed uncomfortably to untangle himself from the horrible woman he was now praying would become his brother's wife.

Love must be in the air, Isabel decided as she peered into Trilby's Mercantile and saw her son embracing pretty Clara Trilby. What a bold lover he was! She hadn't pegged Roy for the overtly affectionate type, but you never could tell about these things. The two of them looked happy—that was the important thing.

She had honestly thought that Roy would favor Ellie, with her wonderful flaming hair. So dramatic! But it just went to show, didn't it, that love was unpredictable?

If anyone should know that, it was her. Her first husband she'd married young, for love, but it seemed that virtually overnight their marriage had turned sour. Fights broke out over matters large and small. The farm was isolated, and she felt, despite the fact that Abner's brothers lived with them, so alone. She was impatient and restless, but tried to make the best of things…until Abner turned violent.

First it was a slap. Or a shove when no one was looking. But his nastiness escalated.

Even then she'd stayed as long as she could. She'd blamed herself for angering him, for not being able to please him. But finally she'd had to face the fact that the man she had thought was so gallant and handsome was a wife-beater, and wasn't going to change.

Leaving had been the hardest decision of her life, especially since he wouldn't let her take the children. There were no courts to speak of in Nebraska at that time, and in any case no one would side with a woman who wanted to abandon her husband. If it hadn't been for Abner's brother, Ed, and his assurances that he would look after Roy and Parker, and keep them safe, she wasn't sure she would have been able to leave.

Of course, it had also been because of Ed, and because of her growing affection for him, that it was especially imperative that she leave Nebraska. Ed, so young and handsome, yet sensitive and sympathetic to her, had been her champion. He had made her smile on days when she didn't think she could get up in the morning. And he had made her feel appreciated, cherished almost, when Abner made her feel worthless. She'd fallen in love with him, and she half suspected he returned her love.

But to declare her feelings would have torn that house apart, and pitted brother against brother. Even if she and Ed had wanted to run away together, Abner, both for spite and because he seemed to genuinely care for his sons, wouldn't have let them take Roy and Parker. It was only the prospect that the boys would be under Ed's supervision that had made her able to leave them with Abner.

And so she'd left, and steeled herself to accept her hard choice, and tried to make the best of her life. But for years every morning she awoke wondering if the bargain she'd made—living without her sons and Ed, yet living—was worth its tithe in sorrow.

Her second husband she had cared for deeply but married for security, but after he was kicked by a horse, an accident that paralyzed him, she'd spent years supporting both of them, both in body and in spirit. Through the constant effort of trying to cheer him, to console him, she'd learned patience, and how to find reasons to be happy even when the reasons weren't always in evidence.

No, love had rarely turned out as she'd thought it would.

That thought made her frown. Now faced with the prospect of what she had hoped would be her third marriage, she found that she was as timid and confused as a flustered schoolgirl. How to start?

Of course, a part of her thought perhaps she should simply remain a singleton. Being a working widow had its appeal. It gave her a certain amount of freedom. And there was much she wanted to do—work, mostly, but she would also cherish the opportunity to finally spend more time with her boys.

She chuckled to herself. They certainly weren't boys anymore, but men on the verge of having their own wives and families. She was glad of that.

And maybe that's why she knew she wouldn't remain unmarried. Jolly as it was to be independent, she now had the opportunity to finally find what she'd always most wanted in her life—true, deep love. Not simply to be one of two, but to love another so much it would seem more like two as one. That's what she hoped for, at least.

She turned away from the mercantile and headed back toward her new house—she would be moving into it this week. And maybe when she had her home set up, she would work up the courage to make her move toward matrimony!

Chapter Eight

"A big tree branch fell in Whitman's Pond. Wind must have knocked it in." Roy stood in the middle of the living room, waiting for his brother to respond. When he didn't, he added emphatically, "Guess we should go pull it out."

Parker barely looked up from his book, which he and Ellie were taking turns reading aloud. Seated on opposite sides of the fire, they appeared, as Clara might have said, dangerously companionable.

"I suppose it will keep till later, won't it, Roy?"

Roy frowned. "I wouldn't want to wait too long. For instance, till afternoon."

Parker narrowed his gaze on him. "Is there some schedule for pulling limbs out of ponds that I'm not aware of?"

He was smirking. And what was worse, Ellie was also grinning at Roy as if he were being boyishly unreasonable. At the same time, she was twiddling her fingers, inciting the kitten in her lap to play.

Roy felt his cheeks heat. Granted, it was a Sunday, and he and his brother sometimes gave themselves a day of rest, but in emergencies they always did what needed to be done. "I would call a fine oak branch lying in the water going bad with winter coming on a circumstance that needs to be dealt with.'' He became so indignant as he spoke that he almost forgot the oak branch in question was purely a figment of his imagination. ''We'll be grateful for that branch come January.''

Parker began to stare at him as though Roy had lost his mind. ''Come January we won't remember whether our firewood stayed in a pond one day or two.''

Roy crossed his arms, barely holding back a churlish wave of irritation. He hadn't reckoned on Parker being so difficult. But now, as if the matter had been settled, Parker was back to reading to Ellie.

Ellie looked more beautiful than ever, with her hair braided around the green hair ribbons he'd bought for her yesterday at Trilby's Mercantile. He'd imagined—correctly—that the green would exactly match the color of her eyes. He'd held off on the plaid fabric, thinking that it would be a more suitable gift once they were better acquainted, but, daringly, he'd gone ahead and purchased the stockings and received a becoming blush when he'd given them to her.

He couldn't tell whether she was wearing the stockings today. Her skirts modestly covered the tops of her boots at all times. Maybe if they were outside…?

He grumbled to himself. Slim chance he would ever have of getting Ellie alone outside when she and Parker were so toasty here in the parlor! They looked as comfy as two peas in a pod, and that book they were reading was as thick as a dictionary. It would take them a coon's age to finish it. And unfortunately, it was an absorbing story. Roy had only been half listening yesterday evening as they read, yet all night long he'd been unable to keep his mind off the crazy tale of a woman who seemed to be in love with three men at once, none of them very suitable. And of course the silly heroine was bound to pick exactly the wrong one. Probably already had. People always did, it seemed.

He stood up quickly and stretched. "Well *I'm* going out to the pond." The announcement only caused a ripple of a disturbance in the dramatic reading.

"Whatever you think best, Roy," Parker said.

An indignant harrumph built in his throat, but he swallowed it back. His brother never would have spoken to him that way before Ellie's arrival. Oh, a woman changed things all right! More evidence that they should be avoided. But how could you avoid them when they were in the same house, serving as a corrupting influence, turning brother against brother?

How could you keep them from being so damned *companionable?*

With a melodramatic lift of his head, he stomped from the room, heading outside.

But once he did, he immediately regretted it. It was cold, and there was nowhere to go except to Whitman's Pond to meet Clara Trilby—a singularly unappetizing proposition.

There was no use trying to concentrate on Thomas Hardy. "I hope we haven't upset Roy," she said, interrupting Parker's reading in midparagraph.

"How?"

She felt silly bringing up the branch in the pond again—and yet Roy had seemed unnaturally irritated that Parker didn't want to go extricate it. "You don't think Roy would go to Whitman's Pond and pull the tree out himself, do you?"

Parker shrugged. "He might ask Ike."

"But Ike's not here."

Really, she was surprised at Parker! Since the weather had turned colder, and they'd started spending their free time reading by the fire, his personality had altered, and not for the better. He seemed more gloomy, less talkative, and oftentimes she'd catch him staring into the fire and swear there was something like a moan coming out of him.

"Oh, I forgot Ike went off to check on Uncle Ed," Parker said.

Ellie had heard about Uncle Ed in letters, but so far, this was the first mention of the older gentleman since she'd come to Nebraska. "His house is near here?"

"About five miles. Ike should be back by evening, no doubt with a wagonful of apples."

"Apples?"

Parker smiled. "You could say apples are Uncle Ed's vocation."

She smiled, uncertain what he was talking about—but she remained too preoccupied with Roy to question Parker more thoroughly about his uncle. "I hope Roy won't do anything foolish. It would be terrible if he reinjured his toe."

She was tempted to trot after him, but she didn't want to appear forward. Nor did she want to get them into another untenable position.

Perhaps after their kiss she should have left the McMillan farm. Although Roy had seemed apologetic, and even brought her gifts as a peace offering, including a warm pair of stockings she was thoroughly grateful for since she could ill afford them herself, she feared her remaining after their disgraceful conduct in the kitchen was leading him to have wrong ideas. People said all sorts of things about widows...especially in relation to bachelors.

And yet she was still faced with the same problems

as before. Money, money, and finally, lack of money. Other than that one kiss, the brothers had been so kind to her. And then there was the possibility that the kiss hadn't been an insult. Maybe he really was attracted to her. It was a possibility.

Unrealistic, perhaps. Unproductive, certainly. But tantalizing.

She wondered if she should approach Parker now about the possibility of her staying on as their housekeeper. She needed to say something soon. If she didn't, they would certainly begin wondering when she was going to leave. She had already been there a month—a long time for anyone to put up with a visitor.

And yet, with Roy so unpredictable and Parker so mournful and faraway looking, she wasn't sure how to broach the subject. She wasn't certain they would think she was irreplaceable.

She jumped up and began to pace restlessly, with Polly batting at her skirts as she passed. "I feel like taking a walk. Why don't you come with me?"

Parker shook his head. "No thank you."

"Are you sure?" she asked, wanting to make it absolutely clear that she wasn't going out to meet Roy. Which truly she didn't intend to do.

Not purposely, anyway.

"Don't worry—I won't read ahead while you're gone, Ellie."

She grinned, grateful that he wasn't making jokes about a rendezvous with Roy. "See that you don't! I'll be back soon anyway," she said, donning her coat. "Just going out for a stroll."

He laughed. "No destination in particular?"

She shook her head, realizing with sudden disappointment that this was in fact the truth. Even if she did want to accidentally bump into Roy, she didn't have the slightest notion where Whitman's Pond was.

Parker got up and poked at the fire. "If you'd enjoy a scenic view, you might try taking the path behind the barn."

She nodded. "Thank you."

As she walked out the door, she could have sworn she heard one of those moans.

Wrapping her coat around her against the cool wind, she strolled across to the barn, where she found the path Parker had spoken about. As she walked, her mind drifted back to that moment in time, so brief, when she'd found herself in Roy's arms. She shivered just at the memory of the swell of feeling his kiss had caused within her, and tightened her coat around her even though her brisk pace had taken the chill out of her bones.

But she had to be wary of Roy. She'd been so luckless in love, and Roy seemed so unpredictable; theirs was a bad combination. She didn't want to create a scandal in Paradise, the place she'd come to with the purpose of giving her baby a start with a clean reputation. Carrying on with Roy McMillan, without knowing his intentions, would be a sure way to tarnish that reputation.

For both her sake and the baby's, she needed to resist the temptation Roy posed and put him out of her mind.

As she arrived at that noble determination, she crested a swell in the landscape and took a deep breath, ready to set forth on a plan of romantic self-denial. So it was very surprising to her when she looked down the slope and saw a picturesque small pond surrounded by trees, and a man and a woman embracing. The romantic tableau was all the more stunning for the fact that the man was none other than

Roy! The woman he cradled in his arms she recognized vaguely as the pretty but hostile blonde from the store in Paradise.

For a moment she stood frozen, visually eavesdropping on what was apparently a very emotional moment between the two lovers. She was too far away to hear any of their conversation, but from the frantic way the woman clung to Roy, she guessed that this must be a reunion of some sort.

Fire seemed to circulate through her veins. Roy, the man who had bought her hair ribbons and stockings and given her a kitten, who had kissed her so passionately, the man who half a minute ago she'd vowed with such self-sacrifice to renounce, was standing before her in an intimate embrace with another woman! He'd kissed her when obviously he'd been involved in some romantic to-do with this blond girl.

Ellie spun on her heel and scurried back down the hill, hoping to escape detection. The last thing she wanted Roy to know was that she had seen his little love scene by the pond!

She frowned. Was that Whitman's Pond? If so, he'd made quick work of that branch!

Then again, judging from sly Roy and his romances, the man was a pretty fast worker all around.

"How was your walk?" Parker asked when they were again seated by the fire.

"It was fine," she said, trying to compose herself. Her mind was still in a tizzy.

Parker frowned. "You didn't see anyone?"

"No, of course not. But then I didn't go far."

"You didn't go to the pond?"

"Pond?" She batted her eyes in all innocence. "What pond?"

He shook his head. "I thought maybe you'd walked out that way."

She shrugged and tried to stroke Polly slowly to seem as if nothing was amiss. "Perhaps I did, but I must not have walked far enough." What a liar she was! "Aren't you going to read?"

Parker gazed at her, and for a moment she feared he could see right through her. But then he opened the book and began reading. He had a wonderful voice, and he did characters very well during the dialogue passages. But though the story had until this morning absorbed all her interest, it was no use now. Parker might as well have been reading in Japanese.

She interrupted him after less than a page. There was no stopping herself. She knew she had no claim on Roy, but that fact did nothing to cool her burning curiosity. "I was just curious…I saw a woman in town the other day."

Parker smiled patiently.

"A young woman. With blond hair."

His smile disappeared. "You saw her at the mercantile, I suppose."

The town of Paradise, it appeared, was not bursting at the seams with youthful blond women. "She was quite attractive…in a way."

Now that she'd had time to reflect on the young woman's appearance, she decided she hadn't really found her so pretty. She was thin to the point of being wraithlike, and her clothes showed a passion for showiness without any sense of particular style. Not that Ellie knew too much about clothes, of course. But she did think the girl's partiality to frills and gewgaws, along with a nose that was too turned up, only added to her already haughty manner.

Well. Not just haughty. When Ellie had seen her in that store—her natural habitat, she assumed—the woman had been downright belligerent. In fact, the more she thought about the woman, the less and less she liked her.

Parker didn't appear to care for her, either. She'd never seen such a sour look on his face. "She's Mr. Trilby's daughter. He owns the mercantile."

He didn't seem inclined to give her any more information than that.

"Oh." Ellie smiled. "Thank you. I'm sorry if I sound overly inquisitive. It was just idle curiosity on my part. Please go on reading."

Parker read another paragraph, and it was another paragraph that was completely lost on Ellie. Try as she might to picture Thomas Hardy's rural England, the only country tableau in her head was that of the pond, with Roy and the fair-haired girl embracing.

Before she knew it, she was blurting out, "What is her name?"

Parker flicked his gaze up from the page, thinly veiling his annoyance. "Trilby."

"I meant a Christian name."

He swallowed. "Clara."

There was that look again—as if he'd just bitten into a sour persimmon.

"I'm sorry for interrupting you, Parker. I was just wondering…" Parker tapped his fingers impatiently. Which was strange. Parker was usually the soul of forbearance. "…I was wondering about Roy. Doesn't it worry you that he's been gone for so long?"

Parker seemed surprised. "It's barely been over an hour since he walked out the front door."

"Has it?" She felt a blush creep into her cheeks. "It seems longer."

Naturally it would, since she'd spent the entire time moping over Roy. She'd come to some startling realizations. Yes, he'd kissed her, and given her little

gifts, but he'd never told her he loved her or made
any promises.

Was Roy in love with Clara Trilby?

The question stung far more than it should have.
"Parker—" she blurted out before she could remind
herself that she wasn't supposed to waste her time
moping over Roy. And even though Roy was nowhere near the house, she crossed to the settee so that
she could speak to Parker more confidentially. "Has
Roy ever had a sweetheart?"

Parker laughed.

Ellie blinked. "Well, has he?"

Parker folded his arms. If he thought her question
was bold or transparent, he didn't indicate so. "I'll
just say this. I've never seen my brother show any
more interest in a woman than he's shown…" he
grinned, "…than he's shown for you."

Ellie gasped in surprise at his answer—and then
gasped again when the door flew open and Roy appeared, followed quickly by a chill in the air. As if
by reflex, she jumped away from Parker and back to
her straight-backed chair. How much darker Roy's
glower would be if he knew they were having a *tête-
à-tête* about him!

She tried to compose her expression to look a shade
less guilty, but when she looked into Roy's dark eyes,
she immediately thought of him standing by the pond
with Clara Trilby clasped to his bosom. In fact, she
realized, causing a flush to heat her cheeks, she'd
spent practically the entire day so far either thinking
about Roy, spying on Roy, or trying to squeeze information out of Parker about Roy.

Behind Roy came Ike, who laughed at Roy's im-
mobile stance in the open doorway. "Get a move on,
Roy, you're lettin' the chill in and I was hopin' I'd
be able to thaw out."

Roy shuffled aside, never taking his piercing glance off Parker and Ellie.

He knows, she thought. He probably spotted her running down the hill after she'd seen him at his trysting place. Or perhaps he simply guessed that she was gossiping about him. She felt red with shame. Also, she was still shaking with excitement at Parker's words. *I've never seen my brother show any more interest in a woman than he's shown for you.*

But how could that be, given what she'd witnessed at the pond?

She jumped up, eager to flee the tension in the room. "I'll help you thaw out, Ike, by getting you some tea."

Ike grinned. "That'd be better'n a warm blanket, Ellie."

She rushed to the kitchen, where she threw herself into the process of making tea. Now that she was alone, she could let her thoughts focus on Roy and what Parker had told her about him.

"...never show any more interest in a woman than he's shown for you."

Parsed more closely, the answer that had bolstered her spirits now seemed like something vague and unsatisfying that she could chew on forever and never understand the meaning of. Perhaps it meant Roy was interested in her. Or perhaps he was interested in her, but had shown equal interest in several other women. Or more depressing still, maybe Parker was simply trying to indicate that he paid very little attention to his brother's affairs and therefore was surprised to see Roy show an interest in any woman.

How could she know?

Ike came in bearing a bushel of apples. "From Uncle Ed," he announced, setting down the basket and then sprawling into a chair. He laughed. "I got away easy this time."

Ellie tilted her head, wondering about this Uncle Ed. From people's comments, he seemed rather fond of apples. "Should we make a pie?" she asked. "I've never done that."

Never done it particularly successfully, she amended.

Ike nodded. "We could at that. Make a fine finale for a dinner tonight—and it's my turn."

"I'll help you," Ellie said, then added suddenly, "...if you'll help me."

Ike's eyes widened with interest. Especially when Ellie pulled up a chair close to him. "What do you need?"

"I'm trying to find out something about a woman I saw in town...a woman named Clara Trilby."

At the mention of the name, Ike flapped his hands for her to lower her voice. "Shhhh! You want to bring the roof down over our heads?" He leaned closer to her, his grizzled face tensed in warning. "Whatever you do, don't mention that name around here!"

Ellie was shocked. "Why on earth not?"

"Because that gal's been the source of misery here for a year! And it's especially bad with winter coming on." Ike's voice dropped in volume until it was barely audible. "Haven't you heard the moaning?"

So that was it! Ellie straightened, shocked. That strange, heartrending sound that she'd been hearing wasn't just her imagination. And no wonder Parker had looked so sour when she'd asked him about Clara Trilby. The woman had broken his heart, no doubt...betrayed him with his own brother. And no wonder Roy had seemed so long-suffering as the woman had clung to him.

She frowned. But Roy...why was he kissing her

one day and then running off to meet Clara Trilby two days later?

She cleared her throat, daring only to ask one question more of Ike. "Roy...?"

His face clouded in warning. "Roy especially doesn't want her name spoken here."

Ellie's heart wrenched painfully. That was it, then. She'd stepped into a gothic novel worthy of the Brontë sisters, complete with tragic love affairs, jealousy, and a mysterious mother who vanished and then reappeared. And at the center of it all was a brooding, handsome man who, despite everything, seemed to have her completely enthralled.

Chapter Nine

It was Roy's night to sleep out in the barn with Ike, and as if the cold and Ike's earsplitting snoring weren't enough to contend with, he just plain couldn't sleep. He tossed and turned on the lumpy mattress in an agony of wakefulness till he was exhausted.

But even though he was exhausted, he still couldn't sleep. Every time he closed his eyes he saw Ellie as she'd been that afternoon, practically sitting on Parker's lap! The second she'd heard the door open and seen him standing there, she'd vaulted away from his brother and gaped up at Roy like a child who'd been caught with her finger in the pie. If guilt had a face, it could have been either hers or Parker's.

What had they been doing? Talking lovey-dovey? *Kissing?* Ellie hadn't seemed so pleased to be kissed by him the day before yesterday!

The thought provoked him more than it should have. Here he'd been out doing his level best to get Parker sidetracked, and all he'd actually wound up doing was giving Parker more time alone with Ellie.

Now Roy was stuck with more aggravation than one man could dig himself out of—a big lump of it coming from Clara Trilby. That infernal woman had nearly suffered a nervous collapse when Parker didn't show up at the pond today, and she'd spent a half-hour crying into Roy's lapels, which in his estimation was about twenty-nine minutes too many.

What was the matter with his brother? Couldn't he see that there was a woman eating her heart out for him? Granted, she was an annoying woman, but heck, last winter Parker had been eating his heart out for *her*. Not to mention the moaning had started up again. He didn't know how a man could moan about one woman at the same time he was kissing another.

He needed to do more than keep an eye on Parker. He needed to make certain that Parker and Ellie weren't left alone in a room again. If anyone was going to be kissing Ellie in this house, it was going to be him.

He flopped over on his stiff bed, suddenly consumed with another worry. What if Ellie preferred Parker? What if companionability had turned into something very serious in the short time it had taken him to be mauled by Clara at the lake?

Horrible thought.

What he needed to do, and soon, was make his intentions clear to Ellie.

As far as he could tell, he had two choices. He could plan a shameful immoral seduction that would be wonderful but nevertheless would end up ruining both their reputations because Paradise was a small town and people's more interesting deeds never did remain secret for long. The second option was, he could marry her.

At the mere thought of the word, he shivered.

How could he even be considering contemplating such a move? He wasn't even certain Ellie liked him! In fact, the one time he'd kissed her, she'd seemed shocked.

Hell, *he'd* been shocked. Never had he been so obsessed with a woman—and such an unlikely woman. A pregnant widow who in all likelihood preferred his brother's company!

"Damnation!" he cried out loud.

Ike bolted up to sitting. "What goes on, Roy?"

"I can't sleep, that's all."

Ike chuckled. "You're just spoiled by feather beds and such. Why, I can remember a time when everyone lived simple. Just like that uncle of yours. I was over at his place today, and Ed was still the same as ever. No frills. Dyed-in-the-wool bachelor, he is."

Uncle Ed.

Suddenly, Roy glimpsed a glimmer of sanity on the horizon. Uncle Ed would get his head back on straight! Ed would look once into his lovelorn eyes and tell Roy to get to work and forget all about female foolishness. The McMillan bachelor tradition would continue.

"Good old Uncle Ed," he said, breathing more easily. He'd go visit for a few days. Set out first thing in the morning.

That way he wouldn't see Ellie and forget all about his bachelor credo again.

"Gone?" Ellie blinked into her coffee cup. "When did he leave?"

"This morning," Ike replied. "He's gonna visit his Uncle Ed for a few days."

The idea of Roy's being five miles away made her feel unaccountably sad. There was no reason for her to miss Roy, particularly, and maybe now that he was gone she could stop thinking about him so much. Why, last night she'd barely slept a wink for wondering about him and that girl, Clara Trilby.

But out of sight, out of mind, the old saying went,

and now perhaps she would be able to consider more important things.

Namely, her immediate future.

"How's the weather?" she asked Ike. "Could I walk into town?" She wanted to make some discreet inquiries about families who might be looking for a hired girl. If someone were desperate enough, they might take her. And she was beginning to doubt the wisdom of staying at the McMillans' much longer. It was good that they had taught her so much, but given her confused feelings for Roy, it was wrong to stay on. She should have left long ago.

Ike's eyes rounded as if she'd just asked him if she could walk to the moon. "Lordy, no! Looks like snow, as a matter of fact."

"When?"

"Soon," he answered, the authority in his tone counterbalancing the vagueness of his answer. "'Sides, if you'd wanted to go to town, you should have gotten yourself out of bed early and hitched a ride with Parker."

"Parker's gone, too?" Good heavens—she'd slept until eight-thirty, and now she felt as if she'd missed an entire day's worth of activity.

"Gone at the crack of dawn. I don't know what for." He leaned toward her and commented in a confidential tone, "There's strange doings in this house, if'n you ask me. The whole of last night, Roy tossed and turned and cursed and complained till I thought I was gonna have to pour some liquor down him to get him settled."

"What happened?"

Ike shrugged, grinning. "Durn if I didn't finally mention his uncle, and suddenly Roy was sleeping like a baby."

The old farmhand, mindful of just having spoken

the word *baby* in front of a pregnant woman, and still keeping up the ruse of pretending that he knew nothing of her condition, went pink in the face and looked quickly away. "Anyways, it looks like you've got the house to yourself today."

"Where are you going to be?"

"Oh, I've got a fence to mend, then I thought I'd start breaking sod for a winter cover crop out in the vegetable garden."

She smiled. "I'd be glad to help, if you'd show me what to do."

"It's fieldwork, not for you."

Ellie wanted to argue with him. Except for being a little tired at both ends of the day, Ellie had never felt better in her life. The queasiness she'd taken pains to hide at the Sternhagen house had subsided. Within her, especially in the mornings and at night as she settled into bed, she could feel the stirrings of the little one, which made both her pulse and her thoughts race feverishly. Occasionally the kicks filled her with hope; at other times she feared she would be eaten alive by worry. But she had far more energy during the day now than heretofore.

"It's a job for one, anyhow," Ike said.

"I think I'll bake today while I wait for Parker to get back."

The minute Ike left the house, Ellie marched into the kitchen and set about making bread. She was still a little unsure of how much to make, so she poured what she considered to be a generous amount of flour into the big mixing bowl.

While the bread was rising, she got out a dustrag and began to polish every wood surface available to her. From long practice, when she cleaned she was able to let her mind wander without detracting from the quality of her work. And so she spent the whole morning thinking about Roy, and what had really driven him to Uncle Ed's.

After noon, bootsteps sounded at the door and Parker appeared, his cheeks flushed and his blue eyes shining from the cold. He took one look around the sparkling-clean parlor with a fresh fire crackling in the hearth, and smiled at Ellie.

"For a fine lady, you certainly do know how to dust." There was a mischievous twinkle in his eye that made her very uncomfortable.

"Well…I've been practicing lately," she said lamely. "I've been baking bread, too."

She hoped Parker wouldn't go into the kitchen, though, and see that she'd actually baked enough to feed an entire army. She could dust with her eyes closed; baking, however, could still be a hazard.

"You shouldn't be working so hard." Parker frowned. "Where's Roy? His horse wasn't in the barn."

"He's gone to your uncle Ed's."

"So suddenly?"

She nodded. "Ike said he just decided to go in the middle of the night."

Parker stared into the fire, his brow creased with worry.

Come to think of it, though Parker had been perfectly cordial, he had a distracted manner.

"Is something wrong?"

He shook his head. "No, just tired, I suppose. I left early. I went to see my mother."

The subject of Isabel was usually studiously avoided. "Is she all right?"

"Yes, in fact, she's settled in quite nicely…right next to the mercantile. In fact, she said she saw Roy thereabouts Saturday. In the mercantile…"

His words trailed away, but his face looked pained.

"Anyway, Mother sent her regards." He smiled.
"And she gave me this message for you. She said,
'Tell her I might have picked the wrong one for
her.'"

Ellie paled, realizing that Isabel must be referring
to having told her that Roy and she would make a
good couple. Stricken at first by the assumption that
Isabel now realized this to be impossible—no doubt
from witnessing Roy in town with Clara Trilby—Ellie
was soon flooded with embarrassment. Could Parker
see through the transparent message?

The sympathy in those blue eyes told her he could.

Poor Parker—in love with his brother's sweetheart!

Oh, she wanted to escape! She'd thought life would
be so much easier, so much more straightforward
here. But she seemed to have stepped into a situation
much more complicated than anything ever dreamed
of in New York!

But all she could think of was seeing Roy again,
of looking into his eyes again and making certain that
there wasn't love in them…or if there was, that it
wasn't for her. Then she could go on with her life
without a qualm or backward glance.

"I'd like to see your uncle's farm," she said.

Parker looked alarmed. "It's a little late, and the
weather's bad."

"But I could get there on horseback fairly quickly,
couldn't I?"

Parker thought for a moment. "Yes, I suppose so.
But I'm not sure…"

She smiled determinedly. "Whether Roy would
want me there? I'll just have to see about that when
I get there!"

"Look at that snow comin' down," Uncle Ed said,
peering up through the kitchen window.

The kitchen of Ed's house felt like a basement, and was actually the original soddy that the McMillans had resided in in the first decade they'd lived in Paradise. When they'd added on to the house, the brothers had simply built a wood-frame structure atop the soddy, cemented the floor and plastered the sod walls. In the autumn and winter, when Ed used his stove nonstop, the whole room warmed up like an oven.

"Glad I got all the apples picked before this blew in!"

The stuff coming down was thick and fluffy—the first snow. "It's too early for this. Hope it doesn't mean a cold winter," Roy muttered.

"They're all cold," Ed observed.

But for some reason, Roy couldn't help linking the early snow to Ellie's arrival. The woman seemed to have brought trouble with her—and this troublesome weather had followed. "Anyhow," he said with a sigh, "I hope this snow doesn't bury the roads."

Only half a day into Roy's open-ended visit to his uncle, he was already considering escape. Only, with Ellie at home and his mother in Paradise, it was hard to know where to run. That's why he'd come here, thinking he would feel at home in his uncle's solitary bachelor existence.

But as he began to peel his third bushel of apples for the day, Roy began taking a hard look at the McMillan bachelor credo. And he also took his first solid gander at Uncle Ed, trying to see him through the new perspective he seemed to have acquired since Ellie came to town. What he saw surprised him. All these years, he'd thought his uncle was a gloriously happy, solitary character, but now he just seemed like an eccentric.

Ed still had his tall, lean figure; more than one source had told Roy that in his heyday, Ed had been considered quite a gent by the ladies—even back in the time when women were as scarce on the prairie as waterfalls. He still had a handsome patrician face, with dark brown eyes the color of rich chocolate, and he wore the long mustache he'd sported in his younger days, only now his mustache drooped on him in the same manner his clothes hung on his lanky frame. His blond hair had turned gray and retreated down his skull, leaving him bald on top. His movements weren't as spry as they used to be; he now seemed awkward and slightly bent, as if his body, so often hunched in work, had forgotten how to move freely.

He wasn't his old self; but for that matter, how young and normal could any man seem when he ran around in an apron most of the time talking nonstop about apples?

The fact of the matter was, Roy perceived with sudden clarity, his uncle wasn't just an eccentric, he was a nut. For apples. Apples were his vocation. A self-proclaimed Johnny Appleseed of Nebraska, Ed McMillan had dedicated his life to the apple when he was young, planting and replanting, cross-pollinating and grafting, always battling bugs, rabbits and the elements. Now he was literally reaping that harvest of his life. In fact, the little seedlings the bachelor had cared for so tenderly and vigilantly in his youth and had pampered through drought, blizzard, and flood had flourished more than anyone, including Ed, could have imagined. Now the trees produced far more than other orchards in the area; in fact, the orchard put forth more than Ed could comfortably handle even after he had sold part of his crop, sending him into a fruit-induced frenzy every year. The strain of picking then selling, preserving, and storing his crop lent him the frantic demeanor of a man who was always a few bushels behind.

"Where'd I put my knife?" he asked now, pivoting on his heel and inspecting every surface of the kitchen.

But every surface was already devoted to apple business, and so the place was loaded with peels and cores waiting to be thrown into slop buckets for the hogs, jars awaiting sauce, and piles of peeled fruit awaiting their destiny. The kitchen probably looked this way from September through December every year, but Ed always managed to seem confounded by the chaos.

Roy sighed. "It's in your left hand."

His uncle's eyes bugged in surprise to see the utensil precisely where Roy said it was. "Aha!" he cried with the shock of Columbus discovering the New World. "It might have hidden there for years. See what a help to me you are, Roy?"

Roy grinned, trying to make his uncle feel better, but the truth was, he suspected Ed was never more absent-minded and fluttery than when he had company. Ed moved and worked in the way of a man accustomed to being alone and doing things his own way, so that the mere sight of a stranger in his kitchen threw him off his stride completely.

He was even more distracted than usual today, but that might have had something to do with the fact that he'd had another visit from Ike just yesterday. Two different people two days in a row would be a novelty. Though Ed usually went into Paradise every two weeks, he rarely spoke to anyone except to conduct his business at the mercantile and the feed and seed warehouse. He never socialized, claiming that all the noise of people caterwauling made him nervous now that he was a solitary old bachelor.

"Ike told me about your mother—" Ed blurted out now, choosing the wrong moment to start a conversation, just as he was transferring a heavy pot of stewed apples to one of the crowded tabletops.

Seeing his gray-haired old uncle careening around the kitchen with hot pans and sharp objects set Roy's nerves on edge; having him careening *and* talking about Isabel nearly made him apoplectic. He got up and tried to stay a few steps behind Ed, watching him warily as if the man were balanced atop a ladder instead of moving around his own kitchen.

"She arrived a few weeks ago."

Ed's brown eyes bulged in surprise. "As much as that? No one told me!"

"You've been busy since the harvest."

Ed laughed. "Yes, of course—busy time of year. How does she look?"

Roy looked around the kitchen. "Fine, except that you've got too much filling and not enough crust made."

Ed's gray eyebrows shot up in alarm. "I was referring to Isabel."

"Oh!" Roy naturally assumed his uncle had been talking about his work, which he usually spoke of as lovingly as he would of any woman. More lovingly, even. "I suppose she looks all right. I don't exactly remember too much of how she looked before."

"No, naturally!" Ed laughed nervously again, and tugged at his mustache in thought. "Do you really think I shorted on the crust?"

Roy shrugged. "You've got a better eye than me for these things."

Ed frowned. "No, no—it's good to have you here, Roy. Good to have your opinion on the pies. You say Isabel looks well?"

"I said I guessed so." He wished his uncle would

pick a topic instead of trying to talk simultaneously about apples and his mother. Of course, Roy knew which topic *he'd* choose.

At first it seemed Roy would get his wish.

"Well, the apples will keep, but I hate to see crust go to waste," Ed said.

Roy couldn't see how a crust could go to waste here when there were apples everywhere that looked ready to leap into the nearest pie pan.

"And what's she doing?"

Roy blinked, distracted by the question. They were back on his mother again. "Oh, she's…well, she's setting up a store of some kind. Hats, I think." Roy laughed in disgust, now that it suddenly struck him how odd a choice of profession that was. "If you can imagine trying to make a living from that!"

Ed clucked his tongue. "Well she's done pretty well up to now making hats."

Roy fingered a pippin absently. "Oh, sure, up to now…" He frowned and turned on his uncle. "How would *you* know how she's been doing?"

Color rose in his uncle's cheeks. "Oh…we kept in touch through the years."

"She's been writing to you? For how long?"

"Ever since I tried to find her."

Roy was stunned. "When was that?"

"'Bout fifteen years ago. A few years after your Pa died, I wanted to know if she was faring well…you know, didn't want her to starve."

"Why should anyone in the McMillan family have cared?" Only once the question had registered in his uncle's eyes did Roy realize how callous his words sounded.

"Of course we would have cared, Roy," Ed lectured. "She was your mother and our brother's wife."

"She abandoned us!"

Ed turned and started rattling pans at the stove, pulling off lids and sending plumes of fragrant steam into the air. "Things are never so cut-and-dried, you know. People are hardly ever just one thing or the other. Fellows learned that in a war, I guess. Least-ways, I did."

Like his older brother, Roy's father, Ed had served in the Union army. Roy's father, however, had married and come home after two years with a young bride he'd met during leave in Philadelphia, just before the entire clan up and moved to Nebraska in response to the new Homestead Act. Ed hadn't come to Nebraska till he was mustered out in May of 1865, the year Roy was born. Roy had always wondered how his father's siblings must have reacted to his hauling a woman home from the war.

Ed, apparently, hadn't minded as much as Roy had assumed.

"Your pa and your mother didn't get along so well."

"Because she couldn't stand it here."

Ed nodded. "That's what Abner always said. But the fact of the matter was, he mostly couldn't stand being married. Didn't like it. He and Isabel didn't get along."

Roy frowned. Ed was taking Isabel's side? "She couldn't stand it here, and she left," he insisted, placing the blame squarely back where it belonged.

Didn't it?

Ed shook his head. "She didn't jump, Roy, she was pushed."

"You mean Pa told her to leave?" Ridiculous!

"Not in so many words, but he made it unbearable enough for her here that she couldn't stay. Maybe you were too little to remember how things were back then, or at least to understand. Things got ugly, Roy.

Then, when she told him she was going back to Philadelphia, back to her folks, he wouldn't allow her to take you boys. I've never seen a woman so broken up.''

His mother? He couldn't imagine her ''broken up'' about anything. Roy bristled. ''Sounds like she's had your ear, all right. Why haven't I ever heard this before? Why haven't I heard from *her?*''

''Out of respect for Abner, my brothers and I didn't take sides or interfere. That just wasn't our way. Then, after Abner died and I tracked her down, I discovered she'd married again.''

''So you see,'' Roy pointed out, ''she could have gotten in touch with us then.''

Ed looked doubtful. ''Except that her husband had had an accident and was an invalid, and Isabel was working hard at her shop to support them both. She didn't feel she could waltz back into your lives after all that time, especially since she had such a hard financial burden to bear. She didn't want you to feel responsible for her in any way.''

Ed shook his head. ''Women's lives aren't always easy, Roy—and they especially weren't back when Isabel was a young woman. What do you think her folks made of her coming home after marrying and going out west? You think they were glad to see her when they already had five other children to support?''

Roy tried to digest all this information as best as he could, but he was still skeptical. ''All I can see is that Pa never should have gotten married.''

''I guess that's right,'' Ed said, obviously glad to be back in agreement on something with his nephew. He looked around in complete befuddlement. ''Have you seen a wooden spoon around here, by chance? I know I had it....''

Roy picked it off the spoon rest and handed it to him.

"Abner maybe should have never gotten married," Ed agreed, stirring a pot of applesauce. "He should have stayed a bachelor like the rest of us. Life's sure simpler this way."

Roy couldn't help looking around the disaster area of a kitchen overrun with apples and apple products. Back when his other uncles were alive to temper Ed's passion for fruit, things around here had seemed a little saner. Now Ed's life appeared to be not only turbulent, but one-dimensional.

Yet productive, he added loyally. An orchard might make life difficult for a few months of the year, but it was nothing compared to the problems his father had endured during five years of marriage.

Roy frowned. What had Ed meant by "ugly"?

"Of course," Ed reminded him, "if Abner hadn't married, then you and Parker wouldn't be here. There's that."

Roy nodded. His father had been a curt, taciturn man, but less so with his children than other people. Maybe that's why Roy had a difficult time believing Isabel could have had such a rough time...except that he'd seen his father rail against other people, and sometimes against his own brothers.

"And then there's something else, too," Ed added, sprinkling crushed cinnamon from a shaker into his pot. "Maybe if Abner hadn't married, he would have always been thinking about that pretty gal in Philadelphia he should've married. Maybe he would have had regrets. There's nothing in the world worse than that."

Roy's brows lifted in surprise. "Why, Uncle Ed, sounds like there's a pretty gal hidden away in your past somewhere!" He laughed. "Where is she, in

Omaha? Or maybe you left somebody back east during the war? Is that why you've turned into such a bleeding heart all of a sudden?''

Ed's face turned pink, and he fluttered his hand at his nephew to shut him up. ''That's none of your business!''

Roy chortled. ''You can't fool me. You're the happiest man alive here on your little farm with your orchard. Your life's turned out just the way you wanted it.''

Ed nodded thoughtfully. ''Just the way I wanted it when I was a young man.'' Then he looked up. ''Only I never expected all my brothers to be gone so soon. Or…'' His words broke off as a lid over a bubbling pot started making threatening noises.

Roy wasn't used to seeing his uncle so introspective. Ed was a busy man, and usually didn't have time for such foolishness as looking back and worrying about regrets. ''That's the female influence, all right,'' he muttered. ''That's what they do to a man. Start making him think about all sorts of things that are best left alone.''

''What woman are you talking about, Roy? Isabel, or that woman that's over visiting Parker?''

''Both!''

Ed laughed. ''Ike told me about her. Said she was real pretty.''

''Did he tell you she was pregnant?''

''Widow, isn't she?''

Roy nodded.

''Well, now, I have some sympathy for widows,'' Ed said. ''I reckon they have a harder time than most folks, on account of they're grieving and trying to figure out how to make their way in the world at the same time.''

Roy rolled his eyes. This visit was supposed to be

helpful. It was supposed to remind him of the bachelor paradise his world used to be. He put his hands on his hips and informed his uncle, "There's been no end of trouble since she arrived. Ike's practically in love with her, Parker's in such a funk I can't tell what he's thinking, and did I tell you I broke my toe?"

Ed looked down at his boot. "Looks fine to me."

"Oh, sure, *now.* When it happened, Doc told me I was going to have to stay in bed for months."

Ed frowned. "But you didn't."

"Of course not," Roy said testily, "but it was touch and go for a while. And it never would have happened if it weren't for that Fitzsimmons woman."

"What did she do?"

Roy stubbed the toe of his uninjured foot against the wide-plank floor and shrugged. "She was helping me one night."

Gray eyebrows arched. "Helping you where?"

"In my bedroom." Roy blushed. "Well, actually, it's hers now. I was just getting some things down and…" He let out a ragged sigh, remembering how Ellie had looked that night in nothing but her nightgown, with all that cloud of red silky hair framing her face. Was it any wonder he had taken a fall? "Anyway, it wouldn't have happened if it weren't for her."

Ed nodded. "Looks like you've got a problem."

"The foot's better now."

"But your heart's sore, isn't that it?"

Roy felt heat burn his cheeks. "Of course not! I'm just worried that she's never going to leave—that things won't be the same back at the farm again. You know how happy we all were."

"Happy? Just last month when you were over here helping me with the picking you told me that Ike was driving you crazy. Said his constant talking was getting on your nerves. You said you didn't know if you could stand another winter locked up with Parker and his moaning. Said you were considering running off to Alaska or someplace.''

''Did I?'' he asked in amazement, only having a vague recollection of his complaints from last month; his woes now seemed so much stronger. He muttered in disgust. ''I just didn't know how good I had it then.''

''You just didn't know how love felt,'' his uncle corrected.

Roy opened his mouth to refute the implied accusation, but Ed cut him off.

''Hand me that potholder, won't you, Roy?''

Feeling numb, Roy did as he was told. He wasn't in love!

''Uh-oh,'' Ed said, looking out the window again.

''Is the snow bad?''

Uncle Ed shook his head. ''It sure is—but not as bad as the news I have for you.''

Roy looked up, alarmed, and joined his uncle at the window. He had to lift himself up to peer through the opening. Outside, through the driving white powder falling through the sky, they could just make out the figure of a small woman with red hair peeking out from beneath her scarf, riding up the disappearing path to the house.

''That would be the Widow Fitzsimmons, I suppose,'' Ed guessed.

Ellie? *Here?*

Muttering a curse, Roy spun on his heel, slammed his hat on his head and ran outside. Squinting against the driving flurry of ice and snow, he ran till he reached Ellie and her horse and grabbed the reins from her.

"What are you doing here? Have you gone plumb crazy? You shouldn't be riding."

He looked into her face, making sure she still had color. "Nonsense!" Her cheeks and nose were pink, and her lips pulled back in a big smile. "I brought you some bread!" she said through chattering teeth.

Roy rolled his eyes. "Good, good. We aren't exactly hurting for baked goods here, you know."

She looked offended by his less-than-welcoming tone. "No, I didn't know."

"What was Ike thinking, letting you come out in this snow?"

At the sound of a door slamming, Roy turned and saw his uncle running out toward them.

Ed hadn't put on a coat, only a hat and gloves, and he was banging his hands against his arms to keep the heat circulating in his long limbs. "Hello, ma'am, my name's Ed McMillan."

"Pleased to meet you," Ellie said. "I'm Ellie Fitzsimmons."

That, apparently, was all the conversing Ed was capable of with a woman. He pivoted toward his nephew. "Don't keep her out here, Roy. Come inside after you take the horse to the barn."

Roy watched as Ed helped Ellie down from her mount and escorted her inside. It was a good thing his uncle had a firm grip on her arm, because he slipped on the ice and nearly fell more than once in their dash inside. As they disappeared, Roy couldn't believe his rotten luck.

He'd come here to get away from Ellie—but now he was stuck in an even smaller house with her. Was there just no escaping this one troublesome, beautiful widow?

Chapter Ten

Ellie was never so shocked in her life as when she walked into Ed's kitchen and found a bakery. The smell alone nearly knocked her out, but nothing prepared her for the shelves and shelves of preserved apples and bottles and jugs of apple vinegar, apple-jack and apple cider. Apples were practically piled up to the rafters.

"You do all this?" she asked, half in awe, half in horror. No wonder the man had a distracted look. She wondered that he had time to sleep!

His cheeks colored ever so slightly, and he raised his head with modest pride. "Well now…I wouldn't say *all* by myself. My nephews and Ike come over when they can and help me with the picking. That's the onerous part, especially for an old soul like me."

She smiled. "You're not old—I'll bet you're the best picker of them all."

"No, that would be Roy," Ed said with a reverent nod toward his nephew, who was caught in the middle of the act of busting into a jug of applejack.

Roy had taken no pains to conceal the fact that he wasn't exactly thrilled to see Ellie. Now, apparently, he was going to try to drown out her presence with alcohol.

"Roy does a heap of work for me at harvest time," Ed said.

Ellie folded her arms and grinned with just a tad too much sweetness. "And how nice it must be for you, Uncle Ed, to be able to tell Roy to go climb a tree."

Roy popped the thick cork out of the applejack, scowled and stalked away.

Ed laughed. "Here, I'll show you the pie he helped make just this morning."

In a cool closet dug into the wall just off the kitchen, Ed revealed his real treasures. There were several pie safes bulging with the fruits of his labor—pies, loaves of bread, even strudels. Her mouth watered, and she realized that she hadn't had a bite to eat since Ike's breakfast that morning.

"I'll be taking most of these into town. I sell a few things at the store there."

Ellie thought of Clara Trilby behind the counter of the mercantile. "I see. I suppose Roy is an eager volunteer for that duty, too."

Ed's blue eyes blinked at her in incomprehension. But then, Ed was so caught up in the bounty of the apple he probably didn't have time or inclination to worry about his nephew's romantic life. In fact, Ellie would have given anything not to have to worry about it herself.

Why had she come here? It was certainly the most harebrained idea she'd had since...well, perhaps since her decision to come to Nebraska. Her next move would be smarter; she would go to town and tramp door to door and beg for a job if she had to.

Yes, beg. Doing so wouldn't be any worse of an idea, or more humiliating, than coming here and throwing herself at Roy McMillan had been. And it certainly couldn't be any less successful!

A wave of queasiness washed over her.

Ed squinted at her. "Are you all right?"

She shook her head, suddenly realizing it would be pointless to lie when she felt as if she was going to faint. "If I could just lie down…"

She darted out a hand to brace herself as her body sagged against the wall.

"Roy!" Ed cried out in alarm.

In a moment, she was swept up by strong arms—Roy's, she discovered. She tried to take comfort in that, at least. It might be the last time she ever found herself in Roy's arms.

"These are the finest pies you've ever brought in, Ed," Cora Trilby observed. "Just look at how beautiful the crust is!"

Ed regarded his creations as an artist might view a canvas—with love but with inescapable acknowledgement of his work's flaws. "There's a jagged strip on the lattice crust there. You might want to discount that one."

Mr. Trilby hovered nearby. "Why don't we take that one home ourselves, Cora? We haven't had a pie since…"

His wife frowned at him. "Since the last time Mr. McMillan was here!" She turned to Ed with a laugh. "My husband's going to eat us out of the family business one of these days."

Ed nodded and forced a smile. Usually he enjoyed talking with the Trilbys—he spoke to so few people, and as business partners, they seemed to appreciate his work more than anyone else. But today he couldn't seem to build up much enthusiasm for idle conversation.

He cleared his throat. "I was wondering..."

Mrs. Trilby tilted her head with interest.

It was all Ed could do to keep himself from stammering and blushing like a schoolboy. "I've heard that a woman named Isabel Dotrice is in town. Do you know where I might find her?"

The store proprietors' eyes widened with curiosity. Of course they would find his question interesting, since everyone in town would know of his family connection to the woman. They probably wondered why he didn't ask Roy or Parker where Isabel lived. He wondered that himself. His only answer was, he didn't want his nephews to see how eager he was to visit their mother.

And Roy—if he hadn't noticed Ed pumping him with questions about Isabel, it was only because Roy was too in love himself with the Widow Fitzsimmons to notice. He'd never seen his nephew in such bad shape over a woman, although when he saw the woman he certainly understood that she would drive a man to distraction. The unfortunate thing was, she didn't seem to know it. In fact, she seemed to be eating her heart out instead of just plain eating, bringing herself to the brink of collapse.

It was an object lesson for anyone in love, he decided. Try to avoid it, let it fester, and you ended up with one woman sick in bed and a man guzzling applejack. Ten feet apart, crazy in love, and neither seemed to know it.

And so he'd left them. Loaded up his wagon, left a note in the kitchen, and driven off on his own quixotic mission.

Now he was so nervous he wished he was back guzzling applejack with Roy.

Mrs. Trilby's face lit up with a polite smile. "Of course you'd want to know," she said, her voice just hiding the fact that she was trolling for gossip, "she was your late brother's wife, wasn't she?"

Ed nodded. "They divorced."

As if the whole town didn't know that. The breakup of Abner's marriage had been the talk of the town— heck, of the whole county—for years and years.

Sensing that Ed was not going to say any more, Mr. Trilby leaned over the counter. "Says she's going to open a dressmaking and millinery shop."

Mrs. Trilby *tsk*ed loudly. "Can you imagine? There's no call for any such establishment in Paradise! Why, we sell perfectly fine ready-made hats right in this store. I haven't heard any complaints."

Ed squinted over at the hat rack in the corner. He was no expert on women's fashion, of course, but looking at the faded felt, limp trim, and drooping feathers that adorned the goods for sale there, he couldn't imagine that Isabel's enterprise could possibly fail.

"And she's rented the building right next door!"

"Next door?" So close!

Cora nodded curtly. "The building with the red door. I think she's living upstairs. Maybe you can talk some sense into her, Ed, but she doesn't seem to listen to anybody. In fact, she seems a most peculiar sort of individual."

He strained to hide his anger at that description. "If you mean that she's rare, I'd certainly agree."

He thanked them and bid them good-night, then had to hold himself back from running out of the store.

Just next door!

He scurried toward his wagon, not stopping until he had his hand on the basket he'd prepared for Isabel. His fingers shook as he checked each item. In the package he'd gathered all his best goodies. A pie with a perfect crust, an applique apple made of dough adorning the top. Two jars of sweet applesauce with ribbons tied around the lids. A little jug of his best cider, and a loaf of quick bread baked that morning. Cushioning his goods were apples themselves—the most perfect he could find in his cellar, with drying leaves still on their stems. He tucked his best cloth napkin around the goods, and fiddled with the bow tied around the basket's handle until it looked just the way he wanted it.

And all the while, he was aware of the fact that Isabel was right next door. So close she could see him if she looked out her window.

So close!

Why hadn't she told him she was coming? Why hadn't she written? He would have met her at the train....

He nearly laughed. Meeting her at the train seemed so insignificant after all the years they'd corresponded. Maybe she didn't understand what her letters had meant to a man living alone. Certainly, he hadn't poured his heart out to her, or anything near it. They'd always just written of everyday things. He'd been giving her reports on her children for fifteen years, until he felt almost foolish informing her that Roy and Parker, now grown men, seemed to be doing well and washing behind their ears, eating fine and all the things a mother might worry about.

In turn, she wrote him of her life in Philadelphia, of her shop there, and about her husband's slow decline. The last time he'd written, it was to express his sympathy over the death of Mr. Dotrice.

He picked up the basket and carried it not toward her red painted door, but across the street, where he stood on the sidewalk and gazed at her new dwelling, trying to imagine her inside. His skinny legs practically trembled beneath him, and he felt ridiculous for behaving so much like a young fool. He had every reason to simply walk up to her door and knock on it. No one, least of all Isabel herself, would think it odd. The whole town knew of their connection through Roy and Parker.

But no one could know what was in his heart. Any more than anyone could have guessed how he felt when, twenty-eight years ago, as a young man returning from what had seemed sometimes to be an endless and endlessly brutal and ugly war, he had finally stepped foot into the depressing sod house in the strange treeless land his family had moved to in his absence and found the most beautiful woman he'd ever laid eyes on smiling up at him.

And how he'd felt in the next second when he'd realized that she was his brother's wife.

His brother's marriage had been a kind of torture to him. He supposed he was actually in love with Isabel then; her smile brightened his days while she was there, and seeing her unhappy tore him apart.

Now she was free. And after twenty-four years, no one could say that he had horned in on his brother's marriage or that his attraction for Isabel was unseemly. He'd waited. He'd been patient. Now he couldn't wait another moment.

What's more, he didn't have to. When Ed looked up, he saw her, standing in the window by a gas lamp. He sucked in his breath, shocked by her appearance.

She hadn't aged a minute! She was just how he remembered her—tall and slim and stylish. Beauty like hers could take a man's breath away, as it had when he was a soldier coming back from war. As it did now. His eyes weren't what they used to be, but even from this distance, he could see that her dark hair had the same soft sheen to it. Her blue eyes still looked out at the world with humor and barely checked impatience, and her wide mouth was forever turned up in a wondering smile.

So much emotion flooded through him that he had to dart away from her line of sight. Though she hadn't been looking his way, he suddenly felt terrified that she might have caught him staring at her. He stood in the shadow of a darkened building, clutching his apple basket and breathing heavily.

To see her so unchanged, so like the memory he'd held in his thoughts all these years!

The vision was humbling. She was the woman of his dreams, and now there was only a layer of brick and mortar and a few panes of glass standing between them. He was awestruck.

He was terrified.

He'd waited. Long years he'd waited. Years that had apparently glanced off her like water off a duck's back. While he…

He looked down at his old hands holding his basket and suddenly made a quick assessment of the ravages time had taken on him. He was fifty-six years old, and looked it. No longer could he pretend to be her young and dashing McMillan ally. Years of living alone and doing farmwork showed: his hands were rough and brown. Under his old hat, his gray hair clung to the sides of his bald pate in unruly scruffs. Old, unstylish and unpressed clothes dropped off his lanky stooped frame. His moustache had gone untrimmed for what seemed like months—though surely it wasn't that long? He couldn't remember. That was another thing to make him shudder; his memory was going.

He was in the autumn of his years; not the gnarled old tree he was sure to become, but turning. Definitely turning. While Isabel—she still looked like springtime to him, as fresh and as blooming with life as ever. She'd even come here with plans to start a new business. Hats! Still trying to make the world gayer, prettier. She would never be old.

He, on the other hand, already felt like Methuselah.

What could he do about that now? He couldn't knock on her door looking like a rumpled old fool.

Slowly, he finally crossed the street. His heavy footsteps were not those of a romantic suitor now, but a condemned man. He reached the red door and hesitated a moment, staring at the doorknob her hand had touched probably a hundred times now.

He didn't touch the knob. He didn't even knock. In the end, after twenty-four years, all he could do was place the basket in her doorway and turn away.

When he was safely back in his wagon, heading away from town, away from Isabel, his hands still shook, but he felt better. Relieved. After all…he and Isabel…after all these years…

Well, it was a foolish notion. Why, everyone knew he was a dyed-in-the-wool bachelor, and happy that way. What did he know of love? It was all very well to lecture Roy about regrets and whatnot, but could he honestly say that he regretted having lived alone, free, creating his beautiful orchard? Isabel was beautiful, and he had happy memories of her. There were all sorts of things they could talk about, but that wasn't love, was it?

Certainly not!

And when you came right down to it, love was damn painful. Look at poor Roy and that Fitzsimmons woman. Suffering? He was the one who had been suffering since Roy came for his visit. The boy had moped and growled and put too much cinnamon in the sauce, all because his heart was sore over a woman. Ed had recognized the symptoms immediately. Roy had been acting exactly how Ed had on those days when he'd been sure a letter from Isabel would come, and none arrived.

He gasped. Now that Isabel was in town, he supposed there would be no more letters.

What hope would punctuate his days now?

There wouldn't be any more disappointment, though, when the letters didn't come. That would be a consolation, a relief.

Relief, he repeated to himself. That had to be what was left when all the excitement was sucked out of him—had to be why he drooped even more than usual as he headed toward home.

"This is quite a switch."

Ellie's green eyes stared up at Roy as she accepted the mug of warm milk from him. "What?"

"Me bringing you hot liquids."

She laughed, and as always, the laughter worked a kind of magic on his system. He steeled himself against the silly grin that wanted to tug at his lips. "I'm perfectly fine, you know. I could easily get up and fetch it myself."

"That's what I used to think when I broke my toe and you were pestering me with tea all the time."

"And was it true?" she asked him.

Suddenly the kitchen seemed unbearably warm. "Maybe," he answered, his voice dropping a notch. "But if I'd gotten it myself, I wouldn't have been able to be alone with you so much."

Ellie blushed to her hair roots, and he turned away, got up and poked at the fire. He didn't look at her, but he could see her behind him in his mind's eye, sipping at the milk mug cradled in her two hands, a blanket draped over her thin shoulders, those green eyes staring up at him.

What was she doing here? Was it some madness, some perverse pleasure in seeing him suffer that had brought her here at exactly the worst possible time, during a snow that had covered the road so that he couldn't possibly send her back?

And where was Uncle Ed? He'd been gone for hours! Why the heck hadn't he at least waited till tomorrow to go to town, when Ellie would have been feeling better, and he could have dropped her off at the farm for Parker to deal with.

To Roy, it suddenly seemed as if the whole world were conniving against him. In cahoots. Parker, by bringing a woman into his world who he couldn't have. Ellie, by not leaving him be. Ed, for leaving him with Ellie. Ike…

Well, he didn't know what Ike had done, but he wasn't going to let him off the hook just because of that. He was sure there was something.

He punched a red log with the poker and it collapsed in an explosion of brilliant sparks. He stared at the display with a vicarious relief—he felt as though he might explode that way himself if he spent much more time around Ellie. When he turned back around, Ellie was gazing at him.

Why did she look at him that way, with those dewy green eyes of hers? It was almost as if…

Well. He didn't dare think it, but it was almost as if she loved him.

Ha! That was a perfect bit of wishful thinking.

He gritted his teeth. "I'd better go out to the woodpile, get another log."

To his dismay, she hopped up, too. "I'll go with you."

"Are you out of your cotton-pickin' mind? Sit down."

She put her cup down impatiently. "Nonsense. I've

been penned up in here all day. I'd like some exercise.''

''Your foolish five-mile trek through the snow wasn't enough exercise?''

She glared at him now, her hands in fists by her sides. ''It wasn't foolish. I made it, didn't I?''

''Yes—and now you can't leave!''

Her cheeks turned a shade redder. ''I'm sorry. But if I can't leave, shouldn't we make the best of it?''

''The best of it would be you staying put. I don't want you to die before Uncle Ed gets back.''

She laughed. ''Don't you know? I wouldn't die for anything now, Roy. I wouldn't want to give you that satisfaction.''

His lips flattened into a thin line. Is that what she thought? That he would be happy without her? He couldn't help himself. He blurted out, ''If that's how you think I'd feel, you're not as smart as I thought you were!''

And then he turned and slammed out of the house, feeling like a damn fool for his outburst.

He might as well have told her that he was burning up inside with love for her and be done with it!

Wouldn't you know it, the door opened and shut behind him and he heard the light crunch of footsteps coming upon him. He turned, surprising her so that she slipped and almost went flying past him. He grabbed her arm, at once stopping her and holding her upright. She still had that blanket draped around her, only she had draped it over her head, too, like a scarf, so that her green eyes blinked up at him as though through the opening of a red plaid tent.

''Go back inside,'' he told her.

Her chin darted up defiantly. ''I'm going to help you, Roy, whether you want me to or not.''

He sighed. ''Fine.'' Keeping a firm grip on her

arm, he marched her over to the woodpile between the house and the barn. Once there, she dutifully held out her blanket-draped arms, and he began stacking logs—the smallest ones he could find—onto them.

"Did you really mean what you said just then, Roy?"

He picked out a larger dry log for himself to carry and put it aside. "Mean what?"

"That…you wouldn't be happy if something bad happened to me."

"Of course I meant it!" he said gruffly, glad that she couldn't see his face, which was probably as pink as a baby rash. "I'm not an ogre."

She smiled up at him, one of those smiles that could melt a glacier. "I know you're not."

In fact, if he were a glacier, he would be half a lake already. "I wouldn't want anything bad to happen to a friend of Parker's."

"Is that how you think of me?"

"Isn't that what you are?" he asked. "Parker's friend?" The words *Parker's sweetheart* steadfastly refused to come out of his mouth, though that would have been a much more helpful question to ask.

She seemed to understand, though. "Parker's friend, yes. Did you think there was anything more?"

His mouth felt dry, and it was all he could do to lift a piece of wood that was practically a twig into her arms. "Of course…what else can I think when you two seem so…companionable."

Two red stains appeared in her cheeks. "Parker and I seem companionable?" she asked with indignation. "And so we are!"

He frowned. "I don't see why you should be so angry about it."

"Because you—" She stopped, taking a deep

breath. "Because you seem to imply there's something shameful between him and myself."

"That's because every time I walk in a room, you two spring apart as if you've been kissing."

"Kissing?" Her mouth dropped open. "We have *never...!*"

"Never?" he asked doubtfully.

"All men aren't like you, Roy," she said. "Kissing me one day and then—"

"Then what?" He tilted his head, utterly and hopelessly confused. This was the first time she'd ever mentioned his kiss again, but she seemed to think he'd betrayed her somehow. "What did I do?"

She lifted her head, collecting herself with some effort. When she spoke, it was in a clipped, incensed voice. "Well, if you must know, Sunday morning I saw you."

"Saw me what?"

"I saw you by the pond with that young woman. Clara Trilby."

That name—it nearly caused him to drop his log. Instead, he tossed it aside and planted his hands on his hips. "What did you see me doing?"

That proud pointy chin hiked up another imperious notch. "I saw you two embracing."

A shudder ran through his body—a feeling of pure, unadulterated joy compounded by relief. His Ellie! It was all he could do not to whoop for joy, or do a celebratory jig, or to bend down and toss snow in the air like confetti. Only by reaching down to the depths of his self-control did he manage to stay composed.

"You followed me!" he guessed.

Green eyes widened, and she shook her head frantically. "No, I swear I didn't. I was just out for a walk...."

He grinned, bouncing jauntily on his boot heels. "Just happened to be out strolling, huh?"

Her frantic head shake turned to a frantic nod.

"And when you saw Clara and me, how long did you stand there ogling us?"

"Not but for a few seconds! I went back to the house immediately, and I foolishly asked Parker who the blond lady who worked at the mercantile was...I didn't know, you see."

He frowned. "Know what?"

"What Ike told me later. That Clara Trilby's name shouldn't be spoken in your house."

"Did he tell you why?"

She shook her head mournfully. "I guessed. There was obviously some sort of love triangle between you and your brother and this Trilby woman."

The very idea made him hoot with laughter.

She looked up sharply. "I don't see what's so funny. Does watching a woman's pain always make you laugh?"

Her pain. *Her* heartache. The idea that Ellie had been eating her heart out for him while he had been pining for her nearly made him laugh again. But he forced a sober expression, and methodically began taking back the logs he'd just placed in her arms and dropping them to the snowy ground.

Her eyes narrowed in confusion.

"Do you know what desperation drove me into the arms of Clara Trilby, Ellie?"

She shook her head.

"The thought of you and Parker together."

Her brows furrowed in disbelief.

"You see, Clara is in love with Parker, but sweet, patient Parker is too darn stubborn and proud to forgive her for an argument they had almost a year ago. I was foolish enough to think that if I threw them together, love would blossom again, and I would have you to myself.''

Her mouth gaped open, and though he eased her burden by picking the last of her logs out of her grasp, she looked as if she were going to collapse. He grabbed her arms, half because he couldn't wait to hold her, half because, like an old building that was about to topple over, she looked like she needed reinforcing.

''Are you saying you don't love Clara?''

Roy smiled ''Not only do I not love her, I can honestly say that Clara Trilby is probably the last woman on earth I would even consider loving. Do you understand? If she were Eve and I were Adam, human life would have slammed to a dead stop back in Eden.''

Ellie let out a laugh, then shook her head. ''But when I saw you—''

''She was upset that Parker didn't show up for the rendezvous.'' He pulled Ellie close. ''She was crying on my shoulder. That's what you saw. And if you had stayed another minute, you would have seen us gladly parting ways.''

She smiled up at him, and tentatively put her hands on his chest. Though there was a blanket and his coat between them, her touch seared him as it might have if she had been touching his naked skin. ''You braved the elements with a woman you disliked on my account?''

She made it sound as if he were unbearably noble, when the thoughts running through his head were anything but. His instincts were to head back inside and make love to Ellie before Uncle Ed came home.

Yet when he looked into those green trusting pools that were Ellie's eyes, he found himself feeling confused, as if all the ways he'd related to women in the past no longer applied. This was no floozy from the Lalapalooza. Eleanor Fitzsimmons was a real lady. There could be no fooling around now.

The strangest thing was, he didn't want to fool around.

He lifted his hands to her cheeks and stared into her beautiful face until he feared his heart might burst. "Oh, Ellie, how could I help loving you?"

Her red lips parted, and she blinked back moisture from her eyes. "I love you too, Roy. So much!"

Lady or no lady, he wanted to kiss her like there was no tomorrow. He brought his mouth down on hers with barely restrained hunger. He didn't want this kiss to end like their last, with her fleeing in confusion. In his mind, confusion was a thing of the past. For now, there was just him and Ellie and a long future stretching before them.

As she clung to him, parted her lips to him, a transformation overtook him. All his life he'd fought against the idea of falling in love. But why? Ellie's lips, her warmth, her sweetness were a miracle to him. He suddenly felt free—free from the loneliness that had been eating at him for years, free from a sadness that had embittered him and made him believe that no woman could be trusted with something so frail as affection.

Ellie's hands tucked around his neck and he groaned at the prickling sensation that shot through his body as she pressed against him. Heat built in his loins, making him ache for her.

He pulled back, feeling as if he were gasping for air.

Her closed lids opened and she looked at him as if slightly dazed. "Don't stop, Roy."

Lord knows, he didn't want to.

He stood torn with indecision for a moment, then scooped her into his arms in one movement. When he looked into her face, her expression was a sweet confusion of desire and love and maybe a little nervousness. Not far from the same confusion going on inside him.

"I've got to get you inside and warm," he said.

"I'm not cold." Her grin held more than a trace of mischievousness. "Anymore."

His breath came out in a ragged, throaty sigh, and he closed his eyes against the tortured wanting building inside him. He'd never known he could want a woman so much.

Yet he wanted to wait. He had to wait. This was Ellie.

This was the first and last woman he would ever love.

Chapter Eleven

Happiness, real happiness, only happened in books. That's what Ellie had believed until the moment Roy told her that he wasn't in love with Clara Trilby. She was still so amazed, so overwhelmed, so flooded with joy that she could barely think. She hadn't even been aware of how unhappy she'd been until the opposite emotion had taken hold of her.

As he strode toward the house with her in his arms, Roy looked like a man possessed—possessed with desire. Her pulse raced as the delicious possibilities before them took hold in her imagination. Shameful thoughts!

But were they really so shameful when the man loved her?

A delightful shiver ran through her as she looked into Roy's hungry eyes.

In response, he warmed her neck with a kiss. "I'll get you out of this cold."

Could he possibly think she was responding to the weather? She nearly laughed, but happened to gaze into those eyes again—blue eyes regarding her as a man dying of starvation might eye a sumptuous feast. Roy looked as if he could devour her whole.

He kicked the door open, causing another shiver to run through her. Was he mad? Was she? More importantly, was she about to be treated to a night of passion right out of Byron?

To her surprise—and not a little disappointment— Roy passed up the door to Ed's bedroom. He also marched gallantly past the sofa and directed them straight downstairs to the kitchen and deposited her lovingly into a cane-backed chair, taking care to tuck her blanket around her. He disappeared into the pantry and returned seconds later with a pie, which he placed in front of her, followed by a plate and a fork.

She blinked up at him, uncertain.

He sliced off a wedge and plunked it down on her plate.

After expecting a ravishing, pie was a letdown. "But I'm not hungry," she protested. In that moment, she'd felt as if she could have lived on air and Roy's smile.

Except that he wasn't smiling now. When he spoke—the first words since declaring his love—his voice was practically a growl. "Now that I've got you, I don't want you to expire from hunger."

"I'm not going to—"

Before she could finish, he jumped up and ran outside, moving as if he had buggy springs in his heels. He was back in nothing flat, with those logs they'd abandoned in favor of a kiss. He dumped one on the fire now, poked it into flames, then returned to the table.

"Why aren't you eating?" he demanded.

She laughed. "Roy, I can't eat. You fed me all afternoon."

He looked at her as if she were mad. "Can't eat? I could eat three of these." And as if to prove it, he pulled the pie pan toward him and began to stab at his uncle's creation as if he hadn't had a bite in months.

And she could have happily watched him eat till the end of time. Gazing into Roy's handsome face would be pleasure enough for a lifetime—as long as he was gazing lovingly back at her, as he was now. Hungry though he claimed to be, she didn't think he'd spared a glance for what he was eating.

"Are you still mad at me for coming here, Roy?"

He barked out a laugh. "As far as I'm concerned, it was the best mistake you ever made."

No, that had been coming to Nebraska. A sense of well-being the likes of which she hadn't known since the days when she was living with her father came over her. Maybe because it had been that long since there was another person in the world who loved her. Tears filled her eyes.

Roy dropped his fork and reached across the table to grab her hand. "What's wrong, Ellie?"

His voice was so low, soothing, and utterly tender that she was nearly undone. She wasn't prone to weeping—hated it, in fact—but she felt a tear spill unbidden down her cheek.

Ridiculous, really, to cry when she was so happy. "That's another thing I thought happened only in books."

Not having been privy to her thoughts, Roy frowned. "What?"

"Crying from happiness."

A slow, gentle smile tugged his lips, and he pulled her into his lap as easily as you please. Though, to be honest, she didn't require much coaxing. She nestled her head against his shoulder, still amazed, and a little unsure, that it was her right to do so. That he was hers.

"What was the other thing?"

She looked into his handsome face and felt a heat stir deep inside her. "Love."

A deep flame flared in his blue eyes. "I guess I need to read more. I never knew anyone could feel like this, even in fiction."

She smiled. "I could give you some titles."

A dark eyebrow arched sensually. "That might take a little time. Why don't you just act out some of the best parts for me…you know, a little demonstration of all this love you've been reading about."

Her gaze took in his full lips before gliding back up to his eyes. Was he asking her to kiss him? A flush swept from the roots of her hair right down to the toes of her stockings. In her condition, she couldn't exactly be labelled an innocent, but in her limited experience, the man had always initiated the kissing. She hesitated a moment, floundering in her own desire and shyness. Then, detecting a challenge in his eye, she bent down and touched her lips to his.

Her bravery was richly rewarded. Roy's mouth yielded to hers, giving her a heady sensation of power, as if Hera had finally triumphed over Zeus. She wrapped her arms around him, snuggling close, all the while testing how bold she could be with his lips, which tasted deliciously of apple and sugar. When his mouth opened and his tongue teased hers, she felt her spine turn noodly, and tilted her mouth instinctively against his, seeking more of this awesome pleasure.

The chair beneath them squeaked as he shifted her slightly, and in that moment she could feel the swelling of his manhood against her thigh. She sucked in a ragged breath at the evidence of his desire for her. Experience told her that men were unable to check desire when it reached this point…no matter whether they were in a linen closet or a cane-backed chair.

Given the desire thrumming through her veins, she would be little able to resist such a temptation.

Roy pressed her to him and her body arched instinctively in response. She had about as much resistance in her as water cascading over a fall. Her hips moved provocatively against the firmness of him, the heat swirling inside her making her feel as if she were about to reel out of control.

He groaned, then put his hands on her hips, anchoring them.

She glanced questioningly into his eyes, which were hooded and dark beneath heavy lids. She felt dizzy and confused by his stopping her. Had she gone too far? Been too bold?

He swallowed. ''Those must be some books you've been reading,'' he rasped.

Before she could decide whether the best response would be to laugh or to beg him not to put a halt to this delicious new kitchen activity, bootsteps sounded on the porch and she sprang out of his lap.

Ed shuffled into the kitchen, his face drawn. He looked beyond tired. Of course he'd driven to town and back through the snow, but something about the difference in the man she'd met this afternoon and the one she was looking at now made Ellie frown. His bleary eyes first took in his nephew then her with a look that made her wonder if he knew exactly what had been transpiring in his beloved kitchen.

''Looks like you feel better,'' he said to Ellie. ''In fact, your cheeks are glowing with health.''

They glowed even more after his observation. For a moment Ellie considered what Ed might have found going on in his kitchen if he'd come in ten minutes later! ''I feel fine. Thank you for all your help, Mr. McMillan. I don't know why I fainted earlier....''

"A woman in your condition has to eat," he observed.

His was one of the few direct references made to her pregnancy since she'd arrived, and it threw her. Her mouth dropped open, her face felt as if it were on fire, and there was no earthly way her eyes could meet Roy's.

Her baby. In his words of love, Roy hadn't mentioned the fact that she was now two.

Could he love another man's child?

Roy changed the subject. "How was your trip to Paradise, Uncle Ed?"

Ed reached down to pick up the pie pan off the table. He busied himself with cleaning up. "Oh, the same as always."

In the silence that ensued, Ellie wondered how soon she could slip away and be by herself. She picked up her uneaten piece of pie and followed Ed to the pantry.

Roy tagged after them. "You sure did leave in a hurry. I could have helped you load the wagon if I'd known you were going to town today."

Ed laughed nervously. "I could tell you had your hands full with your patient."

Ellie blushed. Had he left the house to give them time alone?

But surely he couldn't have known how they felt about each other before they'd even realized it themselves! Why, when she'd first arrived this afternoon, Roy's bearish manner toward her had nearly driven her to walk back to the farm.

"Still, you hadn't mentioned leaving," Roy insisted.

Ed frowned, and looked slightly disoriented.

"Is something wrong?" Roy asked.

His uncle shook his head. "It's just a feeling I can't shake."

Roy looked alarmed. "What feeling? Aren't you well?"

"When I came through that door and saw you two sitting at the table, it reminded me of something."

"What?" Roy asked.

"Gettysburg."

Roy and Ellie exchanged glances. She gathered from the worried look on Roy's face that the war was not a subject Ed usually chose to dwell on. And why would seeing her and Roy in the kitchen together, their faces flushed from kissing, remind a man of a battlefield?

Ed hitched his baggy trousers and shook his head mournfully. "Isn't it strange, Roy? I made it through some of the worst battles a man could imagine, yet I never knew till today just what a coward I am."

When Roy walked into the kitchen the next morning, the place was in utter chaos. At least the usual apple madness wasn't under way, but there was now paper everywhere—on tables, on the floor, spilling out of cabinets.

Roy froze in the back door in amazement, till a strong wind blew in, sending a tornado of loose paper flurrying around the room.

Ed glanced up. Roy hadn't even seen him in all the clutter, but now he spotted his uncle kneeling by a cabinet in the corner of the room.

"Mornin', Roy!" He greeted him casually, as though nothing was amiss. "Shut the door and come on in and have some breakfast." He picked up a sheet of paper lining one of the little drawers in the cabinet, then tossed it aside. "Sleep okay?"

Roy sloshed through the sea of papers to the table,

where a fresh loaf of apple quick bread awaited the knife. "Fine."

He'd found bedding down in a barn much easier to take knowing that the woman he loved slept snugly inside. Ed had slept on the little sofa in the parlor upstairs, but from the looks of things, he hadn't slept much. A man had to get up early to create this much disorder.

"Coffee's on the stove," Ed said, "and help yourself to an apple."

Roy hunted down a coffee cup amid the debris, hoping that a few swigs of the strong stuff would give him enough mental sharpness to begin to fathom what was going on here. Last night his uncle had been mumbling about the war. This morning the kitchen looked like the scene of a pitched battle. Even after downing a whole cup of lukewarm inky coffee, he couldn't figure it all out.

"Uncle Ed...?" He cleared his throat. "Is something wrong?"

Ed, still kneeling and inspecting another piece of paper that had been lining a cabinet, glanced up with startled eyes. "Beg pardon?"

"I said, is there something wrong?"

"'Course not. Why?"

Roy gestured vaguely around at all the disarray. "I just wondered if there was a reason for all this...paper."

Ed looked around the kitchen and parlor as if he hadn't noticed anything out of the ordinary till just now. "Oh!" He chuckled. "Yes, I see. A little cluttered, isn't it?"

"A *little?*"

"Well, you see," his uncle replied, "I thought I'd buy myself a new suit."

That, apparently, was his explanation. He turned

away from Roy and began sifting through papers on the ground again.

"What does this paper have to do with buying a new suit?"

"Oh, well, a few years ago I was spring cleaning and I went through the house lining all the shelves with a Montgomery Ward catalog. So now..." he tossed the paper in his hand aside "—now I'm trying to find the page with the men's clothes on it."

"Good heavens!"

Ed nodded. "I know...it's turned into quite a project. I'm afraid it might be in the bedroom." He looked at Roy worriedly. "Do you think Ellie will be up soon?"

He obviously couldn't wait to start ransacking another room.

"If you're so set on having a suit, why don't you go see if Trilby's has one ready-made?"

Ed shook his head. "I don't want to do that. That Cora Trilby would have it all over town before I'd even handed her the money for it."

"Well good grief, who cares if you're buying some new clothes? You're entitled to, I guess." An idea occurred to Roy. "Or how about asking my mother?"

His uncle's face went slack with horror.

"Why not?" Roy surprised himself by recommending his mother, but today he was feeling generous. In fact, he was beginning to wonder if he weren't a changed man. "She's a seamstress, and I'm sure she could use the work."

"I could never..." Ed's words trailed off as he rifled through the papers with more fury than ever before.

"For that matter," Roy said, feeling a little uncomfortable seeing his uncle in such a state, "I don't see what's so wrong with your old suit. You looked fine in it last night.''

Which seemed strange, now that he thought about it. Did Ed always dress up to take his apples to the mercantile?

''Fine, you say?'' Ed barked out a laugh. ''It makes me look like an old snake who needs to shed his skin!''

Just then, Ellie appeared on the stairway, and seeing her nearly took Roy's breath away. For a moment he forgot about his uncle and catalogs and suits and simply focused on Ellie. She was so beautiful. And she loved him. He'd stayed up half the night marvelling at that fact. Every time he'd attempted to nod off to sleep, her face would swim in his mind's eye, causing his heart to soar.

But this morning, in the flesh, she was much prettier still. She'd dressed in her clothes from yesterday—she hadn't brought any others—and her red hair was mussed from sleeping on it. She looked all the more adorable for appearing slightly rumpled. And her eyes were still muzzy from sleep.

Or maybe they were muzzy with confusion.

He'd almost forgotten he was standing knee-deep in clutter.

''What's happened?'' she asked, her voice slightly croaky.

Roy smiled. ''My uncle wants to buy a suit.''

She frowned. ''But...''

''He lined his shelves with the Montgomery Ward catalog, and now he's looking for the page with men's clothing.''

''Oh!'' Ellie's eyes rounded. ''I saw it last night!''

Ed went rigid with surprise.

She nodded and pointed into the bedroom. ''When

I was fetching another quilt for you, Roy, I saw that very page at the bottom of the chest in the bedroom.''

Ed jumped to his feet, ran over to Ellie, and twirled her in a circle, laughing. "By gods, you are a wonder!'' He winked at Roy. "Hold onto this one, nephew.''

Roy looked at Ellie's pink cheeks and surprised eyes and felt something inside him melt. "Believe me, I intend to.''

"Your uncle said there's going to be a dance in town in a few weeks.''

Ellie could have kicked herself the moment the words were out. It sounded as if she were fishing for an invitation!

Which she wasn't. She wouldn't even know how to behave at a dance if she wasn't there to gather dirty punch cups. But she was curious…did Roy go to dances and talk and flirt with ladies? He would cut a fine figure on a dance floor—or anywhere for that matter. She found herself feeling jealous of women she didn't even know for sure existed—any woman who might have set her cap for Roy.

He took her arm and chuckled, and, as always, his merest touch sparked a fire inside her. She felt girlish, like skipping. Instead, she chuckled too, not even knowing why, and held onto his arm.

"I have to warn you, the dances here probably aren't what you're used to.''

She frowned, realizing suddenly that he had no idea what she was used to. Servitude. Her life hadn't been about dancing and laughing and idle afternoons paying social calls, as Roy probably imagined. "Roy, I should tell you that my life hasn't been all laughter and gaiety, as Parker might have led you to believe.''

He looked down at her, his eyebrows raised in mock alarm. "Hasn't it?"

They were strolling on a hillside—Roy called it a hillside, though it just looked to her like a slope—through Ed's apple orchard. The branches of the trees were mostly bare now, and at each step they took their feet crunched and then sank on the blanket of leaves dusted with snow. It seemed appropriate to Ellie that the very surface of the earth she walked on had changed since last night. Nothing felt the same. The morning air after the snow was clearer, crisper, the vista more unbroken and gleaming than anything she had ever seen before. Beyond this little patch of orchard, white fields stretched to the end of the horizon, dazzling her with their blinding brilliance.

She took a deep breath, filling her lungs with the clean air and filling herself with courage. "No, Roy, it hasn't." She didn't know how to begin to straighten the confused record of her past.

He gasped, stopped, then spun her around. "I've got to do something about that!"

"About what?"

"About your unhappy life—from now on I've got to make it a whirl of gaiety!"

His wide blue eyes were in such a comical panic that she couldn't help grinning. *"You?"* she asked, planting her hands on her hips and looked up at him saucily. "And here I was wondering if you even knew how to dance!"

"Dance? Why I can dance like the dickens!" he said, and to demonstrate, he pulled her into his arms and waltzed her around the orchard in steps that were actually great hopping leaps. They turned recklessly and fast, nearly bumping into trees, almost spinning out of each other's grasps. Ellie was breathless with surprise, yet laughter tumbled out of her anyway.

She'd never seen Roy this way, so smiling, so silly, so...

Adorable.

They snaked through the trees into a clearing, where their waltz degenerated into a spin like she hadn't done since she was a child—they practically touched toes, held each other at arms' length and simply whirled around and around and around till she felt dizzy with motion and laughter and looking into Roy's blue, blue eyes.

They finally flew apart, the force sending Roy against a tree and Ellie spinning off into the field until she finally collapsed in a heap on the snow. She was still laughing—so hard her side was beginning to hurt. She needed to stop, but when she looked up at Roy, she began giggling again.

"Told you I was going to make your life a whirl," he bragged.

She groaned at his silly joke, then felt laughter bubbling up in her all over again. In retaliation, she balled up a handful of snow in her glove and lobbed it at him. The white powder splattered on the shoulder of his coat.

His eyes widened in offense at her sneak attack. "Oh, so it's not fun you want, but war?"

Still chuckling, she shook her head—but she was too late; he was already bending down to ready his arsenal. When he came up and chucked a tight snowball at her that whizzed by her ear, barely missing her, she got up with a shriek and began running. Back through the orchard they flew, darting around tree trunks they used as barricades against the snowy missiles they launched back and forth. When Ellie reached the end of the orchard, she had no choice but to make a run for it across the open field to the nearest shelter, which was the barn.

She couldn't remember the last time she had sprinted, or even played outside. Not since she was a girl perhaps. She'd forgotten how wonderful it was to laugh till she was sick with silliness, or to run until she was simply exhausted.

Panting, she ducked inside the barn just ahead of Roy. She stepped to the side as soon as she cleared the door and watched Roy race right past her. He was halfway across the building before a nervous titter escaped her lips, causing him to turn, his expression a study in comic confusion. She barely held back another laugh.

"Trying to hide, are you?" One brow arched up and he took on a little of the stage villain's leer.

She giggled and in return for his efforts assumed the frightened cower of a beleaguered ingenue. Play-acting wasn't difficult with Roy striding toward her, hunched menacingly, clutching his melting snowball as if it were a dreaded weapon. "Please sir," she begged in a quavering high-pitched squeak, "do not bludgeon me with your icy mace."

"I'll do worse than bludgeon you, my pretty," he uttered with a low cackle.

And before she could ask what worse there could be, he grabbed her into his arms and pressed the snowball to her nape, provoking a very real squeal of surprise from her. She tossed her head, sending her hat flying, and pleaded for mercy. Roy, grinning, obliged, dropping his snowball and swinging her up into his arms for a kiss.

One touch of his warm lips instantly undid the snowball's damage to her temperature. She melted against him, cleaving to him as if she were born to have her hands entwined around his neck, her lips pressed to his. Delicious sensations coursed through her, torching to life desires she'd tried so hard to bury.

Such feelings couldn't be wrong. Not when she was so sure that what she felt now was love, and that her love was returned.

His lips left hers and she looked up into blue eyes darkened with passion. His gaze narrowed. "I'm sorry, Ellie—you must be exhausted," he said, pressing her head to his shoulder.

She closed her eyes and was barely aware of the fact that they were moving, covering the length of the barn with Roy's quick strides, past horse stalls and a tack room, beyond a pile of sweet-smelling hay to the very back of the building where there was a small cot. Though breathless, she felt far from tired, and yet she revelled in the feeling of snuggling against him like this, smelling his male scent mixed with the starch in his shirt and the sweet smell of hay all around.

When he stopped, her eyes blinked open. "What's this?"

He placed her gently on the small bed, a mattress tick stuffed with corn shucks.

"This is where I slept last night."

On this tiny bed? She wasn't sure whether to laugh or squirm with guilt. Poor Roy! "How did you even fit here?"

He eased down next to her, smiling. "It was snug, but to tell you the truth, I didn't much feel like sleeping."

"I can imagine!" she exclaimed. "You must have felt like a moose in a matchbox."

He tugged her gently into his arms. "That wasn't the reason I couldn't sleep, Ellie."

She remembered her own night in Ed's comfortable bed, and the restless hour she'd tossed and turned, thinking about Roy. "I understand."

His eyes lit with fire. "Do you?" He shook his

head as he gazed at her face, seeming to try to take in all of her at once. "I wish I could. I feel as if some strange affliction has taken over me. You've bewitched me, Ellie."

She loved it when he said her name, loved it when he pulled her a fraction closer, loved it when his gaze caught on her lips as if he just couldn't wait to kiss her again.

She loved him, period.

It was still so astonishing to think about! She smiled. "Could sorcery coax another kiss out of you?"

His answer was swift and sure. His lips captured hers again with the same hunger as last night. Only now, she realized happily, they weren't by a woodpile, or in a kitchen, but on a comfortable bed. That fact should have shocked her, but it didn't. Instead, all sorts of tempting thoughts circled the periphery of her consciousness.

Nor was she shocked when Roy reached inside her coat and caressed her breast through the muslin of her dress. The mere touch of his hand sent waves of pleasure through her, blocking out all other feelings. As he deepened the kiss, mating their tongues in a sensual dance, she held tight to his shoulders and thought only of *more*. She didn't want Roy ever to stop kissing her, touching her.

The most intimate feminine core of her stirred with heat, and as if sensing her need, Roy shifted his hand underneath her skirts, creating a molten trail up her woolen stockings to that core. He eased her onto her back and she tensed slightly as he fiddled with the plethora of undergarments standing between himself and her hub of desire. She didn't know what to expect—certainly not the gentle massage he lavished on her. His tender ministrations created a ferocious ache within her that could only be relieved by more of his touch. The heat spiraling inside her transported her to a world she'd only known through the exotic accounts of volcanoes and whirlwinds and hurricanes. All those forces held sway inside her, sweeping her feverishly along until her whole body quaked helplessly.

And when the storm ended, she lay next to Roy, mindless and numb, her head spinning as he pulled down her skirts. She'd never known such sensation was possible—never known a man could pleasure a woman selflessly. She was stunned, almost shamed when she realized she was sweating and sticky from her sated desire.

And the terrible part was, she still wanted more. Wanton, indeed!

He smiled down at her, kissing her forehead. His hand, lying on her hip, made a caressing motion and moved toward her middle. To her baby.

Ellie gasped, and shot up to sitting.

She was shocked, but not by her discovery of physical pleasure. Rather, it was Roy, and the realization that he didn't know the true story about the child she was carrying. For the past twelve hours she'd been so caught up in herself and her own desires and happiness, that she had almost forgotten that she had the feelings of another to consider.

There was so much Roy didn't know about her. Roy didn't know about her baby's father. Roy didn't even know that she wasn't a widow. What would he say when he realized that her baby was not the issue of legal matrimony?

How could she tell him?

"Ellie, what is it?" he asked, sitting up next to her.

She looked into his eyes, trying to gauge what his reaction would be. She wanted so to share her secret, to share the truth about the child she loved already though it wasn't born. Yet would Roy share her joy, her anticipation?

Or would he condemn her?

Of course, his actions indicated that he had few scruples about passion outside the marriage bed....

She frowned. Not that he'd whispered a word about marriage. He'd spoken of love, and vaguely of "the future," but she'd read of instances in the west of men and women cohabiting without marriage, calling each other "common-law" wives and husbands.

She didn't want that. For her baby, she wanted a real family. A loving father like she'd had. Yet she didn't want to beg a man to marry her, either.

But she didn't travel across the country to announce her child's illegitimacy to the world. If word got out, and Roy didn't marry her and she was stuck trying to get by in Paradise on her own...

"Ellie, is it the baby?" Roy asked nervously.

"Yes," she mumbled.

She couldn't deceive Roy indefinitely, but now, after what had just happened, didn't seem the right time to tell him her unfortunate life story. But then, when would ever be the proper time to unravel the web of falsehoods she'd woven around herself since coming to Paradise?

He swallowed, looking at her abdomen anxiously, as if an unexploded grenade were buried inside her. In a way, she supposed he wasn't far from the truth.

"I should have been more careful!" He swallowed with effort, and she detected a bead of sweat on his forehead. "It isn't...coming, is it?"

The pallor of his face indicated he would rather face a firing squad than a baby's birth. Heaven knows the prospect filled her with trepidation, too.

She forced a smile, and shook her head. "No, it's a few months away yet." Two months that suddenly seemed like a heartbeat. But surely some time during those two months she could find a better moment than now to explain the truth to Roy. "I just…felt its kick."

Roy exhaled in relief. "We'd better get you inside now."

He helped her off the bed, and she stood uneasily on her feet. She still felt physically spent, but now she was confused as well. Her legs balked at moving, even when Roy tried to tug her back toward the house.

"Is something the matter?" he asked, tenderly tucking a tendril of her hair behind her ear. She couldn't remember where her hat had gone.

She felt a restless stirring inside her just looking into his blue eyes, and a frustration. And a fear that she had been selfish.

Not to mention awe at Roy's restraint. Percy Sternhagen would never have passed up this opportunity to take his pleasure!

Or perhaps the thought of her baby had cooled Roy's ardor completely.

"Don't you…?" She couldn't bring herself to say the words coherently. "I mean, you didn't…"

Roy's face screwed up quizzically for a moment before he finally registered understanding. Then he laughed and pulled her into his embrace. "Not this time, Ellie. But there will be others. We have all the time in the world now, don't we?"

She nodded numbly, allowing the hopeful exuberance in his tone to overtake her trepidation. She put aside worrying that she'd just let an opportunity pass by, and that she was now, through her silence, trapped in a series of lies of her own making.

Chapter Twelve

He'd always thought men in love were the worst kind of fools, but now, as Roy tramped down the muddy sidewalks of Paradise with a spring in his step, he couldn't imagine why. He suddenly felt as if he were Rip Van Winkle awakening from a twenty-seven-year sleep.

Ellie was the best thing that had ever happened to him. Loving her gave him a purpose in life—in fact, thinking about her and their future together made the whole cockamamy idea of family and children finally make sense to him for the first time. Their kisses had unlocked that mystery.

He smiled to himself and patted the bulge in his coat pocket where a small box lay.

Knowing Ellie had changed him. Completely. And to show that he was a different man now, he was going to do something that until this morning he hadn't dreamed he'd do in a million years. He was going to see his mother.

No, more than that. He was going to forgive her, bury the hatchet, and start new. After all, she would be the grandmother to his children!

Roy knocked on her red door and waited. After a

few moments, he heard the light tread of her footsteps, and then the door opened. Seeing her always
surprised him—like being confronted with a specter
from a hazily remembered dream. He took a deep
breath and smiled.

She beamed back at him. "Roy! How nice of you
to drop by."

Her greeting, which almost made it sound as if his
"dropping by" were nothing out of the ordinary, took
him aback. He hesitated warily at the door a moment.

Then he remembered. He was a new man. A mag-
nanimous man.

He stepped across the threshold. "I should have
come before now."

He looked around the narrow, deep rooms and at
first was surprised by their ordinariness. Beautiful
green velvet drapes hung over the front windows, but
otherwise the room was empty. In the second room,
reached through an open archway, the only adornment
besides a worktable and two high-backed chairs was
a basket of fruit over the mantel.

She followed his gaze. "I know," she said with
her disarming, lilting laugh, "it's a very dull house,
so far. The upstairs isn't much better, though it will
be once all my things are shipped from Philadelphia."

"I see."

"Down here is my workroom." She gestured toward the chair. "The fire is nice and warm here, Roy.
Would you like to sit down?"

He couldn't stop staring at that basket, with its apples and jars of applesauce and apple cider. It could
only have come from one source—Ed—but his uncle
hadn't said a word about seeing Isabel the day he'd
come to town.

"Did you buy that at the mercantile?" he asked,
pointing to the basket.

Her eyes widened, and she shook her head. "It was left at the door. I wish your uncle had come in and given it to me in person. I've so wanted to speak to him!"

Good heavens! Was *that* what had had Ed so riled up when he came back from Paradise the other night? The poor man's references to cowardice and new clothes hadn't made a lick of sense to him then, but now he was afraid he was beginning to understand.

Of all things! She'd cast her spell on his uncle— innocent, happy Uncle Ed, who was now a bundle of nerves. He felt his own nerves jangling and came dangerously close to telling Isabel that she might as well give up hunting for husband number three because Ed was too good for her by a long shot.

But then again he remembered that he was a changed man. A man who understood how wonderful a thing love was. In his present mood, he shouldn't begrudge the wonderful feeling to anyone.

Even a woman who had a history of abandoning McMillans.

He took a deep breath. "Uncle Ed's shy, you know."

Her full lips tilted up in a smile. "Yes, I know. I've wanted to go out to his farm, but I was afraid I'd take him by surprise. Now, however, I worry that waiting for him to come see me mightn't be the wisest course, either."

"Oh, I think it is," Roy said quickly. Then he added, "I mean, I'm sure he'll come around again."

Maybe sometime this century!

"I hope so."

Even in her widow's weeds, Isabel was stylish and beautiful. Her skin was still taut, her figure tall and trim. He guessed that she was one of the best-looking older women he'd ever seen. That thought gave him an unmistakable, absurd feeling of pride, and for a moment, he was that four-year-old little boy again, boasting to all the other little boys at a prairie church meeting one Sunday in the McMillan soddy that he had the prettiest mother.

He hadn't been wrong, after all.

Strangely, for a moment, he felt a prick of uncertainty, as if he were a traitor to the little boy who had felt so lost and abandoned and resentful toward his mother all those years...but then he remembered. Now that he was a changed man, he could admit a few of Isabel's good points. He could mull over what Ed had told him about her, and start to see her leaving Nebraska all those years ago from her perspective. After all, Ed had intimated there had been violence in the house, and as much resentment as he'd harbored toward her, the thought of someone raising his hand to strike her made him shudder with anger. It was as unthinkable to him as someone hitting Ellie.

No woman should have to stand for that.

She took his arm and jostled it lightly to get his attention. When he looked down at her, surprised to have been caught lost in thought, she was grinning. "My, I always forget what a serious man you are, Roy. But I must say, you're handsome. Handsomer, even, than Abner was."

He was almost shocked to hear her mention his father—and so casually. "I was just thinking to myself how well you looked."

She smiled happily. "Thank you! We're a regular mutual admiration society today, aren't we? Would you like some tea?"

"Thank you."

The narrow, high-backed work chair she'd led him to didn't exactly make for comfortable seating, but he did his best to settle into the thing. Unfortunately, something was poking at him. He swivelled, then realized that something was his own coat. Remembering his purchase of that morning, he half stood and pulled the box out of the right pocket.

He'd meant to wait a while to bring the subject up, but now that he had the thing in his hand, he didn't see any reason to beat around the bush. Besides, he was too eager to get a woman's opinion on his purchase—a real woman's opinion, since he didn't trust Cora Trilby. She would have told him anything to make a sale.

"Look here—" he said, causing Isabel to swing away from the fireplace, her brows lifted in question. He felt his cheeks heat now that it was actually time to tell her. Heck, he didn't even know what to call this woman. Mother? Ma? Isabel? And here he was about to divulge his biggest secret to her!

Maybe this wasn't such a good idea after all...

Family, he reminded himself. Continuity. "See here, um, Mama," he blurted out awkwardly, jutting the little box toward her, "I've bought this ring for Ellie. I intend to ask her to marry me."

"Eleanor?" she asked, blinking in surprise. "Not the blond girl from the mercantile?"

Good heavens! Had *everyone* been spying on him and Clara? "No, no. Clara is just a…" *Pest* was the word that came to mind, but he let it drop. "Ellie and I are in love."

Isabel clapped her hands together in obvious delight. "Oh, Roy—how wonderful!"

He shrugged modestly, though inside he felt proud and absurdly puffed up by her approval. "I haven't actually asked her yet, but I intend to tonight. I was hoping you would give me an opinion on the ring. I've never bought a woman jewelry before."

She opened the little box and pulled out the silver

band and gasped in delight. A flower pattern of tiny pearls and diamond chips adorned the band. "How perfectly beautiful!"

His pulse kicked up and he scooted closer to her. "Do you think I should have picked something simpler? They didn't have much, and I didn't want to wait to go to Omaha."

"Absolutely not, Roy. You couldn't have chosen a better engagement gift. Any woman would be delighted with it, and I'm sure Eleanor will be overwhelmed."

Roy frowned. "I hope so."

He hadn't seen her wear jewelry—probably she'd left all her valuables in New York, assuming that Nebraska was not the place for flaunting wealth.

Isabel pushed the ring onto her little finger and admired it, and looking at his purchase adorning his mother's long elegant hand made Roy feel more sure about his choice. It was pretty and unique. Like Ellie.

She smiled at him. "So you're going to be a married man!"

Her tone made him feel as though getting married was a huge accomplishment. "When will the wedding be?"

Roy shook his head. "It's hard to say. Ellie might want a long engagement."

Isabel laughed. "Oh, I doubt that! I'll wager she's more eager than you are."

"But you see, we come from such different backgrounds, and I've never met any of her folks...."

His mother tilted her head doubtfully. "I was under the impression that she'd left very few people behind."

"True, but I still don't want to rush her into anything. Moving clear across the country will be a big step for her." Just the thought of moving Ellie from

Park Avenue to his farm had him tied up in knots. "It will be a big adjustment for her, although she's made quick progress learning all about the farm, and doing housework."

His mother laughed. "I don't wonder!"

"Of course she'll probably want to make quite a few changes out on the farm. New furniture and such. I'm ready for that."

Isabel shook her head and gazed on him with something like awe. "Roy, I have to say I so admire what you're doing for that poor girl!"

He smiled and was about to raise his shoulders in another modest shrug, when suddenly he felt a prick of apprehension. "I wouldn't call her that." He frowned. "Unless you know about…"

She sighed. "I know it all."

The baby. He and Ellie had barely discussed the matter, but Roy was certain of one thing. "I'll raise the child as if it were my very own."

His mother gazed at him in an admiration that went straight to his head, swelling it a few sizes. "How wonderful to hear you say that, Roy."

"Heck, I'm glad she'll be having a baby right away," he said. "I hope we have dozens."

She waved a hand dismissively. "It wasn't just the baby, it was everything. You should thank me, you know. I played matchmaker with you two!"

Roy frowned quizzically. "No you didn't. You told me there was something brewing between her and Parker."

She laughed. "I knew that would make you look twice at her. You see, I so wanted to do something nice for you—and her, too.

The poor girl was practically begging me for a job, but from some sort of intuition—call it unearned maternal wisdom, if you will—I sensed something would happen between you!''

Roy gaped at her. Even after chewing them over a second time, her words were incomprehensible to him. ''Ellie asked you for a job?''

''Yes, that day I visited you after your toe accident. She felt she'd already caused too much trouble and asked me to take her in. But of course she'd had no experience.''

Roy frowned. ''Of course not! Her life hadn't prepared her to make hats. My wonder is that she'd even want to!''

Maybe that silver mine investment was even more disastrous than she'd let on....

Isabel laughed. ''Well it's a certain bet she'd have a hard time finding a position like the one she had before, unless she went to Omaha or at least Kansas City. Certainly no one in Paradise is in need of a serving maid.''

The blood rushed through Roy's temples creating a roar inside his head. *Serving maid?*

Had his mother gone mad, or had he?

''Look, the kettle's ready!'' she said, hopping up spryly and taking two cups out of a small cabinet shelf. ''I'm so glad you've come, Roy. I'll admit I've been in rather low spirits lately.'' She hummed to herself as she took the kettle from the fireplace.

Roy barely heard her. He was still so stunned about Ellie. A maid? Surely his mother was wrong! He bolted out of his chair, startling the words out of her. ''When did Ellie tell you about herself?''

She poured water from the steaming kettle into a waiting pot. ''That same day. I guessed the truth.'' She laughed. ''Anyone could from those sad little weeds of hers.''

Roy breathed a sigh. She'd guessed—wrongly, no

doubt. His mother, who always dressed like a fine lady, though she wasn't one, probably wouldn't understand the mentality of a rich woman who didn't care about clothes. "She dresses like a maid."

Isabel *tsk*ed pityingly as she filled a tea strainer. "Yes, and then when I told her that it was obvious she wasn't the grand lady she was pretending to be, the poor thing just sagged in relief, and out poured the whole sad history of that snooty young ne'er-do-well she worked for who seduced her, and then her being fired in such a humiliating way, and her desperate decision to come here. She's quite a talker, your Ellie—so entertaining, though. The way she described it her life seemed like something straight out of a novel."

Roy's head was reeling. She hadn't been mistaken. Ellie had told her—told *Isabel,* whom she barely knew. But not him, her would-be husband. The man Isabel had told her to try to wrap around her little finger!

Novel? It didn't surprise him that Ellie's life would seem like a novel, since she'd apparently done nothing but plot it out since coming to Nebraska! His face burned as he remembered it all—a deception that had begun since before she'd stepped off the train. Her widowhood. The far-fetched story about a husband who'd drowned in the ocean. He'd been such a gullible fool, he'd spent half an hour teaching a maid how to change bedsheets!

What an actress!

Of course he'd known all along…or, at least, he'd certainly suspected her from the very beginning. From the moment he saw her at the railway station, carrying nothing but a few dusty bags, he'd had his doubts. That's how he'd broken his toe—checking on her to make sure she wasn't up to no good with his brother.

His trouble was he should have kept a closer eye on her and not have been swayed by her coquettish ways and pretty green eyes. Those honeyed kisses...

His head pounded. He couldn't speak. Anger roiled in him, especially when he heard his mother next to him, humming as she poured out two cups of tea. Humming! Because she was happy that he had just been duped. In fact, she'd encouraged Ellie!

At the sound of a cup rattling toward his back, he stiffened, then pivoted on his heel.

His mother's eyes widened. "Aren't you going to have your tea?"

His jaw clenched so tightly he was afraid he would grind his teeth down to dust. His voice came out as a bare rasp. "I'm sorry, I can't."

Her face fell. "Is something wrong, Roy?"

He wasn't going to cry on Isabel's shoulder about this, that was for damned sure. He wasn't going to cry, period. He wasn't such a damned fool that he didn't know a bit of luck when he saw it. Isabel and her little revelation had just saved him from attaching himself to a scheming woman.

"Nothing's wrong," he said stonily. "I'm just eager to get back to the ranch. To talk to Eleanor."

"Oh, don't forget this!" She pulled the ring off her pinkie finger and turned to drop it in its little box. When she handed it to him, her brow was furrowed. "Are you sure you won't stay and take something to drink? You look feverish."

He stuffed the box into his pocket. "No, it's important that I go now."

In fact, he had to hold himself from hitting the door running. Gathering his wounded pride around him like a second coat, he said good-night to his mother and strode quickly down the sidewalk. The sound of his boot heels against the pine planks echoed in his ears. *Deceived. Deceived. Deceived.*

So much for being a changed man!

"I don't think I've ever seen a woman so happy."

"That's because there never was one." Ellie grinned at Parker, hesitant to bring up a taboo subject. She decided to throw caution to the wind. "You must feel pretty good yourself, knowing that Roy isn't in love with Clara Trilby."

A slight smile tipped at his lips. "I'll admit I was worried. My mother had me convinced that wedding bells were ringing."

Ellie laughed. "Appearances can be deceiving— thank heavens!"

He nodded. "You know what the most amazing thing is? I've never seen *Roy* so happy, Ellie."

That observation meant all the world to her. More than her own happiness, even, she wanted good things for Roy.

And she was going to make those good things happen. Starting now. She had her sleeves rolled up over a steaming laundry tub in the kitchen, filled with his clothes. She was going to show him that she was someone who could work hard and stick by him through thick and thin. She was going to show him....

That she loved him. Every time she thought about it—and about the miracle of his loving her back—she felt her body go as limp as one of her overcooked dumplings.

Parker laughed. "You're both a sight."

She felt like dancing, but instead concentrated on scrubbing an old work shirt against the washboard. "Wouldn't it be wonderful if feeling like this could go on and on?" she mused. "It's like being lost in a good story—only it's real."

He stretched out his legs, leaned back, and gazed at her long and hard. "You mean you don't think your story will have a happy ending?"

"Oh, it's not that!" She shook her head, chuckling. As long as she could share her life with Roy, she would be happy. "It's just that there are always a few bad days, little bumps on the road, trials no one foresees."

He nodded. "Sometimes we create those bumps ourselves."

Some brittle undertone in his words made her straighten up warily. His blue eyes pierced right through her, right down to her soul, and she felt her stomach flop. "What do you mean?"

He cleared his throat. "I haven't wanted to say anything, seeing how happy you two were, but before Roy gets back, I wanted to ask you."

"Ask me what?"

"When you're going to tell him."

She relaxed slightly. "About the baby? We've talked about that. He said days and days ago that he knew about it—that you all knew from the very beginning. I felt like such a fool, but you all have been so kind, so circumspect..."

He shook his head. "Not the baby, Ellie. You. When are you going to tell him about you?"

Her mouth felt as if she'd swallowed a sand dune. "You mean...?"

His head jerked in a curt nod. "I mean telling him you're not a lady."

"But..." Her neck and cheeks were aflame with embarrassment. And shame. "How long have you known?"

He tilted his head. "I've had my suspicions. Things here and there that you would do—calling one of us "sir," for instance. Or the fact that your clothes had crooked seams, as though you'd made them yourself.'' He nodded toward the washtub. "And that you sometimes pick up things like doing the wash instinctively, as if you've watched a lot of housework being done in your time.''

"I…'' She hardly knew where to begin. "Why didn't you say something?''

He chuckled gently. "I didn't mind, for myself. I got a kick out of wondering how long you could keep it up. Heck, I might never have mentioned it…except for Roy.''

She felt stricken.

"You *were* going to tell him, weren't you?''

She frowned. "Yes, of course—except to be perfectly honest, I haven't been exactly keeping up appearances lately. That is, I haven't been putting on an act with Roy, if that's what you mean. I've become so comfortable here, most of the time I forget all about pretending to be a rich lady.''

"So you think he's come to love the real Ellie Fitzsimmons?''

The thought of that not being the case made her quake with fear. "Of course! Don't you?''

He nodded. "I don't think he's marrying you for your nonexistent fortune.''

No, Roy wouldn't do that. Even if she had been rich, she knew that would make no difference to him. "He's honorable to a fault. That's part of why…''

He smiled, almost pityingly. "You love him?''

She lifted her chin. "Yes.''

"And you don't think a man who's honorable to a fault will look askance at your having lied?''

Now that she saw how it must look when she did confess, she was mortified, ashamed. "But I swear, my having no money—''

"It's not the money,'' Parker said, interrupting

firmly. "It's the fact that I suspect there was never a Mr. Fitzsimmons, was there?"

Oh lord. This was it then; her tarnished reputation had chased her all the way across the country. Her face burned, and she shook her head and admitted in a barely audible voice, "No."

"Your baby is fatherless."

The words were like a punch to the gut, and just as she'd wanted to argue with Mrs. Sternhagen months ago, she felt the same reflexive anger kick in now. But she couldn't yell at Parker, either, because, in terms of what society thought, he was correct. Her baby would be illegitimate.

How she hated that word! How could anyone she cared about so much be dismissed so derisively, so callously? Her feelings for this baby weren't illegitimate. His or her life would be just as long, just as full of challenges and hardship and joy as the child of the most respectable couple in the country. Why couldn't the rest of the world accept a child into their midst without blaming it for the fault of its mother?

She sighed. Her efforts to shield her child from stigma had brought her to Nebraska, had made her lie to the very people who were offering her their hospitality. And now, because of her lies, she had failed her child in her first endeavor to protect it.

"I'm sorry," she said, but she wasn't sure she was speaking to Parker or to the young life stirring inside her.

"I'm sure you intended no harm," Parker said. "I don't think you have a mean bone in your body. But as much as I like you, Ellie, I can't stand idly by while my brother is taken in by a lie."

"No of course not," she said. "I'm sure I would feel the same way. I'll tell Roy the moment I see him."

"Tell me what?"

Ellie whirled toward the door, startled by Roy's deep voice. "Roy!"

Caught in his thunderous gaze she could tell that something was very, very wrong. "When did you get back?"

He stood smack in the center of the doorway, his arms folded. "Just now."

Her heart sank. He wasn't looking at her hungrily...except maybe with the gleeful hunger of a cat about to toy with a mouse.

"Sounds like you two were having a cozy little discussion here," Roy observed, looking from Parker to Ellie with exaggerated interest.

Parker smiled as if there wasn't anything in the least wrong with Roy's demeanor. "Ellie's practicing on your wash."

"I'm sure she would need practice. She probably hasn't done wash for people in..." Roy's lips turned up in something between a snarl and a sneer. "How long has it been since you've done wash for people, Eleanor? One month? Two? Or did your employers boot you out of your job longer ago than that?"

Ellie shuddered. Oh, Lord, he'd found out—found out before she could tell him the truth! But how could he have found out? Did he guess?

If only she hadn't been running around like a fool in paradise for the past two days, she would have had the sense to know that she should tell him about herself. She was so ashamed she could hardly speak. She licked her lips, her eyes trained on the floor. "I was let go a few weeks before I came here."

"Came here to...what?" His blue eyes glittered darkly when she hazarded a glance up at him. "Marry one of us because your rich sweetheart would bed you but not wed you?"

She gasped. He'd been talking to Isabel! She was the only person in Paradise who could have given him information like this. That it had been muddled in translation just made it all sound more sordid. "He was not my sweetheart!"

"That's right—there was some sad story that went along with your misfortune. Rich man, poor girl. Mother said you'd made it sound like a novel."

Parker frowned. "Roy, don't."

Roy was too focused on Ellie to hear his brother. "Did you come here hoping Parker would marry you? Or did you think your chances were better with two brothers in the house?"

"No," she said, her voice barely a whisper.

"Then why did you lie about being rich?"

"That masquerade began a year ago," she confessed, "when Parker and I first started writing. In his letter he addressed me as the lady of the house, and I played along, because it seemed more interesting than having to write him that I was just a maid."

Parker nodded. "You had me fooled, all right. I thought I was writing to Mrs. Vanderbilt."

Roy shot him a quelling gaze. "It doesn't take much talent to report what she saw through a keyhole." He fired his gaze on her. "I knew all along something was strange about your coming here. I sensed you were a fraud from the very beginning."

Every word he tossed at her stung like a dart, and the worst part was, he was right. She *was* a fraud. She had taken people who'd meant only kindness, and played them for fools for her own ends. "I'm sorry, Roy. I just wanted to give my baby a fresh start and clean name. That's why I lied. Not to trap you."

He laughed.

It took all her courage not to turn tail and run out the back door. But she knew she could never live with herself if she didn't try to explain to him how real her feelings were. "But you have to believe that the past two days weren't a lie, Roy. I wasn't masquerading when I told you I loved you."

Parker got out of his chair quietly and attempted to make an exit, but was stopped by Roy.

"Don't bother sneaking away, Parker. There isn't going to be any tearful reunion."

At his harsh words, Ellie panicked and ran up to Roy. "Can you just dismiss everything between us so easily? Kisses? Words of love?"

His lips flattened to an intractable line. "I wouldn't mention those things right now. Being reminded of them doesn't exactly make me swell with longing."

His sarcasm hit her like a blow. What a cool customer he was, how unforgiving! But of course she'd known that. He'd spent nearly a quarter of a century harboring a grudge against Isabel.

He brushed past her, and she grabbed at his arm, nearly wincing at the hardness of the tensed muscles beneath her hand. "Roy, where are you going?"

He turned, and the look he sent her chilled her to the bone. "To Uncle Ed's. This time, don't follow."

Yanking his arm away, he stormed out the doorway, leaving nothing but a blast of cold air where he had been just moments before.

Ellie stood frozen, stunned.

Parker patted her on the shoulder, but the gesture brought her little comfort. She knew she deserved all the vitriol Roy had hurled at her.

She looked into Parker's kind eyes, then took in the rest of him. She was surprised to see that he'd put on his coat.

"I'll go after him," he explained. "I'll talk sense into him."

She shook her head violently. "Please don't—it won't do any good."

"He's just angry."

"He has a right to be angry."

Unbelievably, Parker grinned. "Watch out. You're starting to think like him."

Anguish kept her from smiling back at him. "You warned me, Parker. I only wish I had been smart enough not to need the warning. I wish I—"

He put his forefinger to her lips. "Wish all you want—but Roy's getting a head start and I have to go." He put on his hat. "Besides, knowing Roy, he would have felt just as aggrieved no matter when you'd told him."

But she would have felt better about her own behavior, she thought. She wouldn't have been so clearly in the wrong.

"I'll be back in a blink," Parker promised her.

Maybe, she thought as he closed the door after him. But she doubted Roy would be coming back with him.

Chapter Thirteen

"Roy, don't be a damn fool."

Roy leaned on his saddle horn and looked impatiently into his brother's eyes. A bracing wind was sweeping across the prairie, but the moon was bright and clear. "Is that the message Ellie sent you thundering out here to deliver?"

Parker shook his head. "She didn't send me. She didn't want me to come."

"Then she has more sense than I gave her credit for."

His brother gazed at him steadily. "You've got less than I gave you credit for, Roy."

Roy sputtered indignantly. "Why should I stay back there when it's obvious she's been manipulating us?"

"How? By pretending to be rich?" He tilted his head. "You weren't planning on being a millionaire, were you, Roy?"

Roy squinted. "'Course not."

"It was a harmless charade, born out of desperation."

"Harmless? Does her desperation make it any better that she used us, staying in our house posing as something she wasn't, while all the while she was angling for one of us?''

"How do you know she was angling?"

Roy laughed bitterly. "Look what happened!"

Parker smiled one of those wiser-than-thou smiles at him. "Are you sure you fell in love with her because *she* wanted you to and no other reason?"

"It certainly didn't happen the normal way."

"What way is normal?"

"I don't know...." Roy shifted uncomfortably. "All I know is that nothing has been normal since that woman came to town."

"You're right. It's been better."

"Better for you, maybe," Roy shot back. "I'm the one who's been ground through the mill like a juicy piece of sorghum. You've just been sitting back enjoying the show."

"You know what I've really enjoyed? Seeing you look happy."

"Happy?" The word came out somewhere between a yelp and a howl. "Ever since she came here I've been sleeping out in the freezing cold with a man whose snores rattle the barn walls. I've had my toe broken. I've been running around on fool errands when there's work to be done." Even in the heat of the moment, he decided it best not to mention his travails with Clara Trilby. "Is *that* your notion of happy?"

Parker smiled wistfully, as if he'd just described something wonderful. "These past weeks, it was like seeing a bear come out of hibernation. You came back to life."

Roy winced. Just this afternoon he'd been thinking the same thing. That he'd come out of a trance. He didn't like being reminded of how good that felt—of

how much his old bachelor suit seemed to pinch and
tug at him now that he'd put it on again.

"Well look at me now and tell me how much you
enjoy seeing me like this," Roy said heatedly. "Because she's responsible for this, too—and this sure as
hell isn't happiness."

Parker sighed. "If you leave now, Roy, if you don't
even give her a chance…"

"A chance to what? Twist me around her pinkie
finger again?"

"Is that why you resent her so?" Parker asked.
"Or is it really because you now know she gave her
heart to someone else before you?"

The suggestion made Roy practically roar with indignation. "That's a very interesting question you
raise! How can we be sure this sob story she's told
is what really happened? She might have had a hundred men in New York, for all we know."

Parker looked skeptical. "You don't believe that."

"Ha! As far as I'm concerned, we shouldn't trust
a word she says from now till doomsday."

His brother was silent for a moment. Then he
looked at Roy with his piercing blue eyes and asked,
"What's going to happen to her?"

Roy blinked. "Happen to her?"

"How's she going to get by?"

"She earned her living before."

"But now, with the baby on the way…."

Roy fought the uncomfortable sympathy threatening to overcome his ire. "We aren't responsible for
her problems. If she needed my help, she could have
asked for it instead of trying to trick me into taking
care of her for the rest of her life."

Parker stared at him with those blue eyes so intently that Roy had to look away.

"If she has any decency, she'll leave our house."

"And go where?"

Where could a woman like that go? A woman with a baby and a shady past didn't have a lot of options. Especially in these little towns—although, frankly, the cities weren't much better. He could think of only one option, and it was decidedly unsavory.

Sweat broke out on Roy's temple as anger built inside him. Parker and his incessant questions! If they sat out here in the cold mulling over the problems of the world much longer, he was apt to do something entirely foolish, like gallop back to the house and take Ellie into his arms, common sense be hanged. Pride be hanged.

Damn!

He reached deep into his pocket, pulling out part of the money Cora Trilby had given him when he'd returned the ring. He handed it to Parker. "Here," he said gruffly. "If it makes you feel better, give her this."

Parker stared at the money in his hand. "Twenty dollars?"

"She should be able to get to Omaha on that. Omaha's a big place." The words seemed to tumble frantically out of his mouth. "Something will work out for her there."

"Do you really think so, Roy?"

Roy bridled indignantly. "How should I know? I'm a farmer, not a fortune teller. Just send her on her way."

"Are you going to stay with Uncle Ed?"

"Until she's gone, yes."

Parker nodded, his expression almost mournful. "All right, Roy." Without another word, he turned and spurred his horse back to the house.

Roy was glad to see him go. But though he no longer had his brother's knowing gaze pinned on him, he *felt* as if he did. Guilt mixed with anger mixed with something else again waged a mighty battle inside him.

But what did *he* have to feel guilty about? He hadn't made Ellie any promises! He'd given her hospitality, more than his reason told him he should have, and she'd repaid him with deceit.

Still, Roy stared after Parker's retreating horse, fighting the urge to follow him. But that would be sheer folly, he knew. Ellie was a woman who made him forget his better judgement. She'd cast some sort of spell on him, and the best thing to do would be never to see her again.

Ever.

The look on Parker's face when he came back into the house told Ellie all she needed to know.

Roy wasn't going to forgive her.

She held up her hand, silently pleading with Parker not to give her the grim details.

He doffed his hat and combed his hand through his light hair. "I'm sorry, Ellie. I thought I could bring him around, but I couldn't. That brother of mine has a head like a mule's."

"He's angry, as he has every right to be."

"But if he'd just see the thing from your angle...."

"It wouldn't change the situation. I made a mistake and now..." Now there was an aching pain inside her that felt as if it would never go away. She wished she could throw herself on her bed and cry for about twenty years. "Believe me, Parker, if I'd known the trouble I was bringing to your family, I would have stayed in New York."

Even her pathetic existence as Mary O'Malley's unwanted houseguest was preferable to feeling as if her heart had just been split in two.

She stared at Parker. He appeared to want to say something more, though she wasn't certain she had the mental strength for further conversation. There was nothing left to say anyway.

Ike came bursting in from a long day mending fences in the south pasture, his face florid from the wind and cold. "Lord 'a mercy!" he cried, banging the dust off his boots on the threshold. "Such goings-on! Roy's galloping away, Parker's galloping away, then back. I didn't know what to make of it all. Is Ed okay?"

Parker nodded. "Far as I know."

Ike's smile faded as he registered their expressions. "Oh. See, I saw Roy headed toward Ed's and I wondered…" He looked at the washtub in the middle of the kitchen, as if it might hold some answers, then hazarded a glance up at Ellie.

Her face turned pink; she wanted to run and hide. "I finished the wash, but I'm afraid I didn't have time to empty the tub…."

For some reason, having left the dirty water there made her feel all the more miserable. As if she would always be leaving messes too big for herself to clean up.

Ike jumped in before she could dissolve into a puddle of self-pity. "Don't bother your head about it, Ellie," he said kindly. "I'll take care of it."

"Thank you, Ike. I'm sorry."

He chuckled. "Nothing to be sorry for!"

Which only drove home the fact that he'd missed out on the last hour's drama. Ike picked up the tub as if it weighed nothing at all and hauled it outside.

When he was gone, Parker cleared his throat and reached hesitantly into his pockets. "Roy gave me something for you…."

For a moment, Ellie's heart picked up. Had Roy

written her a note? Even if it was a letter berating her again, she still wouldn't have minded. Perversely, she savored the idea of hearing more from him, of finding out that it wasn't so easy for him to dismiss her from his heart.

She ran over to Parker like a kid hoping for Christmas candy—only when she held out her hand, he placed twenty dollars in it.

She looked at the bills and felt as though the blood were draining out of her, leaving ice water in her veins.

Money? For some reason, it was the last thing she had expected from him!

"He must be desperate for me to leave."

Of course he was; while she was in his house he wouldn't live there. She nodded, seeing how selfish she was to think that she could even stay there another day. And she didn't want to. It's just everything had happened so quickly, she hadn't thought about the future....

"I'll go tonight," she promised.

Parker shook his head furiously. "No, Ellie. Wait."

"Wait for what? For morning?"

"No, I meant..."

She smiled, understanding. He thought she could stay indefinitely, hoping Roy would come around. "You know as well as I that he won't change his mind."

Ike came in through the back door again, more quietly this time. Ellie looked up at him and forced a smile.

"Could you take me into town, Ike?"

"Now?"

Parker interceded. "Not now, Ellie—wait till morning, at least."

The two men stared at her. If she insisted, they

would do as she asked. But Ike looked exhausted after his day—none of them had even had supper, she remembered—and Parker just didn't appear inclined to help her leave the farm at all.

She sighed. "All right. In the morning then."

Taking his cue from Parker, Ike even looked reluctant to do that. But he finally nodded. "All right, Ellie. You just say when."

"Thank you, Ike."

She smiled, feeling as if she would burst into tears if she stayed in the kitchen with these two kind men for another minute. She slapped Roy's twenty dollars on the table and left them quickly.

In her wake, Ike and Parker fixed and ate their late meal in mournful silence.

A night spent tossing and turning—in Roy's bed, of all places—didn't make Ellie feel any better, but it firmed up her resolve. She didn't have enough money to get back to New York, much less start a life there. So she would just have to swallow the last shreds of her pride, accept Roy's money, and stay in Paradise. Seeing Roy again from time to time would just be the price she would pay for what she'd done.

She still burned with humiliation. For the second time in as many months, she was being bundled up and thrown away like old fish bones in newspaper, but this time she had only herself to blame. How long would it take her to learn that she couldn't dream that her life would suddenly transform into a magnificent fairy-tale ending? For her baby's sake, if not her own, she needed to start being more realistic.

And to women like her, that meant getting a job.

She loaded up her bags and went out into the parlor to face Parker and Ike. She'd turned down Ike's offer of breakfast already. She didn't think she would ever eat again.

In the parlor, Ike was waiting for her, his hat in his hand.

She breathed a sigh of relief that things were moving quickly. She looked around for Parker. She couldn't leave without saying goodbye. "Where's Parker?"

Ike's face was almost beet-red. "He's, um, out."

She glanced around, confused. "Is he in the barn?"

"He went out for a walk because I told him I wanted to speak to you," Ike blurted out. "Private-like."

Ellie shifted uncomfortably, uncertain where this was all leading. "What's wrong, Ike?"

"Oh, nothing's wrong, ma'am—I mean miss."

So…he'd heard the story.

Ike hesitated, then beat his hat against his leg. After a moment of fidgeting and twisting, he glanced up at her shyly. "What I mean to say is, I was wondering if you would marry me."

Ellie's jaw dropped.

"If you would do me the honor," Ike added in a rush.

For a moment, she was purely speechless.

Now that the question was out in the open, Ike appeared a little panicky. "Don't worry, Ellie, I'm not fool enough to think you might love me or anything like that. Heck, that'd be akin to a doe fallin' for a leathery old steer."

"Oh, Ike, it wouldn't be like that at all!"

He craned his head. "But you see, I like you real well. I guess you're the finest lady I've ever known since my mama, and it don't matter to me none where you came from or what you did. You might not be a lady, but you always treated me like a prince. I know you didn't mean no harm.''

A lump built in her throat.

Ike shrugged. "I'm just a crusty old farmhand, Ellie, and I'm sure I always would be a bachelor, exceptin' I can't think of drivin' you into Paradise and maybe you catching a train and then my not knowin' what'll become of you and that little baby.''

Last night she had cried until her head ached. Cried until she thought she'd dried up every drop of moisture in her. But now, amazingly, she felt new tears sting her eyes.

As the tears streamed down her cheeks, Ike looked stricken. "I'm sorry, Ellie. I didn't intend to set you off.''

She shook her head. "These aren't tears of unhappiness, or self-pity. Just gratefulness.'' She took his hands. "You *are* a prince, Ike. That's the nicest gesture anyone's ever made me.''

He cocked his head doubtfully. "Then your answer's yes?''

She dabbed her eyes with her sleeve. "No, Ike. My answer's no.''

At the look of relief that came over his face, she had to laugh. "And don't worry about my getting on a train and not knowing what's become of me. I'm staying in Paradise, so you'll know.''

A wide grin broke out across his face. "That's wonderful, Ellie.''

Seeing how relieved he was when she turned him down only made her all the more grateful to him for offering her marriage in the first place.

"I'm glad you're stayin' in Paradise, Ellie. This town could use a few of you.''

She chuckled. "Really? I'm not certain it's ready for just one of me.'' She let go of his hands and leaned back on her heels. "But whether it's ready or not, are you ready to drive me there? I swear that's all I really need."

He nodded and put his hat on. "Sure enough. I'll go get the horses hitched."

After he was gone, Ellie took a last turn about the house, checking that she hadn't left anything, fighting the melancholy that filled her as she looked at the familiar surroundings that she would in all likelihood never see again. Polly, the kitten, was batting a toy she'd made for him—an old sock stuffed with straw—around the rug. She remembered Roy presenting her with the kitten, the joy she'd felt, and now felt a stab of pain at having to leave him behind.

But the kitty might not be welcome where she was going. She would just have to ask Ike to make sure Polly was given his corn mush every day, and a few leftover tidbits from the table at night.

When she finally pushed open the front door, she was surprised to find she was stepping out into a day that reminded her of springtime. Sitting on the old weathered rocker on the porch, apparently enjoying the break in the weather, was Parker.

He smiled at her. "I gather from Ike that you're not in a marrying mood today."

She shook her head. "Poor Ike. He was ready to give up all his freedom just for me."

"It's not such a bad trade-off."

"I couldn't do that to him."

His brow cocked humorously. "Well then...would you consider doing it to me?"

She was stunned. Everybody, it seemed, was willing to marry her except the man she truly wanted! "Oh, Parker. You know it would never work. I'm in love with Roy and you...well, I have a feeling that there's a certain someone in Paradise who you'd rather spend the rest of your life with.''

"Actually, I was just thinking we could get engaged. That would do just as well.''

She let out a gasp of surprise, then laughed. ''Why would you want to do that?''

"Well…for one thing, people aren't above wanting something they can't have. Roy included.''

"Oh, no.'' She flapped her arms in front of her to let him know she wanted no part of trying to lure Roy back into her life. ''I've caused enough trouble around here, Parker. My days of deception are over.''

"It wouldn't be a real deception.''

Her lips twisted into a wry smile. ''And here you were lecturing me just last night on how you couldn't allow your brother to be misled!''

He leaned back and grinned. ''It's not just my brother I'm trying to fool.''

Clara Trilby came to mind again, and she suddenly understood. ''You'd like to use me as your bait to catch a sweetheart?''

Parker grinned. ''You make it sound awfully cold and calculating.''

"It is!''

He laughed. ''Maybe. But you know the saying, to catch a mouse you have to build a better mousetrap.''

She shook her head. ''I'm sorry, Parker.'' And she genuinely was. She owed Parker so much, she would have done anything for him…almost. But this she couldn't do—she was going to be on the up-and-up from now on. No doing anything that Roy could interpret as duplicitous.

Not that she was trying to impress Roy—an impossible task in any case. She just didn't want to sink any more in his esteem.

"You won't help me?''

"I'm through pretending. I just came crashing down from seventh heaven like Icarus with his wax wings, remember? From now on, my feet are going to be treading on solid ground."

He nodded. "I understand."

She smiled. "But of course, you're free to visit me as much as you like. I can't be responsible for how other people interpret your visits."

His brows raised with interest.

"You would be in full view of everyone at the mercantile," she promised him.

"You mean you're going to try to get a job there?"

She shook her head. "Next door. You might have to ask your mother for permission to call on me."

The news brought Parker to his feet. "That's wonderful."

"It will be if your mother will give me a job. But I think she will." She opened her purse to check on the money she'd taken from the table last night after everyone had gone to sleep. "You see, I've decided to put Roy's money to good use and offer myself to Isabel as an apprentice. Do you think he'll be pleased?"

Parker grinned. "I think he'll be livid."

"Good."

She straightened her shoulders, silently gratified by the prospect of still being able to get under Roy Mc-Millan's skin.

Chapter Fourteen

God, it felt good to be back at the Lalapalooza!

Roy gazed around the old barroom with its polished oak bar, the long fancy mirror and girly picture above it—holdovers from the good old frontier days, when the world was populated mostly with homesteaders and soldiers, with no women to offend. He swivelled on his stool and took in the old familiar tables, where a few men were starting up card games and talking excitedly about the capture of the Dalton Gang a few weeks back in Coffeyville, Kansas, not leaving out gruesome details.

The outlaw talk warmed his spirits. That's what men should be concerned with—poker and shootouts and crop yields. Not women. The only female in the place was Flouncy, a regular here, who was flirting with Jim Campbell. Jim seemed more intent on cards and vigilante massacres at the moment than buying Flouncy a drink, and Roy could understand the sentiment. He was so grateful to be back in a world of rotgut liquor and gambling and the real spirit of male camaraderie, his eyes felt almost misty.

Or maybe he was tearing up because he wasn't used to the tobacco smoke....

He tossed down a glass of whiskey and smiled to himself. One week without *that woman*—he didn't dare think her name—and he was fine. Just fine. He was back at home, back in his comfortable room in the house, back to his old routines. Ike was driving him crazy, Parker was moaning again—Roy couldn't have been happier.

Except, of course, if *that woman* had done the decent thing and cleared out of Paradise.

But of course, being the pain-in-the-neck creature that she was, she hadn't. Instead, she'd chosen the place where, next to his own house, he would have wanted her least. His mother's!

It probably never occurred to her to consider how he might feel knowing that she was right there in Paradise all the time, and that he couldn't even go to the mercantile anymore without having to worry about bumping into her, which he was determined not to do if he could help it. But a woman who would go to the lengths that she did to trick a man would never think about going to the same lengths to make amends.

It wasn't as if he'd been asking for much.

He just wanted her gone.

And while he was at it, he wanted her out of his memory. He wondered if drink could remedy that problem.

The bartender wiped up a spill nearby. "Another whiskey, Carl," Roy said.

Carl, a redhead who was so tall and skinny he practically had to double over to pour a drink, nodded. "Makin' up for lost time, Roy? We haven't seen you for a while."

They'd missed him! "Good to be back, Carl. Just leave the bottle."

He poured himself a big one and felt it burn its

way right past the place that had been hurting. His idiotic heart.

The drink warmed and relaxed him, so much so that he fought against a wave of sleepiness. He remembered that he hadn't had a decent night's sleep in over a week; even in his old soft bed, the mattress he'd been missing all those weeks, he'd been tossing and turning, restless.

Some nights as he lay awake, he wondered whether Ellie was blinking up at a dark ceiling, too, remembering their kisses and murmured words of love. Whether she could remember playing chase through the bare orchard, and laughing themselves silly when he'd caught her. He hadn't ever laughed like that before, certainly not with a woman.

He sucked his glass dry and hung his head.

Parker had warned him that it would be awful not knowing what happened to Ellie when she left Paradise...but then she hadn't left. And it was still awful.

Now he had a pain in his chest *and* a thorn in his side. His own mother had taken her in, so it felt as if the two of them had ganged up on him. If Ellie had left, maybe he would have been able to forget her. At least he wouldn't have to tiptoe around his own town, worried about turning the next corner. He wouldn't have to fret about the talk that would erupt when Ellie had her baby. He wouldn't have to see that baby, either, while inevitably he would if she stayed here.

His glass slopped over, making a small crash as it crashed against oak. Roy jolted back to awareness, shrugging sheepishly at Carl as he uprighted the tumbler.

"You better take it easy," the barkeep advised.

Roy forced a smile. "Slippery fingers—I guess that's my trouble."

Someone snickered behind him. "Or slippery women."

Stiffening, Roy swivelled around on his stool and found himself squinting at Jim Campbell. He was seated with a few other top hands who'd come to town to start their Saturday night a little early. "What's that supposed to mean?"

Jim grinned. "I guess you'd know."

Roy jutted out his chin stubbornly. "No, I don't."

A friend of Jim's piped up, "Heck, everybody in town's talking about that woman your mama's taken in. A hen can't hide her eggs forever, you know."

To have Ellie be the subject of barroom gossip got his blood fired up. The legs of his stool scraped angrily against the rough floor as he got to his feet. "So? Haven't you ever heard of a woman having a baby before? Nothing wrong in that."

"Nope," Jim agreed. "But it's not the baby everyone's talkin' about so much as the lack of a husband."

"She's a widow."

That assertion was met by a hearty round of guffaws.

"C'mon, Roy. She's no more a widow than she's the rich lady everybody was sayin' she was a couple of weeks ago. A rich lady who begged for jobs at the hotel?"

Roy's face turned red. She'd tried to get a job at the hotel? Had the whole world known more about Ellie than he had?

Someone else chimed in, "Heck, I'd bet my next payday that she's no more an heiress than Flouncy here."

Flouncy tossed her dyed red hair back and struck a snooty pose, bringing hoots and jeers from the men around her.

Roy's blood boiled.

"C'mon, boys," the saloon girl said with a wink, "won't somebody spare a drink for a poor widder woman?"

Her pantomime of a demure pregnant matron brought down the house.

"Ask Roy!" Jim hollered. "He'd give you the shirt off his back and let you live with his mama!"

In a heartbeat, Roy was flying toward Jim and all hell broke loose. He grabbed Jim by his shirt collar and yanked him out of his chair. Before he could give his actions a second thought, he answered with his fists, clipping Jim on the jaw.

In return, Jim's poker buddy whirled Roy around and smacked him in the chin, sending him backward against the bar. Several chairs tumbled as the two men just plowed through them, and glass shattered as Roy's whiskey bottle smashed to the floor.

Flouncy screamed, and Carl jumped over the bar and picked Roy off the floor. "Get a hold of yourself, Roy!" he said, walking him toward the door. "They was only teasing you."

"Tease me, then," Roy announced, yanking his arm free and slamming his hat onto his head. "Just leave the woman out of it."

He glared at the men standing around, quiet. Jim was still on the floor, rubbing his jaw. Then, without another word, Roy turned on his boot heel and stomped out of the Lalapalooza.

Out on the sidewalk, he cursed himself for being all kinds of a fool. For letting that woman get to him again. He'd been fine, just fine, until they'd brought up her name.

Then he remembered. He hadn't been so fine. He'd been moping into the bottom of a whiskey glass.

This had to stop. Now!

With new resolve, he straightened himself and marched toward the center of town. He was going to confront her once and for all, and this time he wasn't going to turn tail and run like he did last time. No siree! This time he was going to see his task through till the very end.

Till he got Eleanor Fitzsimmons back on an eastbound train.

He snorted. Heck, it didn't matter if the train were eastbound or westbound, or if the train went all the way to China, for that matter. He just wanted her out of his hair.

He nodded at the people who said hello to him, but tried not to let his concentration be broken. He sensed he would need all his mental acuity for the coming confrontation.

Oh, he knew women, all right. Eleanor would probably bat her eyelashes at him and simper and apologize. His mother, no doubt, would take her side, berating him for being a cruel insensitive brute. Between them, they'd do their best to play him like an old fiddle, plucking and sawing at him until he sang the tune they wanted!

By the time he reached Isabel's door, he was in a regular swivet, so that even the color he was staring at incensed him. Red! Was his mother trying to be conspicuous? She might as well hang a big sign outside the place reading Shady Ladies Within!

He took a deep breath and banged on the door.

In two seconds his mother swung open the door, her expectant smile quickly turning to wide-eyed concern. "Roy!" She grabbed him by the arm as if she expected him to topple over, then tried tugging him over the threshold. "What happened to you? You look terrible!"

He dug in his heels. "Just a little altercation at the Lalapalooza."

Her nose twitched. "Good heavens—you've been drinking!"

He laughed. "That's what goes on at the Lalapalooza, I'm afraid."

Sweeping him with a head-to-toe glance, she frowned and asked, "Does rolling on the floor also go on there regularly?"

His jacket and pants were covered with dust. Roy slapped self-consciously to get rid of some of it, and Isabel gave him another tug.

"Come inside, I'll brush you off."

He squinted into the doorway. "Is Eleanor here?"

She nodded. "Yes, she's upstairs right now."

"I want to speak to her."

To his surprise, his mother suddenly burst into tears. Tears!

Roy was stunned. He looked quickly behind him to make sure no one was watching and rushed inside, shutting the door firmly behind him. "For heaven's sake, Mama, what's wrong?"

She lifted a perfectly pressed lace handkerchief to her eye and sniffed. "Everything is wrong! I'm so sorry, Roy. I feel so responsible for busting up your engagement."

"Well you shouldn't. You only tried to tell me the truth."

"Oh, I know...but I had no idea you didn't know about her."

Roy tilted his head. "Ellie didn't use guilt to make you give her this job, did she?" He wouldn't put it past her!

"Oh, no! I needed the help anyway. And she paid me money for taking her in. Twenty dollars."

Roy rolled his eyes. *Twenty dollars?* His twenty dollars?

He felt sick.

"You should have turned her out on the street. I can't imagine she's much help to you."

"Oh dear. I suppose you heard about Emily Crouch's shirtwaist."

He raised a brow. "What about it?"

"Oh, well…there was a little trouble with Mrs. Crouch at the drugstore this morning. It seems that the shirtwaist Ellie finished wasn't…" Isabel sniffed. "But I still say it wasn't *all* Ellie's fault that the front buttons popped off."

Roy had a hard time not laughing, but the thought of Mrs. Crouch's calamity just seemed to set off Isabel's tears again. "Oh, why does it seem that I just can't make anything work out right, Roy? For Ellie, for you…."

He'd never expected contrition from her, but now it seemed to seep out of her every pore. "I've always felt so horrible for leaving my two little boys on the prairie, Roy. You don't know how a thing like that tugs at a woman's heart. For years, every time I closed my eyes at night, I saw those big blue eyes of yours blinking up through your dark lashes. Times were that I thought I could have walked all the way back to Nebraska to see you, my heart ached so."

The desperation in her eyes and the emotion in her voice embarrassed him. He always thought he'd savor seeing her repentant, but he didn't. "Please, that's all in the past…."

She shook her head fiercely. "No, Roy, in my heart I don't think I'll ever be able to put it in the past. I know you thought I was heartless, Roy, but I wasn't. And when I first came back a month ago, and saw your blue eyes staring at me again, I realized how guarded I had become. Instead of falling apart all those years I missed you boys so, I tried to get on with life by making it as pleasant as I could.''

"Good, I'm glad...."

She grabbed his hand. "But I did want to do something nice for you, to make up for all that hurt I had put in your heart. Ellie asked me for a job a month ago, and I sent her back to your house, hoping to play matchmaker.''

He sighed raggedly. "You told me about that. It's okay.'' He'd expected Ellie's tears, but not his mother's. He wasn't prepared for this encounter at all. "I forgive you everything,'' he blurted out, backing toward the door. "I think I'll be going...."

She held firm on his jacket sleeve. "No—I'm sure you came here to see Ellie.''

He shook his head frantically, trying to cut her off, but she was already turning toward the small back stairwell. "Ellie! You have a visitor!''

Roy's heart thundered in his chest as he waited to hear that familiar voice.

Instead, Ellie answered with a laugh—the bright laughter that had first caught his attention weeks ago. "Just a second, Parker!''

"It's not Parker, Ellie,'' Isabel warned, wiping her eyes.

"Oh.'' There was a moment of hesitation. "Just a moment, then.''

Parker? Roy looked at his mother for confirmation. Isabel nodded. "Your brother's been over often.''

So that's where Parker had been getting himself off to! Roy was amazed. He'd noticed his brother's absence a few times, but he'd never expected that Parker was running into town every chance he got to visit here.

"Will you have some tea?'' Isabel asked him, but

before he could say yes or no, she grabbed him tightly by both arms and gave him a little shake. ''Oh, Roy, it would make me feel so much better if you patched things up with Ellie. I do so want to see you happy!''

Happy! That word again!

''Actually, I just came here on business.'' All he wanted to do was speak his piece and clear out.

His mother's face went slack with disappointment. ''Oh.''

He took off his hat and banged it against his pant leg. Just then he heard the floor above him squeak, and a footstep on the stairs.

It seemed like years since he'd seen her, and now he couldn't help watching closely as she made her way cautiously down the narrow staircase. He saw the bottom half of her first, and he was shocked by how much more obvious her condition seemed to him now. What had it been…a month and a half since she'd first come to Paradise? When she'd stepped off the train he hadn't noticed that she was carrying a child. In part, probably, because she'd been trying to hide it.

Then again, he'd been distracted by how pretty she was.

Something similar happened to him now. His first glimpse of her brilliant red hair was a shock, and he froze, unprepared for the onslaught of emotions that began tussling in him again. He dreaded another confrontation and hoped she wouldn't cry and plead to stay with his mother now when he informed her that she would have to go. The last thing he needed was *two* crying women on his hands!

He prayed she wouldn't tearfully ask him to take her back.

He also prayed she would.

She came to the bottom of the stairs and turned,

sucking in a surprised breath when she saw him standing there. "Roy!" Her green eyes sparkled in their old way, only there was doubt and dread mixed in with the old friendliness.

Then she looked over at Isabel's tearful expression and sucked in a breath. "What's happened?" Her face went white. "Has something happened to Parker?"

Parker again!

"No," he bit out, more forcefully than he'd intended.

His mother shook her head. "No, Roy and I were just...talking." She turned to put on a cape and brushed past Roy. "I have to go to the mercantile to hunt for some fabric. Heaven knows they probably won't have anything, but it's worth a try I suppose."

He frowned as she disappeared through the door, then turned back to Ellie with more trepidation than he should have felt.

To his surprise, her expression had fury in it. "What happened?" She tapped her foot like an angry schoolmarm. "What did you say to reduce your mother to tears? Were you berating her for taking me in?"

"No!" Lord knows he would have liked to, but he hadn't even gotten that far!

"Good. Because you have no right to come barging in here and taking your anger at me out on her!"

He tossed his hands out in frustration. "I haven't taken my anger out on anybody yet!"

She jumped on the small opening he'd given her and marched up to him until they were standing toe-to-toe. "But you *intended* to, didn't you?"

He sputtered in confusion for a moment, but before he could spit out a coherent answer, she brayed in displeasure. "Roy, you've been *drinking!*" She stepped back, her hands on her hips. "And look at you! You look terrible!"

He shrugged. "I just got in a fight over at the Lalapalooza."

Her angry stance dissolved as her hand moved to her mouth in surprise. "Oh, no—were you hurt?"

He shook his head, amazed at what a good job she could do of pretending to care for him. He almost believed her. "I nearly got thrown out, though. Thrown out, Ellie," he repeated for emphasis, "of the bar I've been going to since I took my first drink."

"What happened?"

He let out a snort of laughter. "I was defending a lady's honor."

Her face went slack. When he said nothing more, she sighed. "I knew there was probably talk around town. A hush usually falls over a room when I go into the stores here. I was hoping it was because I'm still a stranger, and not because people were being malicious."

Frustration battled with sympathy in him. Even good people could be so damn cruel! He could well imagine the reception she'd been getting all over town.

But then, what did she expect? "Is it malice when people are just reacting to the truth?"

Ellie's round face looked stricken. "No, I suppose not."

Roy shifted uncomfortably. He reminded himself that he was here on a mission, plain and simple, and that he needed to get on with it.

Then he remembered something his mother had said. "Parker's been coming here a lot?"

Ellie smiled that sweet smile of hers. "Do you object to Parker's visiting here for some reason?"

"Of course!"

"He's just being nice to me."

That's what Roy objected to. "He's always had a soft spot for you—I'd hate to see him be taken advantage of."

Her expression turned stony. "He won't be."

"I'm not so sure. It's hard to tell what you'll do—but whatever course you take, it's usually the one most liable to put people out."

"Put *you* out, you mean?"

"Yes."

Her cheeks heated with fresh rage. "Oh, I see! I'm supposed to beg your permission from now on before I see anyone or go anywhere."

"I didn't say that," he replied. "But now that you mention it, it might have helped if you'd left here with the money I gave you."

She laughed. "I've never thanked you for that, did I? It was so kind of you to help me start my new life."

"Then why the heck didn't you start it in Omaha or somewhere else?"

"Because if I'd used the money for train fare, I would have been broke when I reached my destination. So I gave the money to your mother to train as an apprentice for one month, and she graciously took me in."

Roy's face burned. He should have either kept his money or given her enough to send her back to where she came from. In fact...

He reached into his jacket for his wallet and pulled out several larger bills.

Ellie stepped back, clasping her hands behind her back. "No, Roy!"

Her stance only made her belly stick out that much more, and the reminder of her child only made him that much more determined to give her the money.

He jabbed the bills toward her. "You could go back to New York with this."

"I don't want to go to New York."

"Chicago, then."

She shook her head. "I couldn't accept a nickel from you, Roy. You've done too much already."

Too much? All he'd managed to do was wedge her firmly in the middle of his town, in his mother's house, in his brother's sympathies!

If the truth be told, it was that last part that really bothered him. What if Parker went and did something really foolish, like marrying Ellie because he felt sorry for her? Roy would have to spend the rest of his life with Ellie as his sister-in-law. That would be too much! He'd have to leave town himself rather than live with a situation like that, and he had no intention of being the one who was drummed out of Paradise.

"Take the money," he commanded.

She smiled at him. Smiled! "No thank you, Roy. I'm doing very well right where I am."

All he could tell was that she was doing a bang-up job of irritating him. "But you just said you're being snubbed in this town, that no one will talk to you. Rumors are flying around the Lalapalooza, and they aren't pretty."

Her chin jutted stubbornly. "Parker says all that will change after the dance."

Roy blinked. "The dance?"

"At the school," she told him. "It's the fall dance to raise money for a library. Parker's taking me."

Parker was insane. "You can't go to that."

"Why not?"

"Because you're pregnant!" he thundered. "There's enough gossip about you as it is. You don't have to flaunt your condition in everyone's faces when they're already straining to be civil.''

She chuckled. ''That sounds like something Cora Trilby or Munsie Warner would say.''

''It *is* what they'll say, believe me.''

''Parker says that if I hold my head high and go to the dance with him, people will tire of gossiping about us.''

Us—as if she and Parker were an item. Roy felt heat flood his face. ''Parker doesn't know what he's talking about. You two showing up together there will be like throwing kindling on a bonfire.''

Ellie shrugged and let out a wispy sigh. ''We'll see.''

Roy gaped at her, amazed by her complacency. Then he realized that he was still standing there with a wad of bills jutting out toward her. Money that she had no intention of taking.

Mumbling a curse, he shoved the bills into his pocket.

''Are you going to the dance?'' she asked, as if they were having a pleasant social conversation.

''I've always gone to them before,'' he said curtly.

''I'm looking forward to it,'' she said, her eyes twinkling. ''It's been a long time since I've danced.''

''No it hasn't,'' he blurted out. ''We just—''

His mouth snapped shut. For a moment, he was nearly blinded by the memories of holding Ellie in his arms, the two of them turning and swirling through apple trees dusted with white. The whole world had seemed so sparkling and fresh that morning, like a wide-open sunkissed ballroom put there for their pleasure. They'd danced and spun and laughed until they were dizzy.

Didn't she remember?

''Roy? Are you all right?''

He looked back down at her, frowning.

"You were weaving."

Her bow lips turned up at the corners, and in that moment, he knew. She did remember. She was just teasing him, taunting him, and for some reason he wanted to take the bait. He suddenly couldn't help imagining how different things might have been if he'd never found out the truth, if he and Ellie were standing here right now planning on continuing their dance into the future together. He could have swept her into his arms and practiced a few steps right then and there, and held her tight until he couldn't resist stealing a kiss and...

He turned, suppressing a groan. "Tell my mother I had to leave," he said, rushing out the door before he could look into those captivating green eyes again and relinquish all claim to common sense.

As he rushed down the sidewalk toward his horse, it occurred to him than instead of scoring a victory by going to Isabel's, it felt as if he were just barely escaping with his life. Instead of drumming her out of town, he'd only managed to have her reaffirm her intention to stay—and to have her thank him for helping her do it!

Instead of coming out victorious, he'd had to surrender to the fact that Ellie might be here to stay, a constant reminder that love had made a fool of him.

Chapter Fifteen

Clara was wrestling several bolts of cloth, trying to roll them back into some kind of tidy order. Isabel Dotrice had come in and made her take down at least twenty samples one after the other, and had picked over each one for at least five minutes before discarding it, severely testing Clara's patience. If it weren't for the fact that she was Parker's mother....

The doorbell jangled. Clara sighed, vexed. More customers! And she'd just got rid of the last one. They *would* flood in the one afternoon she was stuck here alone. Her parents were visiting her grandmother, who was ill, and had left Clara in charge. If it were up to her, Clara would have just put the Please Call Again sign up and gone for a piece of cake at the hotel's café, but no doubt word would get back to her parents. It always did!

"Oh, miss...?"

At the high-pitched whiny voice behind her, Clara whirled impatiently on her heel, sending three bolts of cloth dropping to the floor. Couldn't whoever it was see she was busy?

Then she saw *who* it was, and nearly fell to the floor herself.

Parker!

He was staring at her with that teasing grin, his eyes practically laughing at the little trick he'd played on her. "Who were you expecting, Munsie Warner?"

At the sound of his real voice, her skin tingled all over. He hadn't spoken to her directly in almost a year—and it seemed longer! She tilted her head, smiling. As always, Parker looked good enough to eat. Tall, fair, muscular—a veritable Adonis.

And finally, *finally* he'd come to apologize for treating her so miserably all these months. He deserved a good tongue-lashing for being so mean to her and so stubborn, but at the sight of him her woman's heart stirred with forgiveness. Love's victory would be so sweet. Maybe now he'd even be escorting her to the dance!

She scooted around the counter, primped her skirts, and looked up at him expectantly. "Did you come here for some particular reason?"

He gazed down at her for a long moment, as if drinking in her every feature. Then, in a warm voice, he replied, "I just came to buy something."

Her mouth, which had been frozen in a smile, went slack. She swallowed with effort. This was hardly the apology she expected.

She tilted her head. "Anything specific?"

He crossed his arms and his brows puckered in thought. "Well…it's for a lady."

She clutched the counter behind her for support. *For a lady?* He'd come here to buy a gift for another woman? "For your mother, perhaps?" she asked sweetly. "She was just here buying the prettiest…"

He shook his head distractedly as he looked around the store. "No, it's not for my mother. It's for someone considerably younger."

"Oh!" She nearly slapped the counter with her fist,

then realized she had yelled. She forced a smile. "I mean, *certainly* we can find something that will satisfy…this woman."

No doubt he was buying something for that Fitzsimmons creature. Everyone knew he was next door practically every day, and not just to visit his mother, either. The final insult! Clara was not only being passed over, but passed over for some woman who was not rich, had red hair the color of rust, and was pregnant to boot! Only the greatest effort kept her from losing her composure.

Oh, but she wouldn't give Parker McMillan the satisfaction of seeing her feathers ruffled! "What kind of present are you looking for?" She led him over to their ready-made clothes and picked up a pair of tiny crocheted blue shoes. She knew she was being catty, but she didn't care. "Baby booties, perhaps?"

He inspected the item carefully and shook his head. "No, those wouldn't fit her."

Clara let out a huff. "Hair ribbons? Chocolate candies?"

"Actually…I was thinking of something more personal." He grinned down at her. "You know, the dance is coming up."

"I know!" she bit out.

He lifted a brow and she tried to keep hold of her temper. But honestly, what did the man come in here for, to torture her?

He fingered a silk handkerchief absently and glanced over at her. "You're going, of course."

"Of course!" She said brightly, lifting her head proudly. "Leon O'Mara is taking me. He asked me months ago, and naturally I said yes right off."

Parker smiled. "Naturally."

She tossed her head. "I wouldn't dream of going

to the dance with anyone besides Leon. In fact, I've promised him every dance!''

"Have you now.'' Parker smiled politely. "I think I'd like to look at your jewelry.''

She turned on her heel and marched over to the jewelry case. "We have some combs with pearl inlay. Those are nice.'' She'd had her eye on those herself.

Parker's lips turned down in distaste. "Aren't they a little…ordinary?'' He squinted down into the case. "What I'm looking for is…there!''

Clara looked down at the beautiful ring with pearls and little diamonds in the shape of a flower. She felt crushed. He was going to buy *that* for some pregnant New York woman who wasn't even rich?

Oh, life wasn't fair!

She couldn't help herself. She took the ring out and slammed it onto the glass counter with more force than she should have. It was painful almost past bearing to think of Parker slipping that ring onto anyone's finger but hers. Was he blind? Couldn't he see that she still cared for him?

She cared for him so much she wanted to shriek.

Curiosity burned in her. "Is this ring for some special occasion?''

"Mm.'' He smiled down at her, his rich blue eyes twinkling at her so much like they used to that she thought she might melt. And then he spoke. "I'm hoping it will be an engagement ring…if the lady says yes.''

Clara felt every ounce of blood drain right into her shoes, and sagged against the counter more than was ladylike. She was so filled with envy and thwarted desire and sadness that she could barely stay upright.

"She'll say yes,'' she assured Parker joylessly.

"You think so?''

"I'm sure of it.''

Because if there's one thing Clara knew now, it was that the woman who let Parker McMillan get away from her was a silly fool.

Ed's clothes made it just in time for the dance. He had that to be thankful for, at least.

The bad news was the suit he'd ordered didn't exactly fit him right. He'd gotten a lot bonier, apparently, since the last time he'd had clothes made, with the result that this suit draped over his body much as his old one did. It looked newer, of course—there was that consolation. And a black wool suit was good for any occasion, even a fall dance. On the other hand, for courting purposes it might have been more appropriate to stretch his imagination a little toward a rich brown or even a lively check that the sports were wearing now, instead of showing up at a party looking like an undertaker.

Behind the schoolhouse, Ed sprang off his wagon and mopped his brow nervously. He was here now. Too late now to worry about his clothes! He set to work unloading the things he'd brought for the buffet—little apple tarts, some sweet cinnamon cider, and spice cookies with dried apples.

Vernon and Margaret Healy pulled up next to him. Vernon laughed in greeting. "Ed McMillan, you old cuss—haven't seen you for ages."

Ed nodded, overly aware of his long neck protruding through a collar that was too roomy by an inch. He'd tried to remedy the problem by tightening his tie, but that had created a rather peculiar effect of material bunching around his Adam's apple, so he'd let the matter be. "Been busy with the harvest."

"Had a good one this year, did ya?" Vernon asked.

His wife chuckled. "Obviously, Vernon. The man's got a shiny new suit on."

Good lord, Ed worried, glancing down, *did it really shine?*

"You look very prosperous, Ed," Margaret went on.

Vernon, who had the round, florid face of a man who spent summers laboring in wheat fields under the hot midwestern sun and winters drinking concoctions from the still in his barn, guffawed loudly and slapped Ed on the back. "I was going to say it looked like the suit was swallowing you whole, but it's the ladies' opinions that matter, idn't that right?"

Ed smiled self-consciously, looked out over the darkened fields heading out of town and seriously fought the urge to vamoose.

"Oh, now Vernon," Margaret scolded her husband, "don't go teasing an old bachelor that way."

Old bachelor. Old fool, maybe.

"See you inside, Ed!" Vernon said, following his wife toward the school.

Ed was sweating so hard now his stiff new shirt was sticking to his back, and he hadn't even stepped foot into the schoolhouse yet. He felt conspicuous and awkward and woefully unprepared to socialize. How good an impression would that make on Isabel?

Gathering his things before his courage could fail him completely, he scurried toward the school building, mindful of others trickling in the same direction down the dark streets of Paradise. 'Most everyone was in their Sunday best, he was glad to see, but somehow his snowy shirt seemed whiter than anyone else's. Perhaps he was just being overly sensitive about his new duds.

He kept a watchful eye out for Isabel but didn't see her. Of course, there was no guarantee that she would even come to the party, though he couldn't imagine the Isabel he knew all those years ago staying away.

The lively fiddle music spilling out of the schoolhouse would surely beckon her like a siren song. She'd been so light on her feet in the old days that she looked like she was dancing when she was just walking across a room. On a real dance floor, she moved like a fairy spirit, as if there were nothing but silvery clouds beneath her heels.

Inside the school, the rows of desks had been pushed back against the walls, and the long teacher's desk was being used as a buffet. Swags of blue fabric decorated the windows, and bouquets of dried sunflowers, mums, and roses were placed along the wall, giving the room the cheery, homey aspect of a parlor. The music, a light jig of a tune, took the creak out of his joints as he ducked his head and moved quickly with his things toward the buffet table. The music reminded him he'd been quite a dancer himself once upon a time and boosted his spirits.

This was going to take two trips. He'd brought the tarts and a bottle of cider, but he hadn't been able to balance the cookies, too. He hurriedly placed the cider on the table, which was filling up quickly, and then, to his horror, looked across the room and saw Miss Munsie Warner bearing down on him.

In all of Paradise, there could be nothing more terrifying. Small, bespectacled Munsie, the outspoken octogenarian and longtime decrier of the town's persistent moral downslide, poked menacingly at Ed's cider jug with her cane, the top of which was shaped as the head of a duck.

"That's not applejack, is it, Mr. McMillan?" she barked at him.

Ed was quick to reassure her. "It's just spiced cider, Munsie. No harm in that."

"Last time you came to one of these socials you brought applejack!"

Ed blushed. Though the incident had occurred eight years before, Munsie had a mule of a memory. She also considered anyone under the age of sixty suspect. "Only by mistake."

"A mistake that threatened to turn the celebration of the election of Mr. Grover Cleveland into a drunken orgy!" Munsie barked loudly, so that all eyes were now staring at him.

"Well, see, the jugs looked so alike—"

Munsie's ranting cut him off. "A mistake that threatened to turn a good example of civic pride for our children into a shameful spectacle of slovenly excess!"

The fiddlers stopped playing their snappy ditty, and the room would have been deafeningly quiet but for the roar of Munsie's accusations. Time seemed to stop, and all Ed could focus on was Munsie's pinched face and her voice braying at him. The cane that had been poking the cider was now poking threateningly at him as she warned him in a loud staccato barrage of the dangers of leading children astray, undermining the efforts of the women of the community to maintain high moral values and encouraging men to indulge their weak, base natures. Ed found himself backing up to avoid being speared by the duck, then, unfortunately, he accidentally swiped the buffet table with his arm, sending a pitcher of lemonade spilling to the floor.

The glass shattered in an explosion of sticky, sugary lemonade, and as he hopped forward to avoid being sprayed by the juice, he ended up falling prey to Munsie's duck anyway, clumsily knocking it out of her hand. Attempting to catch it, he lost his grasp of the tray of apple tarts he'd been holding aloft in his right hand. They fell splat on the floor at his and Munsie's feet, and though he did his best to avoid them, his heel squished down on a piece of cooked buttery apple from one of his tarts, sending his feet flying out from under him.

The next second, he was splayed on the floor— though luckily not in the pool of lemonade. He could hear Munsie still yelling, and see skirts swirling around him as kindhearted yet slightly exasperated matrons scurried to help tidy the area he'd managed to make such a mess of in so short a time. His destructive power amazed even himself.

After a silence that seemed to stretch into an eternity, a slow murmur of voices rose around him, and the fiddlers struck up ''I'll Take You Home Again, Kathleen.''

Ed felt tired and old and foolish; his bones ached from the spill and he was half tempted to pretend he'd broken something so he wouldn't have to move at all. They could just carry him out.

Then again, if he could just get up, he could make a run for it out to the wagon....

''Ed?'' A gloved hand reached down to him, offering help.

He looked up, then froze.

Like a vision, Isabel stood over him, resplendent in a gown of such deep red it was almost purple. A queenly color. And indeed, in the room with its bare wood walls and dried flowers, she seemed like a queen among the commoners.

She grinned down at him, her white even teeth still holding the gleam of pearls. ''You can't stay where you are all night, Ed. I was hoping you would dance with me.''

He chuckled, and clasped her outstretched hand. The warmth of it, the reassurance, coupled with her smile, gave him the spunk to unfold his old knobby limbs and stand. The party going on around them sud-

denly seemed like a dream; there was just Isabel, in
the flesh, picking him up and dusting him off as if
the past twenty-four years had never happened.

He led her out to the dance floor and pulled her
into his arms for a waltz. Surely his feet hadn't moved
in this pattern for over a decade, and yet it felt as
though he'd been practicing all his life. Surely his
hand hadn't rested gently on a woman's waist in years
and years, and yet he was somehow able to hold Isabel with the assuredness of a regular man-about-
town. In a moment, the shambling awkward shell he'd
developed over the years seemed to fall away, and he
felt twenty-five again, and handsome and vital because Isabel's blue eyes were looking up at him.

"I've missed you, Izzy." To his astonishment, the
pet name he'd called her when they were young tumbled easily from his lips.

"Izzy." She shook her head in amazement. "I
haven't heard or even thought of that name in years.
In your letters you were always so formal."

As was only proper. "You were always a married
woman."

She shook her head. "Oh, Ed. It's been a long time,
hasn't it? Half our lives!"

"Not half of yours, Izzy. You'll live forever."

Sighing, she moved closer to him, making him feel
like a king in a ballroom. They circled the dance floor
once, twice, or maybe twenty times, unaware of anyone around them, and rightly so. What person watching them could have understood the miracle they were
witnessing? It was as if autumn leaves had shaken off
one of his beloved trees, giving way directly to apple
blossoms. To Ed it seemed there wouldn't be a winter
this year, or perhaps ever in his life again.

Parker was right, Ellie noted. The stir she had created when she walked into the little schoolhouse

hadn't lasted longer than a hiccup. Of course, Ed's knocking over the lemonade had created a diversion, which had helped.

When Parker had danced with her, the only hostile glare she'd received came from Clara Trilby. After Parker, a man named Rory Jacobs asked to be her partner. After him, there was another man. At the end of a half hour, it seemed that everyone in the room had forgotten that she was the scandalous stranger they had been whispering about for weeks.

At least the men had…with the exception of one.

Roy was there. All the while she was dancing, she could feel those flinty eyes on her, burning into her accusingly, angry at her for appearing to have a good time. It certainly didn't look as though *he* was enjoying himself. Roy hovered at the fringes of the crowd like a bird of prey, watching her so intently that she wondered if he'd come for the explicit purpose of making her uncomfortable.

If that was his aim, the evening could be considered a rousing success from his point of view. Her cheeks felt caught in a permanent flush—and it wasn't from the dancing.

When one tune ended and she found herself without a partner, Ellie felt as anxious and exposed as a field mouse on the prairie with a hawk circling overhead. She made a beeline for the refreshment table, but halfway to her destination a strong hand clamped down on her arm. She twisted and found herself looking into Roy's blue, blue eyes.

"May I have this dance?"

She glanced frantically about her for rescue, but Isabel was on the dance floor with Ed, and Parker was sipping punch and gazing longingly across the room at Clara, who was pointedly snubbing him.

With all the enthusiasm of a prisoner being marched to the gallows, she allowed Roy to take her arm and lead her onto the floor. When his hand clasped hers, she winced; having his arm about her waist was an agony. She could remember the last time he'd held her in a dance; how different that time had been!

His eyes glittered at her. "I've been watching you."

"I've noticed."

He grunted. "You've been popular. With the men, at least."

She lifted her chin. "Does it bother you that people might actually want to be civil to me, Roy? I told you I was sorry for what I did. If I stay in Paradise for the rest of my life, will I spend all those years with you glowering at me?"

"Leave Paradise and you wouldn't have to worry about that."

In the next dance step, her foot came down in a stomp. Roy winced.

"Oh, I'm sorry!" she cried, biting back a laugh. "Was that—?"

His lips formed a grim line, though she could have sworn there was humor in his eyes. "Yes. I forgot I needed to be careful of my toe around you."

"Perhaps you shouldn't have insisted on dancing."

"I needed to talk to you."

"Oh dear," she said wearily, feeling as if their conversation, like their dance, would always travel in the same unyielding circle. "So you could convince me to leave."

"I'll always be here," Roy told her. "This is my home. Do you honestly want to go on having meetings like this?"

She laughed. "*You* were the one who asked me to

dance, remember? I was perfectly content avoiding you!''

His eyes narrowed on her. ''You were content dancing with Parker.''

''Is there anything wrong with that?''

''Only if your designs on him are the same as they were on me.''

She wanted to scream, to shake him. ''I've told you. I had no designs, Roy. It just happened.''

Did he think he was the only person who hurt? Couldn't he tell that her heart felt broken into a million pieces?

''Nevertheless,'' he went on relentlessly, not inclined to give an inch, ''do you think your behavior around Parker is really ethical?''

''How do you mean?''

''I mean that two weeks ago you were on the verge of becoming my wife. I had the engagement ring in my pocket, for heaven's sake,'' he bit out.

His words thrust into her like daggers. His wife? *An engagement ring?*

She had been miserable enough before, just knowing that she had lost Roy's love. Knowing now how close she'd been to forming a permanent bond with him, and seeing in his eyes how completely that bond had ruptured, was devastating.

''I didn't know.''

He tossed his head. ''Of course you knew. I showed the ring to Isabel. She was the one who told me about you.''

Isabel had admitted telling Roy the truth about her past, though Ellie had never felt any resentment about that. How could she? She had been in the wrong, and Isabel had every right to speak openly to her son. But somehow, when Isabel had been telling her about her fateful conversation with Roy, she had omitted the detail that made the story so tragic in Ellie's eyes.

"She never said anything about a ring."

Roy frowned. "Well, it doesn't matter now. Only I don't relish the idea of your becoming my sister-in-law."

Ellie felt as if she were in a daze. She looked across the room again at Parker, whose gaze was still fixed steadily on Clara, and at Clara, who was still glaring at her, and nearly laughed.

How had she gotten herself into this twisted mess?

"What's so funny?" he asked, seeing her smile.

Her eyes flashed at him. "Nothing. Don't ask me to leave again, Roy, because I won't. Someday you're going to realize how wrong you are about me and your brother and everyone, and I want to be around to see your face when you do!"

Chapter Sixteen

On Monday, at a gathering at the Widow Henry's, a pot of steaming tea just happened to spill on Ellie's lap. Tuesday, she was shunned at the mercantile. On Wednesday, Isabel overheard the dentist saying that the word around town was that Ellie was expecting a baby by a notorious outlaw who'd been shot in Kansas last month.

By Saturday, the day Parker had promised to visit her, she was a nervous wreck.

Also, by some odd coincidence, several women—among them Cora Trilby—had simultaneously pressed mending work on Isabel and asked for it to be done by Monday. When Ed had come by to take Isabel for what had become their customary afternoon buggy ride, Ellie had insisted that she could do the work herself. So when Parker arrived for his visit, she had to send him away again.

"Don't you want to come out?" he asked in surprise. "It's a beautiful day."

She remained bent over her needlework. "I saw it through the window a few hours ago."

Really, under Isabel's tutelage, she was becoming a much better seamstress. Of course, she still heard people snickering about Mrs. Crouch's shirtwaist. She doubted she would ever live that down in Paradise.

But perhaps someday she would be good enough to go somewhere else and open her own shop. Maybe New York...

Her eyes began to sting. She didn't want to go back there, but neither did she want to stay here. For a while she had thought that Roy might come around, but a week had passed since the dance, and she hadn't seen him.

Parker stood in front of her, spinning his hat on his finger. "Sitting inside sewing is no way to spend a cool sunny day."

The sun had been shining nonstop for a week, making their early snow of a few weeks ago seem like something that had happened in a dream.

She looked up at him. "The truth is, I'm not sure I should leave this house anymore, Parker. Every time I do lately, calamity strikes." She told him of the weird occurrences of the past week, right down to her conceiving a child by the Dalton Gang. "Next thing you know, they'll say I'm an escapee from Barnum and Bailey's circus!"

He waggled a brow comically and inspected her cheek. "I heard they were missing a bearded lady."

She shook her head, chuckling in spite of herself. "I thought I would stay in this town for the baby's sake, to give it a nice town to be raised in, but I'm beginning to wonder if we'll ever be accepted anywhere."

"Anywhere Clara Trilby lives, you mean?"

She looked into his blue eyes, surprised. Parker had rarely spoken that name in her presence. And yet, all week, at the edge of her consciousness, she'd been fighting back the idea that the young blond woman was at the center of all her troubles. She had been at

Mrs. Henry's tea party and in the mercantile while Ellie was there. Her family was close with the dentist.

Parker chuckled.

"I don't see what's so funny," Ellie said peevishly.

He grinned. "I had an argument a year ago with a woman who flew off the handle so that she said she never wanted to speak to me again. So I haven't spoken to her, except once. Now, instead of merely apologizing, she's going through all sorts of contortions and making several people's lives miserable—including her own—trying to bring me round."

"So you do think Clara is at the bottom of this?"

He nodded. "A woman's mind is a serpentine thing."

Ellie bridled indignantly. "Now you sound like your brother! We aren't all cut from the same cloth, you know." She tapped her fingers impatiently. "If she's angry at you, I wish she would stop taking it out on me."

"She's bound to stop soon. Probably very soon."

Ellie grunted. "Maybe the day a piano lands on my head."

Parker laughed. *Laughed!*

She didn't understand how he could be so calm when she felt as if there were a whirlwind churning inside her, that at any minute she just might fly apart at the seams. Especially one of her poorly sewn seams.

"Be patient, Ellie. If there's one thing you learn living in a small town, it's that people usually get things right in the end."

"Are you sure about that, Parker?" She lifted a brow skeptically. "You're talking to the bearded lady, remember?"

As Roy and Ike plowed up the sorghum rows on Sunday, Roy watched Parker return from town in the wagon. A few minutes later, while he and Ike were taking a break by the water pump, Ed and Isabel waved as they drove past on the main road on their afternoon outing.

"Does it ever seem to you that we're the only ones working around here anymore?" said Roy.

Ike chuckled. "Everybody else has other matters to attend to." He waggled his brows. "Love matters."

Roy grunted.

"It's a funny thing, that story about your ma and Ed." Ike shook his head. "Your uncle was tellin' me about it at the dance the other night."

"Why's it funny?"

"'Cause it's such a shut-and-dried case of missed opportunity, and people workin' at cross-purposes, and yet everything finally working itself out. Say, if she hadn't married your pa...why then, she might never've met Ed. But if Ed had spoken up sooner, maybe they wouldn't have had to wait so long to realize they loved each other."

Roy was still unused to the idea of Ed being in love with anybody. Especially his mother. But, grudgingly, he had to bow to the inevitable. "I guess the problem is, she married the wrong brother to begin with."

"Yup." Ike shrugged. "But how was she supposed to know that at the time?"

Roy hung the dipper back on its nail and leaned against the well. The uneasy feeling he'd had all week was creeping up on him again. In fact, he wasn't sure he'd had a truly restful moment since his dance with Ellie. *Someday you're going to realize how wrong you are...* But he wasn't wrong, was he?

Ike scratched his grizzled chin thoughtfully. "Now you take Ellie. Parker seems to be rushin' her pretty hard—leastways, he goes into town most days. But you'n' I both know there's something that draws that boy to the Trilby girl. Lord knows why—she's thin as a rail. I'll bet she doesn't know how to make good butter!''

Roy sent his gaze heavenward, praying Ike wasn't going to meander down the butter trail for too long. ''You make it sound like Parker's the instigator here.''

Ike's brows rose high on his forehead. ''I don't see nobody holding a gun to his head, do you?''

''Women have other ways of luring men to their doom.''

Ike cackled. ''Roy, you're the hardest case I've ever run into—and I've run into plenty. You're worse off than the man I knew in Dakota territory who froze to death in a whiteout blizzard when he was twenty feet away from his own house.''

Roy didn't see the connection...exactly. Just enough to make him a little more uncomfortable. ''I'm not freezing to death.''

''Oh no?'' Ike chortled. ''You're a walking case of frostbite, in my opinion. Used to be you were cranky, but we had good times. And when Ellie was around you were actually decent company. But now you keep lookin' at Parker as if he's betraying you, and at the dance you glared at Ellie as if she'd wounded you, and you stomp around the farm as if you'd just lost your best friend.''

Roy's breath caught in surprise. That's how he felt!

Really, the source of his misery wasn't that Ellie had lied to him anymore. Or that she'd had a man, not her husband, before him. The sting of those things had ebbed. It wasn't even that she seemed to be encouraging Parker that stuck in his craw. It was that he had lost a friend.

He was shocked to think of her that way. But now that Ike had mentioned it, Roy realized he'd taken to Ellie like he'd made friends in school—instantly and deeply. He'd never laughed so hard or played in the woods since he was a boy. When Ellie was living with them, he'd gotten up in the morning looking forward to the day, to seeing her. Instead of being exhausted and beat at the end of the day, when Ellie was there he'd come back from working with a spring in his step. She'd dug up a piece of his personality that no longer felt comfortable buried—that couldn't be buried. It was like trying to bury sunshine.

He sighed. But now there was Parker....

What was he going to do?

"Yessir," Ike said as he turned back to the field they'd been working, "it's a shame about your mother. If she'd just hitched herself to the right brother to begin with, think of all the heartache that would've been saved!"

Roy walked along more slowly. His problem was, how could anyone without a crystal ball for brains know who the right brother would be?

Ellie was just about to brave going out to enjoy the last of the afternoon when she heard a knock at the door. She opened it and found herself face-to-face with Roy for the first time since they'd danced together.

Her heart performed an uncomfortable flip. How could a man infuriate her and frustrate her past all bearing, and yet still command the power to attract her like no other?

By contrast, he didn't seem at all surprised to see her standing in front of him. Though why would he? She'd been burrowed in these few rooms for days now, dreading the thought of leaving for fear some new calamity would befall her.

He gave her a brief, intense inspection from head to toe and her cheeks burned under his scrutiny. "You look terrible!"

She didn't know whether to laugh or to be outraged. "Thank you very much."

"Haven't you been eating?"

She nodded, wanting nothing more than to get away from him. She might have taken his concerned questioning as sign for hope, but she didn't trust herself enough to be optimistic. So much had gone wrong between them, his very presence made her feel feverish and unstable. She couldn't look into those blue eyes of his without remembering other times... like the breathless moments they'd spent in Ed's barn. Then, too, she'd been flush with hope—hope that Roy's words of love meant that he really loved her.

Could she have been more wrong?

She turned quickly away so that he wouldn't see the flush rise in her cheeks. "Eating enough for two," she assured him.

Silence followed her indirect reference to her baby. She could feel his gaze on her back. Was he scowling at her, or smirking in that way he had? Curious, she spun quickly in hopes of catching his unguarded expression.

His face was unreadable.

"Your mother's not here," she told him.

"I didn't come here to see my mother," he said.

She knew in her heart that Roy hadn't come to pay her a social call, except perhaps to tell her to go back to New York again. That's as far as their conversations usually got these days.

Her hands clenched into fists at her sides. "Then I

don't know what you want here, Roy. I have apologized to you. I don't know what more I can say to make up for the past.''

''You can't say anything. You could do something.''

''I know, I know!'' she cried in frustration. ''I could stay away from your family or hightail it back to New York, or at least Omaha. But I've told you that I *can't* do those things.''

''Actually...that's not what I was going to suggest,'' he said.

A blush rose in her cheeks. ''Oh.''

He took her arm, smiling. ''I was going to suggest a walk. It's a nice day.''

Some reflex caused her to snatch her arm away, even while a part of her wanted to skip out onto the sidewalks with him. But how could she trust that smile of his? ''I can't walk with you, Roy.''

''Why not? You're dressed for it.''

Because it would get my hopes up.

She swallowed and raised her head. Why was he here—and why was he being nice? It couldn't be that he'd forgiven her. She doubted she'd hear absolution from his lips in her lifetime. Which could only mean that he wanted something from her.

Female companionship, perhaps. That's what men generally wanted, in her experience.

She lifted her chin. ''Why don't you go down to the Lalapalooza and ask Flouncy to take a walk with you?''

He shook his head. ''Can't. She sleeps afternoons.''

Her exasperated sigh came out as a huff of fury, and she tugged off her hat and began unbuttoning her coat. Twirling on her heel, she stomped to the back of the store. She heard his footsteps follow, and then he yanked her around to him. The force of his grip sent her smack into his chest, and the contact made her body tremble all over.

"Come on, Ellie. I've been thinking about us. Why don't we bury the hatchet?" he said, pulling her closer.

She resisted. She'd worked hard to try to get Roy out of her thoughts. Ever since the dance, she'd tried not to think about the few days they had been so happy together, because doing so was just torture. But right now she saw the same warmth in those eyes that she'd seen in Ed's apple orchard.

And in the barn.

"I know now that you still want me," Roy said with a grin, "or you wouldn't be so persnickety."

She sucked in a breath, realizing his intent. Everyone knew that Isabel and Ed had been taking long afternoon picnics every day. Roy had come here to see her—probably to seduce her—because he needed to relieve an itch.

She squirmed in his grasp, feeling the maleness of him pressing into her, overpowering her.

"Damn it, do I have to spell it out for you?" he gritted out, holding her fast. "I've missed you!"

"Missed me," she asked, "or missed cavorting on a corn-shuck mattress?"

His face reddened, and for a moment she thought the bells she heard were a prelude to Roy's blowing his stack. But in the next second, they both turned and ran toward the window to see what was causing the commotion outside.

Ellie frowned as she peered past Isabel's thick drapes. "What's that?"

Roy looked alarmed. "Fire bell!" He flung the door open and ran out onto the sidewalk. Sure enough, a small plume of smoke could be seen on the horizon west of town.

Toward the McMillan farm.

Ellie felt nausea rise in her. "Is it a prairie fire?"

Roy looked as white as a sheet. "After snow? Can't be."

"Then…?"

"House fire!" He took off running, and Ellie sprinted after him. He was moving so swiftly she barely had time to clamber onto the wagon in front of the mercantile.

"Stay here," he commanded her.

She wasn't about to do that. "I'm going with you."

"You won't be any damn use."

She squinted at him in a fury. "Never mind that, just hurry."

With no time to argue, he slapped the reins and the horse bolted down the street. They flew down the road toward the McMillan farm, yet the way had never seemed so long. Ellie's breath was caught in a tight ball in her throat. *Please don't let anything have happened to Roy's place,* she prayed silently, over and over. And as they came ever closer to the farm, and the smoke still remained in the distance, she knew that her prayer had been answered.

Yet Roy's face only grew more grim.

"What is it?" she asked in a voice tight with alarm. "It can't be your farm, can it?"

"No," he gritted out, slapping the reins again. "It's Uncle Ed's."

The small house was fully ablaze by the time Roy pulled the wagon to a quick halt a hundred yards away. He jumped down and tossed the reins to Ellie. "Drive the wagon back to where the others are."

Ellie turned toward the other wagons they'd passed on the way in and nodded in agreement.

"And for heaven's sake, stay back," he yelled after her, feeling a flash of dread that something might happen to Ellie or her baby. She shouldn't have come at all, but damn it, he couldn't push her off the wagon.

Several residents who lived in the vicinity had already arrived on the scene and the women and children had formed a bucket-line leading from the well to the house. At the bottom of this line was Isabel, and at its head, dousing the house with water, was the Reverend Jenkins. Ike and Leon O'Mara were running livestock out of the barn and emptying out the chicken house, both of which were, as yet, safe. Men, including Ed and Parker, wielded shovels to toss dirt and old snow through windows and doors. They worked frantically, diligently—and hopelessly.

Anyone could see that the old house couldn't be saved. The structure was already an inferno. Flames from the roof licked the waning afternoon sky and sent fiery bits of ash floating through the air. Even while he worked to save the house, Roy could catch Ed's worried gaze flicking back in the direction of his orchard.

"Don't worry," Roy said to him. "The orchard's far enough away. If we can just get the flames under control…."

Ed shook his head. "I'm worried about your mother."

Roy pivoted, and saw immediately that it wasn't the orchard, but Isabel, who had been the object of Ed's worried glances. More surprising still, he caught sight of Ellie dashing around with a shovel, a muffler wound round her face, heaving dirt through a broken window. *What in tarnation did she think she was doing here?* It was dangerous, foolish, irresponsible….

As he looked on in horror, a section of the roof collapsed, sending an explosion of embers billowing outward. Several shrieks of surprise went up, and men with shovels hopped back to avoid the fiery cinders.

Ellie stood her ground.

He muttered a curse and ran over to her.

"I told you to stay away from the fire!"

His bellowing didn't break her stride. "But I can help!" She sent a spray of dirt toward a window through which plumes of black smoke blew back at her.

"The house is gone," he told her. "Don't risk your life."

He was about to force her to at least go back with the women in the bucket-line, when suddenly her green eyes above her muffler widened with fear. "Roy, look!"

The wind was carrying fiery ashes from the collapsed roof closer to the barn.

Ellie took off running toward the outbuilding, and other men followed. The fight was now on to save the barn, and the bucket-line stretched and concentrated on wetting down its roof. Roy felt relief just to move a few yards away from the raging heat and smoke devouring the house, to be able to look away from the blazing torrent consuming the place where he'd grown up.

What must Ed be feeling, seeing so much of his past disappear in smoke?

What must Isabel be thinking, watching the house where she'd spent so many unhappy days go up in flames?

Roy felt a gargantuan lump building in his throat as he worked alongside the others, and felt hot tears sting his eyes.

He'd lost sight of Ellie right after she'd run to the

barn, and not until the building had been doused with water did he slow down enough to look for her. At first he couldn't spot her in the confused tangle of people dashing about the property, but then he spotted her near the head of a second line that had formed, creating a V running from the well to the barn. Her face was strained as she heaved the heavy wood bucket Isabel had handed her to the next person in line, but she was as fast as any of the volunteers.

Seeing Ellie, the woman he'd been willing to dismiss weeks ago as scheming and deceptive, toiling impassionedly alongside Isabel, the woman he'd written off for years as being cold and heartless, he felt his own heart swell uncomfortably in his chest. Isabel, a woman who looked for all the world as if she'd never lifted anything heavier than an embroidery hoop, and Ellie, eight months along in her pregnancy, labored as quickly and tirelessly as the youngest and strongest among them. And with more heart.

With the unity of movement of a school of fish, the fire-fighting citizenry sensed when the barn was safe and turned back toward the house—a blackened, blazing skeleton now. Nothing would be saved, but the property wouldn't be safe until the last of the flames were extinguished.

Many stayed till the bitter end, and the faces of Ed's neighbors and the expressions of sympathy of those who had come out from Paradise held both relief and sorrow. Fire could and often did kill; this time they had thwarted its deadly efforts. But the flames had taken a house that had stood for over thirty years, one that had been a vital part of Paradise's history.

As people retreated back to their wagons, they could only speculate on what had caused the blaze. Had he not banked the fireplace properly? Left burning cinders in his oven?

Ed looked more distraught than Roy had ever seen him. "Thank God no one was hurt," he kept telling Roy. "I worried about all those people so near that fire."

"'Most all your neighbors came," Roy observed.

Parker, beside them, nodded. "There were nearly forty people here. Someone from every house hereabouts, I would say."

He and Ike were getting ready to go back to the farm. "You could come with us," Parker suggested to his uncle. "We've got plenty of room."

Ed shook his head. "I'll get by here. I want to look after things."

But mostly, he was looking after Isabel, who was still standing by the well.

Parker nodded, then turned to Roy. "See you back at the house."

Roy nodded, distracted. Come to think of it, he hadn't seen Ellie in ages. His heart drummed heavily in his chest.

Where was she?

Parker and Ike set out for their farm on horseback. "I bet it was that oven of his," Ike speculated. "He keeps that thing blazing all autumn long, and you know your uncle—absentminded."

Parker nodded, then frowned. Up ahead, he could hear the sound of a rider coming right toward them, but it was so dark he couldn't discern who it was. No doubt someone coming to see about the fire. But wouldn't the folks heading back toward town have told the rider that it was all over?

The question was just running through his head when suddenly a large white horse came barrelling into sight—and atop the impressive animal was Clara!

"Christmas!" Ike exclaimed as Clara just missed galloping headlong into him.

Parker wheeled his horse and thundered after her, calling her name. They'd travelled several hundred yards before he could catch up to her, and when he did, her eyes looked into his frantically. She sawed on her reins, causing her horse to rear. Parker couldn't tell if she was thrown or simply slid off the horse, but he dismounted quickly to check that she was all right.

"Clara," he said, bracing her by her shoulders, "what's happened?"

She still had a wild-eyed look about her, and her blond hair was flying in all directions. He'd never seen her so out of sorts. For that matter, he'd rarely seen her on horseback.

"I rode all the way from my granny's," she said, her chest heaving for breath. "We saw the smoke!"

"Ed's house burned to the ground," he informed her. He still held her because she looked as though she would collapse without some support. And no wonder! Her grandmother lived almost twenty miles away.

"I thought for sure it was your house—I was wild with worry!"

She looked wild. Smiling, he clasped her to him in a tight hug. "You shouldn't have come all this way by yourself."

As she looked into his eyes, her bow lips turned down in their old familiar pout. "Oh, I know, you've got that Fitzsimmons woman to worry about you now. But I just had to know that you were all right. I guess I just…"

She closed her mouth before she could say more.

"You just what, Clara?"

Shaking off his grip, she stepped back and put her hands on her hips. "I just love you, if you must know!

Heaven only knows why. *My* house could have burned any time in the past year and I doubt you would have come running to see that I was okay.''

''Yes I would have.''

She laughed mirthlessly. ''I doubt it. You've been too busy with that Fitzsimmons woman to notice anybody else. But I notice *she's* not here.''

''She's back at Ed's.''

Clara's smirk disappeared. ''Oh.''

''But she wouldn't have galloped twenty miles to check on me.''

Clara kicked her toe in the dirt. ''Then what do you want to go and marry her for?''

Parker smiled. ''I don't.''

Her lips twisted in disbelief. ''Then why did you buy her a ring?''

''I didn't.''

''Then who—?''

Chuckling, Parker reached into his coat, pulled out the tiny box he'd been carrying with him since he bought it, and dangled it in front of her. ''You never asked me who it was for.''

''You said it was going to be for the woman you were going to marry!''

He stepped forward and pulled the ring out. ''I said if she'd have me.'' Slowly, he took Clara's hand. ''Will you, Clara?''

Her eyes rounded as she saw the ring being slipped on her finger, and then, slowly, tears formed in them. She looked back up at him, her lips still parted in disbelief. ''You mean...you bought it for *me?*''

He nodded.

''And all this time you've just been carrying it around? Waiting?''

''Uh-huh.''

Her eyes narrowed, and she let out a howl of dismay. "Ooooh! I ought to kill you for this!"

He laughed, and pulled her into his arms. "Marry me first. Then you can kill me."

As his head dipped down for a kiss, she whispered, "I'll marry you, Parker McMillan. But be prepared to suffer!"

He laughed. "You don't have to worry about me suffering—your mother will see to that."

At first, seeing his house in flames, Ed had felt as if the very earth were being torn out from under him. His family's house, the place where he'd first met Isabel, where his brothers had lived and died, where he had gone on alone for so many years…it just disappeared before his eyes.

Now, staring at the charred skeleton, he felt strangely composed.

Isabel, on the other hand, sobbed with anguish. "I'm so sorry, Ed. Sorry we couldn't save it."

He put his arm around her and pulled her to his side, pressing his lips to her temple. The soapy smell of her soft hair had given way to acrid smoke, yet to him right now it was a sweeter scent than perfume. "It's all right, Izzy. No one was hurt."

She blinked up at him through tears. "But you've lost everything!"

"I've got my barn, my orchard." He looked into her face, feeling an almost unbearable tenderness overwhelm him. "But I've got a confession to make."

She looked alarmed. "What?"

"Every tree could have burned down, right down to the last cooked apple, and it wouldn't have mattered one whit to me as long as I have you, Izzy."

She sagged against him a little then. "Oh, Ed—who ever knew you were such a romantic fool?"

"Not me," he said, chuckling lightly. "Not me."

"What are you going to do now?" she asked.

"I guess I can sleep in the barn."

"Nonsense," she said, straightening. "You'll come back to Paradise with me."

His eyes narrowed. "People will talk."

"I don't care two cents about what people say."

He looked into her lovely blue eyes and knew it was true. "Then again…I suppose I know a surefire way to stop the gossip."

She grinned. "What's that?"

"Marry me, Isabel." Her eyes registered wariness, and he added in a rush, "Marry me and let's start over. New house, new life together. I know you've been married twice, but never to a man who loves you as much as I do. Never to a man who's waited almost thirty years to win your heart."

Her eyes were wet with tears, and she nestled her head against his chest. "You didn't have to wait. You had it long ago."

For some reason, hearing those words moved him as nothing else that evening had. More than his burned house, more than the idea that forty good people had pitched in to help him. "Then…?"

She looked lovingly into his eyes. "Of course I'll marry you, Edward McMillan. It will be an honor."

He was so flooded with feeling he didn't know how his legs continued to hold him upright, except that having Isabel's love made him strong. And complete. And as happy as a man had a right to be.

Chapter Seventeen

Ellie leaned against the chicken coop, more emotionally than physically exhausted. They had all soldiered so valiantly against the fire, and yet Ed's house was gone.

Staring blankly at its blackened remains in the moonlight, she realized that a house was something she had never known. A home. Ed's house held more memories for her than anywhere. More happy memories. She'd relived every second she and Roy had spent there a million times in her mind. As she stood there now, she tried for a million and one. Images paraded through her mind. Roy meeting her in front of the house as she rode up in the snow. Sitting in Roy's lap at the kitchen table. Uncle Ed and all his loose catalog pages in the kitchen. She and Roy running through the orchard, playing like children. She knew she should banish such thoughts from her mind, but she couldn't. The poignant memories would live forever in her, as fresh as yesterday.

A lone sound caught her ear, and she looked up to see Ed and Isabel leaving in his wagon. Apprehension darted through her. She'd seen almost everyone driving off, but hadn't worried about getting back because she'd assumed Isabel would offer her a ride back to their house in town. Now the horizon was troublingly bare.

She darted toward the house, circled it, then ran back toward the barn. To her relief, she noted one of Ed's two horses and a mule in the stalls, munching happily on newly strewn hay as if nothing had happened. Thank heavens they were there! She at least would have the means to ride back into town.

Sizing up the two beasts, she decided to put a bridle on the old horse, who was small and knobby and appeared much more approachable than the youthful mule. She found a bridle in the tack room, then pulled the horse, Jonas, out of his stall. Slipping the bridle over his head, she prayed she would be able to get up on the horse...and stay up. That might be a problem, too.

Gingerly, she led the animal out of the barn and over to a stump where she might be able to mount him more easily. Just as she was preparing to step up, however, a deep voice called to her out of the darkness.

"Where the hell have you been?"

It was Roy. When he came close enough for her to make out his face, he seemed almost angry.

Her heart pounded uneasily. "I was right here."

"No you weren't," he said. "I looked for you here not ten minutes ago."

"Ten minutes ago I wasn't here. I was rounding up chickens out back."

He let out a sigh. "I didn't look there!"

"I thought everyone had gone." And of all the people who'd remained behind, why did it have to be Roy? She felt so emotionally vulnerable now, she wasn't certain she was prepared to handle his quicksilver moods. "Where were you?"

"I was in the orchard, looking for you."

"What would I have been doing there?"

He didn't answer.

His lack of response told the tale, however. He thought she was reliving the moments when they'd frolicked through the bare trees....

The discomfiting silence stretched into an interminable minute before Roy finally said, "There's no sense in your riding Jonas home. I can take you in the wagon."

"It's no trouble for me to ride back on my own," she said. "I can do it."

His frown deepened. "I'm sure you can. But that would leave an extra horse in town for Ed to take care of."

She hadn't thought of that.

He strode forward to take the reins away from her, but she grabbed his arm.

He stiffened at her touch, and she saw a bone-deep weariness in his eyes that surprised her. She was used to thinking of Roy as tireless, yet the fire must have seemed interminable to him. "You don't need to help me," she assured him. "I can get by on my own."

"Certainly. But for my own peace of mind, I'm going to take you home myself."

"Why should you worry about me?" she asked, lifting her chin. "I'm the woman you've wanted to drive away remember?"

She'd meant to sound haughty and removed, but even to her own ears the hurt seeped through her tone. She felt vaguely ridiculous, and dropped his arm and stepped back to hide her discomfort.

He grabbed her hand, not letting her get too far away from him. "I've tried to drive you away," he agreed, his voice a rasp. "But I failed. My efforts to get you to leave Paradise weren't any more successful than my attempts to drive you out of my thoughts. I can't stop thinking about you, Ellie. What I told you this afternoon was the God's honest truth. I've missed you.''

Feeling some thin shell of control begin to crack, she tugged on her hand; Roy wouldn't let go. ''Please,'' she whispered as he took a step closer.

''Please what?'' he asked.

She shook her head frantically, feeling like a trapped rabbit. But the only thing truly ensnaring her was her own desire for the man in front of her. Even when he'd shown her nothing but righteous anger and contempt, she'd never stopped wanting Roy. What chance did she have against him now that he was confessing his own weakness for her?

The answer was clear. No chance. No chance at all.

He pulled her into his arms with such ease that her feet might have been gliding on ice. Then he tilted her chin up with his thumb. ''I've wanted to do this for weeks now,'' he whispered as his mouth descended on hers.

She expected the kiss to be violent and swift and eager, like the urgent impulses swirling inside her. Instead, his lips coaxed hers tenderly into a response. Her eyes closed, and she wrapped her arms around his neck, unable to mask the flow of desire that flooded through her. Unable to stop herself from showing how much she wanted to hold him close to her, to taste his lips one more time.

She was helpless before temptation, incapable of resisting his kiss. He held her fast, but not nearly as fast as she clung to him. His tongue darted along her lips, teasing her until she allowed him full access. When his tongue entered her mouth, sliding with hers in a mating ritual, she was afraid her feet wouldn't hold her. She felt quivery and loose, as if all her tightly held control had finally cracked and shattered into a million pieces like a sheet of fragile glass.

Roy swept her unwieldy body into his arms as if she were featherlight. As he strode through the darkness, Ellie buried her head against his chest and didn't question where he was taking her. She knew. She knew, and she was past caring about whether it was wrong or right, or if her pride should forbid Roy from going one step further. Pride was a distant intangible idea at the moment, while Roy's arms holding her were astonishingly, powerfully real, as were his passion-darkened eyes and the familiar heat brewing inside her.

When he set her down, she knew without opening her eyes where they were. She'd dreamed of the little cot often enough to recognize the sweet smell of hay, the animal-sweat odor of the horses and Roy's male scent the way she would recognize old friends.

He kissed her again, and though she lost herself in the warmth of his lips, lips that affected her like sweet, strong wine, she was also acutely aware of buttons being undone down her back. His fingers worked methodically, vigorously, and she pulled closer to him to make his job easier. When finally that task was finished, he eased the dress off her shoulders and it spilled to the floor in a puddle of wool. With a whisper of a waistband being untied, her cotton petticoat joined it. Standing now in only a chemise and her undergarments, she felt the cold air chill her, and Roy scooped up a blanket, pulling it over her as he eased her onto the cot. It felt so good to recline, even if she was anything but tired now.

Roy shed his own clothes, all of them, and lay down next to her. Ellie was sure she was blushing down to her toes, and yet she couldn't help staring at the magnificence of him, the sheer power in his muscled body. Though she had been intimate with a man before, she had never viewed one completely un-clothed.

Her wide-open eyes swept up the rest of Roy, tak-ing in snatches of bare flesh that tantalized and aroused her; his broad shoulders, the strong hand rest-ing on her hip, his intent, hungry gaze that was like kindling to her desire. She twisted, nestling closer to him, amazed by the way their bodies fit together even in her condition.

He pushed her chemise back and fluttered a hand over one of her full breasts, causing a moan of need to escape her parted lips.

Roy nuzzled her ear. "I'll be careful," he whis-pered to her.

But rather than soothing her, his words, coupled with the firm pressure of his manhood against her and her recent glimpse at its impressive dimensions, begged questions she feared to ask. *How careful could they be? How did this work?*

Suddenly she was as unschooled and anxious as if she had never known a man before, and, in a way, she realized she hadn't. Not intimately. No one had ever kissed her in the shockingly sensual way Roy now went about kissing her, tending to not just her mouth but seemingly every inch of her. Parts of her that she thought pedestrian and lifeless stirred shock-ing feelings as his lips lavished attention on them. Her eyelids, her nose, the lobe of her ear. She gritted her teeth against sensations he could send racing through her with the merest brush of his lips.

But when his lips moved to her breast, his tongue testing and then teasing her soft flesh into a tight bud, she gave up fighting the whirlwind galloping through her. It was too much for her. All she could do was be swept along, moving against him instinctively, reaching out brazenly to touch that part of him that moments ago had seemed so daunting. Under her hand, however, its hardness seemed more supple, almost velvety. She explored then caressed him, causing a groan almost like pain to issue from his lips.

It took her a moment to realize his response was one of pleasure.

His reaction sparked a thrilling realization. She wasn't just an object, a receptacle for his desire, but a partner fully capable of gratifying him in other ways, too.

A few more minutes of her ministrations, however, seemed to put him on edge. Roy grabbed her hand, and when her eyes looked up his face was tense, his jaw clenched.

Flustered, she blushed. "Don't you like…?"

"Yes," he gritted out quickly. "Too much."

He pulled her to him again and kissed her, hiking her chemise up to her waist and massaging her through her pantalets as he had once before. Then, to her surprise, he tugged her remaining clothes off so that she was fully exposed before him. Despite the cold, every bare inch of her felt red-hot under his sultry gaze.

His eyes were filled with awe. "You're beautiful."

She felt anything but, and she looked down self-consciously at her distended middle, which he cradled gently with his hand.

"Beautiful," he repeated emphatically as he bent down to kiss her.

His voice was so raw, the embrace he pulled her into so tender, that she felt a fierce ache build in her for him. She moved against him suggestively, wantonly as his kiss deepened and his hands roamed her body.

He rolled so that he was poised against the most

intimate part of her. She moved against him, testing, tensing for the intense pain she remembered was imminent. But when he entered her there was only the delicious friction of sensitive flesh. There was only Roy gently moving against her, tentatively at first, then with swifter strokes that fueled the fiery tempest inside her. The inferno licked and crackled at her just as the flames of Ed's house had licked the night-dark sky.

All at once she realized she was losing herself as she had before under Roy's touch, and she gave into the abandon joyfully and eagerly. The dark world around them turned bright with color as fireworks seemed to explode within her. Moments later, Roy shuddered over her, his entire body tensed, and then collapsed next to her with his arm draped over her shoulder.

"Mmm, Ellie..." He groaned and nuzzled his head against her.

Ellie's heart rushed into her breast, and for a moment she was so ecstatic she could hardly think. So *this* was what fired the imaginations of poets and novelists! This was the impulse that spurred musicians to ecstatic bursts of melody and the artist to spread passionate colors on canvas. After Percy, she'd been skeptical about the physical glories of love. But now poems and rhapsodies seemed to flow through her, and all her thoughts had the ringing brilliance of arias. *This* was love in its purest, sweetest manifestation.

And, amazingly, as her imagination thrilled to operatic arias and Keats and Shelley galloped through her veins, something else managed to break through her consciousness, too.

A snore.

She turned. Roy was asleep—so fast asleep that his breath came out in deep heaving snorts.

She felt her brow furrow as the cold night air settled around her, raising gooseflesh. What should she
do now? Wake Roy? Try to sleep herself?

But the bed was too small to accommodate both of
them comfortably, especially when Roy turned
slightly and sprawled his body over more space,
nudging her closer to the edge of the cot. She very
nearly was sent tumbling over the side. She tensed,
trying to breathe lightly in an attempt to make herself
small so that she wouldn't go rolling onto the ground.

The trouble was, she *wasn't* small. And being
squeezed like this was decidedly uncomfortable. The
dead weight of his arm was heavy on her shoulder.
Her arm was falling asleep.

Frowning at how quickly the ecstasy had evapo-
rated, Ellie stared into Roy's face and tried to recap-
ture some of the poetry and music of just minutes
before. She'd been so swept away, so ecstatic just to
be back in Roy's arms, to have it all end so abruptly
jolted her out of her happy thoughts.

Doubts rose up in her. Especially when she tried to
extricate Roy's hand and looked down at the silhouette of her naked, pregnant body lying next to the
powerful male outline of his.

Heavens, Eleanor! What have you done?

Old Louisa Sternhagen's question startled her out
of her love-fogged daze and made her bolt out of bed.

She'd given herself to Roy, heart and body and
soul, and yet did he know? Did he care?

That last thought troubled her the most. Because if
her recollection was correct, he'd never uttered a
word today about loving her, either this afternoon at
his mother's house or tonight after the fire. In fact, at
Isabel's she'd thought he was using her. Both times
they'd been alone he'd only spoken of desire—and

how quickly, how eagerly, how recklessly she'd answered his call to arms!

Her cheeks burned with a fire that was no less hot because her audience was in a deep sleep. She felt mortified, and began snatching up her discarded clothes and donning them hurriedly. She'd lost a stocking—maybe Roy was lying on it. Whirling in a confused circle, she spotted her coat in a heap on the ground, scooped it up, and dashed toward the barn door.

Jonas, the old nag, was still waiting for her, and in her desperation she managed to heave herself up on him in only three tries. She dug her heels into his sides and nearly slipped off again when he bolted forward at a bone-rattling trot; every jounce was a painful reminder of what she'd just done.

The night was dark, and Ellie wasn't even sure of where she was going. There was a path, and she was counting on Jonas's steadiness to get her to town. Right now, as her thoughts spun in a confused, disappointed, heartsore whirl, she just knew where she didn't want to be: in that barn when Roy awoke and his rueful expression revealed how big a mistake he thought he'd made.

Chapter Eighteen

Ellie slept sinfully late. Her whole body felt heavy and sore—unwelcome reminders of her activities of the night before. As if her dreams hadn't been reminder enough! All night, visions of Roy had swirled through her mind. Roy laughing, Roy pulling her into his arms for a kiss. Roy making love to her.

That thought spurred her out of bed. She swung her legs over the edge of her mattress and dressed quickly after giving herself a brief wash from the basin in the corner. She felt unusually disoriented and tired, though she'd slept longer than usual.

Stepping out of the privacy of her curtained-off sleeping area and descending the narrow steps carefully, she immediately knew what had finally awakened her. Ed and Isabel were seated together by the fire, laughing as merrily as they had been when she'd finally come in the night before. When they heard her steps, they looked up and beamed at her.

"Good morning, Ellie!" They practically chirped in unison.

"Good morning," she answered.

She wondered if they had slept at all, or had simply

stayed up talking the whole night. "I'm sorry I slept late," she said quickly. "I know there's work to do."

Isabel jumped up, clapping her hands together. "Not today," she announced happily. "Edward—" She gestured grandly toward him, preparing Ellie for something remarkable. "*My* Edward has asked me to marry him!"

Although Ed sat up taller, his face was tomato-red.

A smile broke out across Ellie's face and she ran over to hug Isabel happily. "How wonderful! Although I can't say I'm surprised...."

Not after seeing them together nonstop since the dance.

Isabel's eyes widened. "Did you hear that, Ed? She's not surprised, either. Only you were."

He grinned sheepishly, though Ellie could tell he was the happiest man alive despite all the other things that had befallen him yesterday. It was remarkable that they could find happiness after a tragedy that would have devastated some.

"I'm still flabbergasted," Edward admitted.

Isabel put her hands on her hips. "Why, you old bachelor, were you secretly hoping that I would say no and you'd be able to hold onto your solitude *and* to me?"

Though she teased him, he looked truly startled by her words, and reached out and grabbed her hands. "No, Izzy, I'm just surprised you'd have me because you're too pretty for me, that's why. Too pretty, too smart, too everything!"

Isabel laughed. "Not too modest, though. No one has you beat there."

Ellie felt herself grinning like a schoolgirl as the two flirted, and she even blushed when Ed pulled Isabel onto his lap and pecked her on the cheek. Amazing that she could blush at anything so innocent as a kiss after last night! But their happiness was so infectious that for a moment she was able to forget her own troubles and revel in their prenuptial bliss.

After a half hour with them, however, a new discomfort set in, especially when she picked up the pattern she had been sewing yesterday and found Isabel blinking at her impatiently.

"Don't bother with that, Ellie. I'm too happy to work, and seeing you toiling away would just make me feel guilty."

Ellie set the sewing aside and looked about her awkwardly. "Is there anything else you would like me to do today?"

"Why don't you take the day to relax?" Isabel suggested. "Or go shopping."

Isabel was truly a generous woman, she knew. But right now Ellie's employer's generosity wasn't completely selfless. As she and Ed sat blinking at her impatiently, it was obvious that Ellie's presence in the little house had suddenly become superfluous.

She cleared her throat. "Thank you. I would enjoy a day to myself to…" Her mind hunted for some activity she might use to occupy herself. "To shop, as you said. Or I might take a walk. Would you mind if I stayed out till this evening?"

The two of them looked as if they couldn't have been more delighted. Ellie hurriedly readied herself for a day on her own, putting on her coat and hat and snatching up her reticule. She left the house in a hurry, too quickly to decide what she was really going to do with all this time she had promised them.

She headed for the mercantile, then turned her steps when she realized she was too exhausted to handle the calamities that might befall her there. She wished Parker had come for a visit this morning, and still half expected to see him.

But most of all, she wished Roy had come.

All during the slow ride from Ed's farm into Paradise last night, she had expected to hear his wagon drive up behind her. But it hadn't. And now as she walked through the town, she imagined him hunting her down to ask her where she had run off to last night. To tell her that he still loved her.

But that, too, was just a wishful illusion.

Tears stung her eyes when she remembered how happy she had felt last night, with so little to base that happiness on. Had she learned nothing from her eight-month ordeal? Another man had used her for his gratification, offering her no promises, and yet she had gone into his arms eagerly, accepting whatever crumbs he cared to give. She had given real love and had received not even empty words in return.

A queer, unbalanced sensation overtook her. She felt like running—yet she couldn't have run if her life depended on it. Abruptly, her steps passed the Lalapalooza and turned off the sidewalk and onto the road out of town. She didn't know where she was headed; all she knew was that she had to be alone. And if her footsteps took her a little closer to Roy...well, there was only one road, and he didn't own it.

She placed one foot in front of the other, feeling better the farther she left the town behind her, and looked ahead to nothing but the fields of burnished brown. Oh, she did love this country—as much as she had on that first day when she'd arrived. She inhaled a deep breath of cool clean air and delighted in a small cluster of coppery haystacks standing sentry next to a rickety log fence. No matter what happened, she was glad she was here, where there was room to breath. Paradise might not be the utopia she'd hoped, but she had no doubt that her child would have a better chance here than where she was.

Her child.

After another quarter mile of walking, she suddenly felt very tired, and stepped off the road to sit down for a moment.

That was a mistake, she soon discovered. When she lay down, she suddenly realized how exhausted she was. And the soreness she felt didn't seem to her a reminder of yesterday anymore, but a very real sensation of pain happening to her right now. Her abdomen cramped uncomfortably, and she leaned over, feeling a sudden flash of heat.

Then, when understanding dawned, a clammy wave washed over her and her mind froze in panic.

Dear Lord, no, she thought. The baby couldn't be on its way. It wasn't time…it was too early.

And she was so very, very alone.…

"Did you hear all the talk last night after the fire?" Ike asked as Roy sat bleary-eyed over a cold cup of coffee.

"No." He'd slept the night in his uncle's barn, then got up this morning to discover Ellie gone. When he'd returned to the house, he'd found Parker had disappeared.

Having his brother absent so suddenly made Roy uneasy, though he didn't know why. Most of his thoughts had been so centered on Ellie, he could barely spare any mental room for Parker. Besides, Parker could take care of himself, while Ellie…

Why had she left him?

He could have kicked himself for passing out last night, but the fire had been so exhausting, and Ellie's embrace so warm, so giving, that he'd simply gone out like a snuffed candle.

When he recalled his time with Ellie now, he felt almost in awe of her. She'd been so beautiful. He'd never known that a woman with child could be so desirable, and yet remembering Ellie lying next to him, he couldn't think of another woman he'd wanted as intensely.

"Well, believe you me, there was plenty of speculating about a McMillan marriage," Ike continued, heedless of Roy's distracted thoughts.

They didn't remain distracted for long.

Roy's weariness escaped him and the gaze he levelled on Ike was razor-sharp. "When?"

"Soon, I guess." Ike shook his head in wonder. "Not to mention, you should have seen this ring Parker showed me. Real pretty thing. Had pearls and diamonds in it, shaped like a flower."

His ring? Parker had bought it?

Suddenly, he was seeing red. And not just because of Parker. Ellie, too!

Of course he'd known that Parker had been seeing Ellie in town every day. At first he tried not to care, then later when he realized that he did care, he'd hoped that Parker's attentions to Ellie stemmed from kindness, not love. Certainly yesterday when he'd been with Ellie, both in the afternoon and after the fire, the subject of her and Parker had never arisen. If she loved Parker—enough to marry him—wouldn't she have whispered some word to him of that fact?

Would she have allowed herself to be made love to by him if she were in love with his brother?

Why had she left him? his mind repeated disturbingly. *What the heck was going on here?*

Damn it, he shouldn't have let her go last night— should have locked the barn or tied her down to the bed if necessary!

"Hey, where are you going, Roy?" Ike asked in astonishment.

He wasn't the only one surprised. Roy was barely

conscious of having jumped up from the table and run for the door like a nervous hare.

"I'll be back!" he thundered, before slamming the door behind him.

He saw the wagon standing where Ike had left it, jumped in, and grabbed up the reins. He didn't know what in the world was going on around him, but he surely wasn't going to let Ellie slip through his grasp now. Not after last night.

He drove the horses quickly and deliberately, his jaw set with fierce determination. He was going to march into his mother's house and tell Ellie that she could just forget about trying to marry someone else. She had no right to be accepting rings from Parker or anyone else after last night!

Plans raced through his head. A preacher. That's what he needed. He'd round one up somehow and drag Ellie through a wedding ceremony whether she was ready or not.

So intent was he on his plans for Ellie, he nearly didn't see the figure on the side of the road as he passed. Only a glimpse of startling red hair made him pull up the reins.

He jumped off the wagon before it had stopped moving. His heart was racing as he saw her slumped form. He bent down and grabbed her by the shoulders. "Ellie, it's me," he said in a rush, "What's happened?"

She was pale and tense and looked at him through eyes glazed with pain. "Roy?" Her voice was dry.

He swallowed. "Is it the baby?"

She nodded.

Without further ado, he swept her into his arms and carried her to the wagon. He took off his coat and put it down for her over a layer of straw that was already there. Then he laid her carefully onto the makeshift bed.

Instinctively, he turned the horses toward home, returning as fast as he could. His thoughts were full of recriminations now, and regrets. It wasn't time for the baby, and yet she was clearly in labor. Had their activities of the night before caused this, or her riding back home on her own? How long had she been there by the side of the road?

Occasionally, she would utter a soft moan behind him, breaking into his unproductive thoughts and spurring him to lap the reins against the horses' backs to speed them.

At the house, he pulled the wagon up to the door and jumped down, calling for Ike. He carried Ellie into the house just as Ike was opening the door.

"What the…?"

"The baby!" Roy cried.

Ike's eyes widened and his mouth gaped like an uncapped barrel. "What are we gonna do?"

"You're going to town to fetch Dr. Webster," he said. "I'm going to put Ellie in my room and try to find the medicine book."

Ike nodded. "I'll start boiling some water and get you some clean sheets before I go."

Roy stopped in midstride and whirled on Ike even with Ellie in his arms. "What for?"

"That's what Mama always said she did for my married sisters."

Finally Ike's mama was coming in handy! "You do that—and hurry."

The trouble was going to be figuring out what to do with that stuff once Ike was gone. Roy didn't know the first thing about how to help a woman giving birth—one of the drawbacks of being from a family of bachelors. For a fleeting moment he even considered asking Ike to stay and going for Dr. Webster himself, but when he looked down at Ellie's pale, drawn face he knew he couldn't leave her.

"Hang in there, Ellie," he said encouragingly, "Ike's going for the doctor. He'll be right back."

Her brow puckered and she looked up at him. "The baby's early, Roy."

He nodded, feeling his stomach go knotty with the same fear that was written in her expression. He forced a tiny smile and said, "He's just eager to see his mother. Can't say as I blame him, since she's so pretty."

She laughed skeptically, then clamped down in pain for a moment. Roy tensed right along with her, and felt his skin go clammy. When she relaxed a little, he sat her up and began unbuttoning the back of her dress. "Let's get you out of this."

She seemed only too happy to go along with his suggestion. When the confining garment was off, she looked slightly more comfortable—enough to encourage him to do more than hold her hand. "You look exhausted already, Ellie. Do you think you could have some water?"

She nodded, and he ran to the kitchen to find the kettle steaming like a dragon atop the stove. He pulled it off the heat, grabbed a mug from the cupboard and ran out to the pump.

Ellie accepted the water gratefully, and Roy spent the rest of the time they were alone alternately giving her sips of liquid, wiping her brow, and running to the kitchen to look out for the doctor and make sure that the water remained boiling hot for such a time as it was ever needed.

His efforts paid off. Though the pain worsened, Ellie began to look a little more up to the task ahead, and she was able to talk more easily, though some of her thoughts were disturbing.

"If something happens to me, Roy, will you find someone to take care of the baby?"

Roy frowned and squeezed her hand. *Something happen to Ellie?* Mostly he'd been pessimistic about the prospects for the baby, and worried about Ellie's pain, but he hadn't allowed himself to consider the possibility of anything terrible happening to Ellie herself.

"Don't talk like that, Ellie. How could anything happen to you? You've come this far."

And he realized suddenly that she *had* come a long way, and sacrificed everything she'd known before, for the sake of her child. And when he thought of the little life he'd felt stirring inside her last night, he felt a fierce possession kick in his own gut. *Nothing* bad would befall that child on his watch.

The minutes seemed to tick by interminably, and as one hour inched along into two, he found himself looking more and more often out the window for an approaching wagon or horse.

Finally, Ike returned with Dr. Webster, followed by another wagon bearing Ed and Isabel. Roy was so relieved to see the doctor that he almost roared at the man as he walked in the door. "Thank God you've come!"

Dr. Webster, however, looked more than usually tense. And gloomy. "This is all very unfortunate, Roy," he said gravely, "very unfortunate…"

Before the doctor could go in with Ellie, Roy grabbed his arm. "Don't talk to Ellie that way, Doc. It's taken me a long time to convince her that all isn't lost, and I don't want your doom and gloom predictions reversing that."

The doctor nodded. "Of course, Roy. Of course." He went into the room with Ellie and closed the door.

Isabel made coffee, and Ike, Roy and Ed started a long, tense vigil in the parlor.

If Roy thought time was going slowly before, it truly began to crawl now. Already he felt exhausted, he couldn't possibly imagine what Ellie was feeling. He gave up the idea of not going into the room with her after thirty minutes; it made him feel better to have Ellie squeeze his hand and speak to him in short bursts. He mopped her brow often and tried to make her laugh. But finally, it seemed that she was beyond laughter and that the time was at hand.

Roy's heart was in his throat as the doctor announced that he could see the baby's head. A few agonizing moments later, as Roy's eyes squeezed shut in tension, the doctor practically let out a whoop.

"A girl—a little girl!"

When his eyes opened, it was to see the little red baby—still attached to her cord and more messy than he'd ever imagined a child could be—kick her legs and let out an uncertain cry.

At the sound, Roy very nearly cried himself. Instead, picked up by his soaring heart, he ran to the door and called out, "A girl!"

A flood of people rushed in.

If Ellie objected, she was past having the energy to say so. When he ran back over to her, she was smiling absently at the activity going on around her. He mopped her brow as they watched Dr. Webster instructing Isabel how to cut the cord and clean the baby. Roy mopped Ellie's brow one last time, then bent down to kiss her lightly on the cheek.

"Congratulations. You're a mother."

Limply, she held out a hand toward her newborn, and Roy rushed over to take her from Isabel, who was attempting to swaddle the squirming infant into a sheet. She handed the child to him carefully, and the moment Roy held the baby in his arms, a rush of wonder struck him. And awe. She was so tiny, so light, and yet she already showed incredible strength in the way her small fists punched at the air, and he could swear the blue eyes squinting out at the world had a little of Ellie's green in them.

As he stared into those eyes, his stomach churned as if he'd just stepped off the edge of a cliff. He'd never known that the feel of a little fist beating at his arm could move him so. But now that he did, he understood what Ellie had obviously known all along: this baby was precious beyond jewels. Maybe he hadn't believed her weeks ago when she'd told him that she'd lied to give her child a good name and a clean start. But he understood now.

"Roy?"

He turned to see Ellie, one brow crooked curiously, still impatiently holding her arms outstretched.

He flushed and moved over to her. "I was just checking out your handiwork," he told her. "She's much better than that shirtwaist you sewed for Mrs. Crouch."

As he handed over the baby, he was treated to one of Ellie's delighted bursts of laughter.

"I like Gwenevere. It sounds so…queenly."

Roy frowned. "It sounds peculiar!"

Ellie looked down to where her baby lay against her breast, her eyes squeezed shut, and was unable to resist touching her downy hair. "All right, how about Annabelle? I always loved that poem about Annabelle Lee. Don't you think that would be pretty?"

His nose wrinkled. "How about something non-literary? A good solid name, like Mary."

Mary O'Malley came to mind, as did her dire predictions about what a terrible end Ellie would come to, and Ellie immediately protested. "Oh, no! I must have something a little more imaginative." And less scolding! "Don't you have any names that you particularly like...say, if she were your own baby?"

Roy looked away, and Ellie immediately regretted her foolish question. Roy had been so good to her during the birth—she didn't know what she would have done without him. And ever since Dr. Webster had left, he'd barely given her a moment's peace. Even while she was asleep, Ike had informed her, Roy stayed by her side, watching over her and the baby. It gave her a funny feeling to know that he had taken such proprietary care of her. So much had happened between them.

After a moment, he surprised her by turning back to her thoughtfully and saying, "Violet."

She blinked. "Violet? Like the flower?"

He nodded. "I remember from when I was a boy, my mother always smelled of violets. I suppose she had some perfumed water, because there certainly weren't any around here. But ever since then, I've always thought violets must be the sweetest flower there is."

Then what better name could there be for a child that Ellie was already certain was the sweetest in the world? She nodded her head, and said the name aloud to test it. "Violet." Out of some impulse that seemed startlingly like recognition, the baby kicked her thin legs. Ellie laughed. "Violet it is, then!"

Roy's expression was proud and pleased, but slowly his smile faded ever so slightly. "Violet Mc-Millan."

Ellie was so surprised she almost fell out of bed.

She wasn't even sure she'd heard him correctly. "What?"

He looked at her with a rueful smile. "That's what it will be, won't it?"

Her heart pounded in her chest. He seemed to be intimating…and yet his miserable expression was anything but that of a lover. "Why would it be?"

"Well, from what I've heard, you and Parker are fairly serious."

Her jaw dropped in astonishment. "Parker!"

He nodded. "I suppose you can count on him to do right."

Every inch of her stiffened. "And why should Parker have to worry about *that?*" she said, jettisoning pride and discretion. "*He* wasn't present in the barn after the fire. He wasn't the one with me on that cot!"

Roy looked startled.

Did he think she'd forgotten their time together in all that had subsequently happened? "Don't worry, Roy, I'm not going to try to entrap you. But if you think you can foist me off on your brother, you're wrong. How could you think I could love another man after you? Though heaven knows I've tried not to think of you at all!"

He looked offended. "You have?"

"Of course! Do you think I *wanted* to be in love with a cranky dyed-in-the-wool bachelor like yourself? Heavens, no—but apparently I have no choice in the matter, for the harder I try not to think of you, the more I do. The harder I try not to care for you, the more I do. It's a terrible quandary."

"Terrible?" He paced in front of her bed.

She laughed. "Yes, but I'm resigned. Because I…" She hesitated, then rushed on anyway. "I love you, Roy. I love you and it doesn't matter if you love me back, because I'll just carry a torch for you anyway.

I'll become as isolated and odd as your poor Uncle Ed before he decided on marrying Isabel, only instead of becoming obsessed with apples, I suppose Violet will be my life's work."

Roy stopped and looked as though he were having a hard time following her words. "Wait—Uncle Ed is going to marry my mother?"

"Of course!" She raised her brows. "Didn't you know?"

His face went slack. "Wait a moment...did Parker ever give you a ring?"

"Good heavens, no." She drew back, unsure what had him looking so stunned. "Is something wrong?"

"No!" A prairie-sized grin spread across Roy's face. "Only I thought...well, never mind what I thought. I'm a fool. It wouldn't have mattered anyway. Because even if Parker had set his heart on marrying you, I wouldn't have let him. Not after all we've been through, Ellie."

Her heart felt as if it were waltzing. "Then...?"

He crossed to the bed, knelt, and took her hand in his. "Of course you can make Violet your life's work, Ellie. She'll be mine, too. But no matter what you say, we're getting married just as soon as I can get a preacher over here. I love you, Ellie."

"Roy!" she exclaimed in surprise, but she couldn't talk for long, because Roy bent down to capture her lips.

She twined her arm about his neck, and suddenly it seemed that she and Roy and Violet were all bound up together, as one. His kiss was as warm and intense as ever, but he held her gingerly, lovingly, as if she, like her daughter's namesake, were a delicate flower easily crushed.

When he finally pulled back from her, his eyes

were so full of love that Ellie felt almost light-headed with happiness.

"At the dance you said you wanted to see my face when I figured out how wrong I'd been—well, here it is," Roy said.

"It's an adorable face."

He held her tight. "I've loved you ever since I saw you step off that railroad car, Ellie. Loved you so much it scared the pants off me. Maybe that's why I flew off the handle when I found out you'd lied. I was too scared and too stubborn to see that your love meant more to me than anything."

"Oh, Roy," she said, sinking down against the brace of pillows against her back. "I've never heard such wonderful words."

He grinned. "I've never spoken any, either. I guess when it comes to love talk, I'm not very accomplished. But now that I'm starting to get the hang of it, I intend to tell you how much I love you at least five times a day."

Ellie was thrilled, but she pretended at least to think over his loving offer. "I think I'd prefer ten times a day. And for every time you say it, there should also be a kiss."

"You've got yourself a bargain." He pulled her into his arms again. "Ten it will be, Ellie."

And to get things started, he fulfilled his first day's requirement in a matter of minutes.

The others were called in to hear their announcement, which was met with smiles and hugs of congratulations.

"Lord-a-mercy," Ike exclaimed, "the McMillan bachelor tradition is coming to a screeching halt, I'd say."

"Good riddance," said Ed.

"Well, wait a minute now," Roy said. "There's always Parker."

Isabel laughed. "Your little brother has beat you to the altar, Roy. He and Clara eloped last night."

Roy's jaw dropped. "Why didn't you tell me?"

Ellie smiled gently at him. "I think you were a little preoccupied."

"'Sides, I know I told you about the ring Parker had bought," Ike said. "What'd you think it was for?"

Roy would never forget his consternation about the ring—only now he couldn't be happier. He let out a bark of laughter. "That's all of us, then. Snagged by devious women despite our best efforts."

Ellie shot him a sidewise glance. "Sure you won't weasel out at the last moment and try to keep the bachelor tradition going?"

Roy squeezed her hand. "I guess some traditions aren't what they're cracked up to be."

"What about the tradition of marriage?" Ellie asked, her brow raised flirtatiously.

He grinned down at her. "We'll just have to see about that, won't we?"

And for the next fifty or so years, they did see—and in all that time, through good times and bad, Roy never regretted switching marital philosophies.

* * * * *

***Don't miss
an exciting opportunity
to save on the purchase of
Harlequin and Silhouette books!***

Buy any two Harlequin or
Silhouette books and save
$10.00 off future Harlequin
and Silhouette purchases

OR

buy any three
Harlequin or Silhouette books
and save **$20.00 off** future
Harlequin and Silhouette purchases.

***Watch for details
coming in October 2000!***

PHQ400

HARLEQUIN
Duets™